"*Stray Aff*   ould come
with a warning label: Do not pick up this book unless you, like Cassie
and the unforgettable characters who are part of her world, are prepared
for a journey that will change your life!"

—CASSANDRA KING, author of *The Sunday Wife*

"Charlene Ann Baumbich takes us to a town populated with characters—so delightfully quirky they must be real—and illustrates the power
of love and forgiveness. Even the tiniest miracle is still a gift from God."

—JOAN MEDLICOTT, author of nine Ladies of Covington novels

"Do you believe in mystery? After reading *Stray Affections,* you will
understand that the Almighty works in mysterious ways! Charlene Ann
Baumbich creates mystical meaning from a snowglobe, canine friends,
and an intriguing cast of characters. A real treat."

—ANGELA HUNT, author of *Doesn't She Look Natural*

"A tender story by a writer who understands the magic of second
chances and the redeeming power of unconditional love."

—LISA WINGATE, author of *Tending Roses* and *Word Gets Around*

"Through a handful of wonderfully imperfect characters, some unforgettable four-legged companions, and one extraordinary treasure—a
simple snowglobe—Charlene Ann Baumbich unfolds a story showing
the strength of hope and faith, of forgiveness and acceptance, and above
all else, the resilience of the human spirit. *Stray Affections* is a heart-
warming, delightful read."

—GAIL FRASER, author of *The Lumby Lines, Stealing Lumby,* and
Lumby's Bounty

Other books by Charlene Ann Baumbich

DEAREST DOROTHY SERIES

Are We There Yet?

Slow Down, You're Wearing us Out!

Help! I've Lost Myself!

Who Would Have Ever Thought?

Merry Everything!

If Not Now, When?!

Don't Miss Your Life!

Don't Miss Your Kids!

365 Ways to Connect with Your Kids

The 12 Dazes of Christmas (and One Holy Night)

The Book of Duh

How to Eat Humble Pie and Not Get Indigestion

Mama Said There'd be Days Like This

Stray Affections

A NOVEL

CHARLENE ANN BAUMBICH

AUTHOR OF THE DEAREST DOROTHY SERIES

WaterBrook
PRESS

STRAY AFFECTIONS
PUBLISHED BY WATERBROOK PRESS
12265 Oracle Boulevard, Suite 200
Colorado Springs, Colorado 80921

Scripture quotations are taken from the New American Standard Bible®. © Copyright The Lockman Foundation 1960, 1962, 1963, 1968, 1971, 1972, 1973, 1975, 1977. Used by permission. (www.Lockman.org).

The characters and events in this book are fictional, and any resemblance to actual persons or events is coincidental.

ISBN 978-0-307-44471-4

ISBN 978-0-307-45829-2 (electronic)

Published in the United States by WaterBrook Multnomah, an imprint of the Crown Publishing Group, a division of Random House Inc., New York.

WATERBROOK and its deer colophon are registered trademarks of Random House Inc.

Library of Congress Cataloging-in-Publication Data
Baumbich, Charlene Ann, 1945–
   Stray affections : a novel / Charlene Ann Baumbich.—1st ed.
    p. cm.
   ISBN 978-0-307-44471-4—ISBN 978-0-307-45829-2 (electronic) 1. Life change events—Fiction. 2. Human-animal relationships—Fiction. 3. City and town life—Minnesota—Fiction. 4. Domestic fiction. I. Title.
   PS3602.A963S77 2009
   813'.6—dc22

                    2009014328

Printed in the United States of America

2009—First Edition

10 9 8 7 6 5 4 3 2 1

Behold, Thou dost desire
  truth in the innermost being,
And in the hidden part Thou
  wilt make me know wisdom.
Purify me with hyssop, and I
  shall be clean;
Wash me, and I shall be
  whiter than snow.
Make me to hear joy and
  gladness,
Let the bones which Thou
  hast broken rejoice.

—PSALM 51:6–8

Part One

September 2008

One

Preoccupied by troubling news, Cassandra accidentally broiled a batch of cookies. She didn't realize her error until after she'd corralled all four of her young sons into a corner of their backyard, away from the assured danger the smoke alarm proclaimed. In the midst of their huddle, it struck her: the problem wasn't in the oven.

Once again, the problem was her.

The commotion caused her neighbor, outside hanging clothes on the line, to stick her head over the fence.

"We're all out!" Cassandra hollered through the blare. "But if you could come over for a minute and watch the kids while I run back in and check something, I'd sure appreciate it!"

Glenda popped the latch on the gate and flew through the opening. Cassandra passed eleven-month-old Bradley from her hip to Glenda's, who wrapped her arm around his chunky waist. With her free arm—and the focused eyes of a herding dog—Glenda set to work funneling the rest of the boys through the gate into her yard, where they turned and stared at their crazed mommy.

"MAYBE YOU SHOULDN'T GO BACK IN THERE!" Glenda wailed as she watched Cassandra's backside disappear into her house, startling Bradley into panicked screaming.

Within a few moments, Cassandra reappeared through the back door, coughing, a charbroiled cookie tray filled with black smoking wads held at arm's length in front of her. She looked angry as she hurled the whole mess, red plaid oven glove and all, to the ground.

"CAN YOU KEEP THE KIDS A LITTLE LONGER?" she screamed over the sounds of the alarm.

Glenda nodded.

"I'LL BE RIGHT BACK!"

Shortly after she reentered the house, a fierce pounding, loud enough to rival that of the smoke alarm, radiated through the open back door.

Inside, wildly swinging the broom handle, Cassandra beat the ear-piercing alarm until it careened off the ceiling, thankfully crash-landing with a silencing thud. Glenda and the kids—plus the neighbor across the street who'd wandered over—watched as one window in the house after another flew open. Each time, Cassandra stuck her head out and yelled, "I'M FINE! EVERYTHING'S OKAY! I'LL BE THERE IN A MINUTE, BOYS."

The way she swiftly appeared and disappeared in and out of the windows, her red hair flying this way and that, reminded six-year-old Chuck, Cassandra's oldest, of that Bop 'em Sock 'em machine at the Pizza Party House, the game where every time you pounded that crazed-looking animal's furry head, it popped up someplace else. When his mom's head next popped out the bathroom window, he broke into a fit of giggles. Chuck's laughter struck Bradley so funny that he finally stopped crying, sniffled, wrinkled up his nose, snorted, and started laughing, setting off the other two boys. They were all still giggling when Cassandra, huffing and puffing, finally trudged up beside them.

"So you think this is funny, huh, boys?" she asked, grin on her face, hands on her hips, trying to catch her breath. She raised an eyebrow at Glenda, whom she could tell was biting her tongue to suppress her own laughter.

"Wait till Dad hears *this*!" Chuck said, doubling over and holding his side.

Cassandra knew there was no point asking Chuck not to tell Ken, for two reasons: honesty, which they always preached in their family, and the fact that the house would no doubt smell like smoke for days, if not weeks. Plus, if she couldn't laugh at herself, she was doomed. Thankfully, a warm fall breeze blew through southeastern Minnesota that day. The house could remain open to air out, and it wasn't too cold for the kids to be stranded outdoors without their coats.

"Were the cookies on *fire*, Mommy?" wide-eyed three-year-old Howie asked.

"No, sweetie," Cassandra said, smoothing her hand across the top of his wavy hair. "They were just smoking."

"Why?" Harry, Cassandra's two-year-old, asked, as he grabbed hold of her leg.

"Because Mommy accidentally set the oven to broil instead of bake, then your brother had to go potty and…"

Howie's face puckered up. He was her sensitive child, vulnerable to every harsh word or errant blame. She noticed the waistband to his pants was torqued. With Harry still clinging to her leg, she leaned over and straightened Howie's waistband, neatly tucking in his shirttail as she went, then hugged him. Harry detached himself, so she squatted down in front of Howie to look straight into his eyes. "It's not your fault Mommy made a mistake," she said, brushing his cheek with the back of her fingertips.

"At's okay, Howie. It was an axiden," Harry said, parroting his parents' words for when he or one of his siblings spilled a glass of milk.

"Thank you, Glenda," Cassandra said, reaching for Bradley. He gladly held his arms out for his mommy to take him; he'd endured quite a bit in the last few minutes and appeared dazed. When the alarm went off, he'd been snatched out of his highchair so quickly that it toppled over, and then he'd been passed off like a hot potato. "Boys, tell Mrs. Caruso thank you, then let's head back inside."

After a chorus of "thank yous" and an "I owe you one, but I promise it won't be from *this* batch of cookies," launched over Cassandra's shoulder, they returned home.

As soon as they entered, with great drama Chuck announced it smelled "too rotten terrible" to stay. Cassandra agreed and proclaimed they should all go to the park for an hour. Ken would be due home from work by then, and he could drag out the fans. One of the perks of living in a small town like Wanonishaw: you didn't have to worry about locking up your house every time you left.

"Can I please have a cookie now?" Howie wanted to know.

"Pwease?" Harry added, shoring up their bid.

"We'll pick some up at Blanchard's Bakery on the way to the park," Cassandra said, reaching for her handbag and the keys to the van. "Thank goodness it isn't a day-care day." She hadn't meant to say that out loud, but there it was. She hated to think what little Megan's mom would have to say about this, although she had no doubt her own little blabbermouth, Chuck, would tell Megan the next day anyway. The only child she knew who delighted in tattling more than her son was Megan. And the only person who delighted in repeating a tattle more than Megan was Kerri, Megan's mother. The downside to living in a small town was there was no such thing as anonymity or hidden error.

But the only person who could—and surely would—make her feel even worse about the incident than she already did was her own mother,

Betty. Cassandra sighed just thinking about the overblown fallout sure to come. She loved her mom, but sometimes…

With Chuck's help, Cassandra got the last of the boys seat-belted in. She looked at her wristwatch. Her mom should be home from work by now. She might as well stop by and get it over with before Betty heard it from someone else. Maybe the boys could even talk Grandma Betty into coming to the park with them. Cassandra doubted her mom would join in; she almost never did *anything* spontaneously. Betty rarely invited them over, and she often declined invitations to come to their house for dinner, even with a week's warning. "I'm just too tired," she'd say.

Betty, at sixty, always looked and sounded tired, truth be told. Cassandra knew that her mom's factory job at Nodina Industries sapped all her energy. So many years on the assembly line running one of those punch presses had taken its toll, but her mother had never been educated or trained for anything else. Like Betty said, it paid the bills. After Cassandra's dad's untimely death, Betty had shored herself up and done what she needed to do to keep the family—Cassandra and her two older brothers—afloat. Her job wasn't hard physical labor, but it took concentration to stay safe while working around machinery. Manufacturing was loud and tedious work. Historically, Betty had taken any and all overtime opportunities, grateful for the extra money, which was always in very short supply, especially when the kids were little.

Nonetheless, both Cassandra and Ken kept trying to pry Betty out of her pitiful rut. There wasn't much they could do about her job, but they wanted more for Betty *and* their boys. With Ken's parents in California and her father deceased, Cassandra longed for her sons to enjoy a solid relationship with their only available grandparent, especially since her brothers lived out of state and remained somewhat estranged from the rest of the family. Before Cassandra entered high school, they'd each graduated and moved on, leaving Wanonishaw and hard times behind them.

"Why don't I just spend my time plucking my nose hairs?" she'd said to Ken after each new disappointment with her mom. He would remind Cassandra that she was a kind and caring person, and that was just *one* of the reasons he loved her so much. "Yeah, well, life might be easier if I were a ratfink," she said once. Ken still teased her about the line.

Things had never been smooth between her and Betty, not even when Cassandra was young. "Wishing doesn't make it so, Cassandra," Betty often sternly said when her starry-eyed daughter began a sentence with something hopeful. "We can't have everything we want" and "*Many* things are not meant to be" rounded out Betty's favorite trilogy of doom.

Cassandra once described her mom to her best friend, Margret, as Our Lady of the No Wishing, Wanting, or Being. She'd laughed when she said it, but in reality the girls both knew there was nothing funny about Betty.

The deeper issue was that no matter how hopeful the young Cassandra had tried to remain, after years of hearing those downers, eventually she began to believe them.

Eventually, hope waned.

Eventually, Cassandra stopped believing, especially for her heart's greatest desire to come true.

Even after becoming a mother herself, Cassandra felt that the loss of her dream was her darkest heartache, one she no longer spoke of.

Perhaps that's why the phone call, the one that caused her to accidentally set the oven to broil instead of bake, had been both devastating and so utterly distracting. Before the call, Cassandra knew she could at least count on one annual event to indulge in the illusion of surrounding herself with animals, even fake ones, but now...

Nonetheless, off to Grandma Betty's house they traveled. Even if Cassandra had stopped believing in the fulfillment of her heart's desire, when it came to the rest of life, she didn't stop doing the stoic, right thing. After all, she was her mother's daughter.

Two

By the time Cassandra got Bradley out of his car seat, Chuck was already beating on his grandmother's door, Howie and Harry on his heels. Betty opened the door to discover the little posse standing there, all yammering at once. They spouted something about a fire, an alarm, the park, an accident, and going to get a cookie.

"Boys, stop!" Betty threw up her hands like a traffic cop as Cassandra approached with Bradley on her hip.

"I can't sort out a thing they're telling me," she said to Cassandra.

Cassandra stared at her mother, shored herself up, and pasted on a smile. "May we come in, Mom?"

Betty stuttered. "I-I was just getting ready to put my feet up." Cassandra didn't move. "Okay, for a minute." Betty's curiosity got the best of her. "What's this they're saying about a fire?"

"Mom, I thought we were going to the park!" Chuck said, as his mother shuttled the children into their grandmother's house.

"We are, honey. I thought maybe Grandma would like to go with us."

"Yeah!" Chuck grabbed Betty's hand. "Come on, Grandma!"

"Not today, Chuck."

He headed straight for the little rusty fire engine his grandmother kept on a shelf. He loved looking at that old toy and longed to play with it, to see if those black wheels would roll.

"Remember, don't touch," Cassandra said. "Just look."

"I know!" he said, tossing her his dagger-eyed stare, the one Cassandra had long ago labeled "Betty Incarnate."

Betty *tsk*ed at the tone Chuck used with his mother, but both Cassandra and Chuck ignored her. Cassandra tried to conserve her strength for bigger issues with the kids *and* her mom, although if Chuck acted this way one more time today, he was in big trouble. As for her mother, Cassandra figured the potential to mend those ancient, broken fences was gone. Betty was Betty. Cassandra had long ago determined that the most she could do now was keep the peace at all costs and love her mom the best she could—which she sometimes felt was not very well.

Chuck tilted his head so he could see the fire truck's headlights. It had belonged to Cassandra's father when he was a boy. Cassandra played with it as a child, but since her father's death twenty-five years ago, Betty had made it a shrine of sorts. It was one of the few visible reminders Betty kept displayed that let anyone know she even remembered Gerald.

"Cassandra," Betty said, picking a piece of invisible lint from her sweater, "what is this about a *fire*? I do believe I smelled smoke in your hair when you passed by."

"Oh, it wasn't a fire," Cassandra said, trying to sound casual. "I burned a batch of cookies is all. While I was in the bathroom, the smoke set off the smoke alarm." No sense bringing Howie into it.

"How long were you in the bathroom?"

Cassandra chuckled. "Not that long. The truth is, I accidentally turned on the broiler instead of the oven." She shook her head to let her mother know she understood it was a dumb mistake.

"Cassandra! I don't know how you can laugh at such a thing. You might have burned down the house."

"But I didn't, Mom. Everything is fine. Actually, it turned into a great opportunity for a fire drill. I learned I can corral the boys and get them out in record time."

"Did you have day-care kids today?"

"Thankfully, no…but they all know the drill too. We practice a few times a year. When the alarm goes off, they know they have to listen to me. The boys were good, weren't you, guys?" Striving to stay chipper in front of her mom was exhausting.

"Let's go to the park," Howie said.

"Come on, Mom," Cassandra said. "Why don't you come with? It's a beautiful day. The boys would love it."

"YEAH!" Chuck yelled, already on his way to the door.

"Not today. Maybe another time."

Cassandra planted an obligatory kiss on her mother's cheek before they left. As usual, Betty stood ramrod straight and accepted it.

On the way to the park, Cassandra mentally tallied the things she'd messed up in the past few days. Today, she knocked her toothbrush off the sink and into the toilet, then the cookies. Yesterday, she ran the dishwasher a second time rather than unloading the clean dishes, and right after that she accidentally tossed a pair of Chuck's red socks in with the white clothes. The day before, she broke her favorite coffee mug, the one Chuck painted for her in kindergarten, and backed over one of Howie's favorite toys. She couldn't even remember all the dumb stuff she'd done the week before. Although she knew she wasn't the brightest bulb on the planet, she was usually not *this* dimly lit.

She felt inexplicably edgy and unsettled, like there was something important she was supposed to do but couldn't remember what it was.

Like she was living on the edge of expectancy or trapped in one of those terrible dreams where you try to scream but nothing comes out. The worst part was she couldn't pinpoint *why* she wanted to scream. She imagined Dr. Phil could make short order of her neurosis. She could envision him leaning in and drawling, *"But Cassandrah, don't you understand why you're so neurotic?"* That's when she'd bolt from her chair and take out the cameraman in hopes her mom had not yet tuned in.

But she didn't have time for self-analysis. Betty had taught her well: too much introspection added up to nothing more than self-indulgence. *"Just get on with your life."*

After they picked up the snacks and arrived at the park—which was, thankfully, not too crowded—Chuck took Howie to the slide, and Cassandra situated the youngest two boys in the baby swings. While alternating pushing them, she used her cell phone to call Ken at work. It occurred to her that if he beat them home, the state of the house might freak him out. She'd left the doors and windows open, the house smelled like smoke, and the toppled highchair still lay on the floor.

He laughed through her entire verbal replay. "Bad day, huh? I'll stop and get a new smoke alarm on the way home. I'm guessing you beat ours to death."

"Highly likely. But that's not the worst of it."

"There's more?"

"It might not seem that bad to you, but Margret called today to tell me she can't go to the Collectors Convention with me this Sunday." *Good grief, I'm going to cry.* She stopped talking a moment and swallowed. "This will be the first time in fifteen years we haven't gone. I am so bummed. Oh well. It's not like I *need* another animal collectible."

"Why don't you just go by yourself? You've had a big red X through Sunday, September 14, since you put up the calendar back in January.

You've reminded me countless times that you're going, so go. Besides, the boys and I have big plans. Pizza, beer, football…" He chuckled. "Seriously, go. It's good for you to get away from the kids and air out your brain, Cass. Just go. The weather's supposed to stay awesome."

"Mmm…"

"Did Margret say why she's not going?"

"She was pretty vague. Kinda weird."

"Must be something big. She seems to like going as much as you do," Ken said. "Wait, come to think of it, today after the meeting Leo mentioned something about them going away. I didn't put two and two together about the Collectors Convention, though. Oh well. Just *go*."

"I'll think about it—CHUCK! STOP THAT THIS INSTANT—I gotta hang up, Ken."

Three

Cassandra left the house for the Collectors Convention at 5:25 a.m., twenty-five minutes behind her and Margret's usual annual departure time. They liked to be at the front of the line when the gates opened at seven since the first one hundred people received a coupon for a free coffee. But last night Cassandra had been awakened twice by her youngest. Since Margret wasn't going to be waiting in the driveway to pick her up at five, she didn't bother rustling Ken for daddy duty. She speculated her tardy departure would cause her to miss the coffee cut, which it did.

Bummer, she thought as she moped her way through the gates, couponless. Then she imagined what Margret would say. *"Buy yourself a cup. It's your big day out. Live* a little, Cassie!*"*

Exactly. She made a beeline for the concession stand.

Since childhood, Margret Anderson was as outgoing and secure in herself as Cassandra was shy and lacking in self-esteem. Throughout their decades of friendship, Margret naturally led and Cassandra followed—even when it meant following Margret into some pretty wild places.

"I'll *tell* you," Betty had said to her daughter every time the girls were caught in another of Margret's harebrained schemes, "that girl is going to ruin your reputation or get you killed or both. I wish you'd spend more time with that Sasha Davis. Now there's a girl with her head squarely anchored on her shoulders."

The truth was that no matter how smart Sasha Davis was—and oh how Betty admired and pointed out anyone who was smart, including Cassandra's very own brothers—unbeknown to Betty, Sasha was also the ringleader for much of Cassandra's youthful social heartache. For laughs, Sasha was the champion of dishing out verbal wounds by "playfully" referring to Cassandra as a dumb Polack. When it was just Sasha and Cassandra, things were fine; but when Sasha got in front of the popular girls, she'd do anything to be one of them, including tormenting Cassandra. But Cassandra would never tell Betty that, or Betty would march right to Sasha's door, and then the teasing would *never* end.

But Margret—now *there* was a good friend. No matter how much trouble Margret dragged Cassandra into, nearly every ounce of it had been worth it. Among other things, and in no particular order, Cassandra and Margret were caught smoking in the shed; daring each other to run across the river's thin ice (caught because Cassandra lost her boot when her leg fell through); passing notes to each other in school (numerous times); skipping school; shaving their legs before their moms deemed them old enough (especially Betty); mooning the football players (only Margret actually bared her bottom, but Cassandra was guilty by proximity); reading "scandalous" books Betty found under Cassandra's mattress; and shoplifting a condom, which, even though Margret was the one who impulsively took it, she errantly decided it would be *high-larious,* one of her favorite expressions, to tell the police the girls had to get it for Cassandra's mom. Needless to say, that lie did not go over well with Betty, who grounded her daughter for a month, including from even talking to Margret on the phone.

But Betty didn't find out about everything. When the girls were fifteen, they got into Margret's dad's blackberry brandy and Cassandra had her first experience with alcohol. After diluting it with orange juice, the only thing they could find to make it tasty enough to swallow, they drank two shots each. Margret filled the pint bottle back up with water so no one would be the wiser—until Carl Bambenek, Margret's dad, opened his closet door. There the girls sat, on the closet floor, trying to screw the lid back on the bottle and rehide it, which neither of them could manage to do before spilling half of the contents into his Sunday shoes. Mr. Bambenek, whose deep voice (deeper when he was angry) sometimes scared the life out of Cassandra, said he'd have to throw the shoes away lest Father Stachowitz get a whiff of him and think he'd been drinking before church on Sunday.

"Mr. Bambenek, I'll buy you new shoes if you don' tell my mom bou' this," Cassandra pleaded, speaking with a terrible slur. Even in her pitiful state, she was afraid of repercussions from home. For a pocket of time in her dad's life, he tried to drown his depression with alcohol. If Betty thought her daughter was heading down *that* trail—and Betty was always on the lookout for the sins of the father—Cassandra knew her mother would come down hard on her.

"You *can't* tell Bad Betty," Margret said, throwing her arms around her dad's neck and giving him a big hug. "You just *can't*!" Margret always knew how to work her dad, who adored her but still reprimanded her.

"Margret, I have warned you before: do not speak disrespectfully about Mrs. Kamrowski!" he said sternly.

"Yessir."

Cassandra couldn't afford to replace her own shoes, let alone his; every penny her family gathered went toward keeping them in their home and putting food on the table. Everyone knew money had always been tight for the Kamrowskis. But five years before, when Gerald

Kamrowski committed suicide, their financial struggles tipped toward desperate. In a wrenching act of surrender, Cassandra's mom had even forced her to give away her faithful and loving dog, Toby, saying there was no money to feed or properly care for him.

Bad Betty, more often thought of as Poor Betty by the community after her husband's death, had reason to be grouchy. She'd suffered and endured much in her lifetime. After her thirty-six-year-old husband took his life, the weight of her responsibilities, an intense loneliness, and her constant unanswered questions drained the light from her eyes. *Why, Gerald? Why didn't you talk to me? Why didn't you let me help you? What was so terrible that you had to kill yourself?*

For whatever reason, Cassandra became the target of her mother's frustrations.

No, Betty did not need to know about the blackberry brandy.

After a long consideration, Mr. Bambenek responded to their pleas for his silence. "I'll tell you what, girls," he'd given them plenty of time to squirm, "I won't tell Cassandra's mom—*this* time—if you promise me you'll stay away from liquor."

"Never again!" Margret gushed for them both, a promise she, of course, would break the very next weekend.

Carl turned his furrowed-brow gaze on Cassandra.

"Promise."

Carl Bambenek was true to his word. Cassandra not only lost any fear of him, but she forever more adored him for his protection. Since her brothers weren't around, her dad gone, and her beloved Grandpa Wonky had died only one year after the suicide, Carl Bambenek became a father figure to her. She loved eating meals at Margret's house just to sit with a normal family and listen to what Margret referred to as her dad's "boring stories about his stupid work." All Cassandra knew was that Carl Bambenek displayed more life in his so-called boring stories then her dad *ever* had when he was alive. Even his deep voice, which used to scare her, became a salve to her soul.

Carl Bambenek still held a special place in her heart. He represented everything dear about fatherhood that her own father, who often seemed absent even when he was present, could not. He and his wife, Irene, helped fill in some of Cassandra's normalcy gaps left by Bad Betty.

As Cassandra stood sipping the strong, dark brew, she decided to shake the *whole* day up and head to the left instead of her and Margret's traditional route down the right aisle.

It was odd, setting out to browse by herself. Nobody to follow. Nobody to chat with. Nobody to talk her into crazy purchases. She wasn't as comfortable doing things by herself as Margret was. *How could Margret have forgotten to put this on her calendar and made other plans?* Margret always set the pace and talked with all the vendors, plus anyone else standing within her earshot.

If Margret were here, they'd stop to "Behold!" all the gawd-awful things, as Margret called them as they walked away. They would privately add items to their pool from which they selected the Worst of Show. This seek, find, and vote was one of their favorite pastimes during their annual outing; Margret had an uncanny ability and determination to root out the uglies, the lunacies, and the downright horrifying. Sometimes before voting, they would have to go back for a second look, just to laugh again. If the item was gone, one of them would say something like, "Maybe someone had to buy a white elephant gift for someone she dislikes." What else could explain such ridiculous taste? On their way home, they'd recap and laugh about every single pathetic, bizarre, outrageous, or just plain-ole-dumb find logged in their CC catalog, which stood for Critically Clueless.

Last year, Margret had even captured pictures of the finalists on her cell phone. She randomly sent them to Cassandra when one of them needed a laugh. (Cassandra still hadn't figured out how to use the camera feature on her cell phone.) If Margret were here this year, on their way home, they would stop at Texicalas for their usual postconvention dinner.

What will I do all day without her? No, the whole event just wasn't the same by herself. It seemed less…festive. *I wish you were here, friend.* As soon as she thought it, she heard Betty say, *"Wishing doesn't make it so."*

"Right," Cassandra mumbled out loud.

She stopped dead in her tracks, shook her head, and made herself as tall as she could. *Stop wishing for stuff, Cassie, and just* make *something* happen. It wasn't the first time she'd delivered this pep talk to herself, but suddenly, she felt more determined than ever. Whatever dumbness spell she was under, it was time to shake it. *Make something happen. Make something happen!*

Even though she and Ken didn't need the money from her day-care job, this event was one of the main reasons she stuck with it: so she could splurge on critter knickknacks without feeling guilty. She'd had to fight long and hard to overcome her childhood poverty mentality, and keeping her own small income helped her avoid replaying it. Along with her birthday money from her Aunt Harriet, her wallet was full, the sun was shining, and she was away from the kids. *Make something happen!*

The announcement blaring over the loudspeakers interrupted her personal cheerleading session. "To everyone in the exhibit halls and out on the fairgrounds, may we have your attention, please. Welcome to the sixteenth annual Casual Collectors Convention. For security reasons, please keep an eye on your merchandise, purchases, and personal belongings.

"Have a great day, and remember this year's new motto: swap, shop, and chomp till you *collect*-ively drop!" No matter how many times or how many different voices repeated that lively mixed-message announcement of *beware* and *good cheer,* he or she always signed off with a chuckle.

What a lame motto. How about something like...hmm...maybe...Oh! May the knickknacks be with you!

Lamer.

By nature, Cassandra was a trusting soul, so she rarely paid attention to the security warnings. (Yes, Ken had said something after the news last night about pickpockets working the Collectors Convention, but what were the odds?) Among countless other unchangeable facts of life, this naive trust distressed her mother. Betty, the consummate door and window locker, repeatedly warned her daughter that one day she was going to get ripped off, or worse yet, *"knocked in the head and left unconscious in a back alley for being so trusting."* Whether Cassandra was five or her current thirty-five—or whether her mom referred to her daughter's trust of strangers (most of whom Betty described as shady-looking characters), stray cats, wounded rabbits, rangy dogs, or, back in the day, new boyfriends—Betty seemed to think any and all of them could, and would likely, yes, knock her daughter in the head one day.

Thank goodness for the verbal protection and softer childhood tutoring of her beloved Grandpa Wonky. *"Jeny Kochany! Betty,"* he used to retort to his daughter, after they'd once again suffered through one of her familiar diatribes. Young Cassandra had no idea what *Jeny Kochany!* meant, and she was never brave enough to ask, but she assumed it was her grandfather's native Kashubian Polish cursing. She also believed if it were *truly* cursing, her mother would have had a heart attack on the spot, right after she knocked her own father in the head. Well, Betty wasn't the type to *actually* knock someone in the head, but she would have certainly determined his offense powerful enough to deserve it.

Whatever *Jeny Kochany!* meant, after Grandpa Wonky unloaded it on Betty—which thankfully silenced her, at least for a time—he would then turn to Cassandra. *"Your mother is just worried. Not everyone is as well intentioned, trustworthy, and honest as you are, my Cassie girl. But then, that's what makes you so special now, isn't it?"*

Nobody had ever made her feel as loved as her Grandpa Wonky, although Ken ran a close second.

Cassandra stopped at one of the outdoor booths and fingered a red bandana that reminded her of her grandpa. He'd always had a bandana sticking out of a pocket or shirt sleeve. After he was confined to a wheelchair, he kept several practical items either attached to him or tucked alongside him, like a hair comb, a pocketknife, and a sweater. When she was younger, she often watched her Grandpa Wonky and tried to imagine what life would be like if she couldn't walk. When Chuck was born, she cried her eyes out imagining her long-deceased grandpa holding him on his lap, wheeling him around. He was such a gentle man.

Before Cassandra knew it, she'd walked in a memory-laden daze clear to the end of one of the rows, without seeing a thing. Odd how memories could be such transporters. Maybe she wouldn't buy anything today; maybe she'd just walk, remember, think, and, like Ken had suggested, air out her brain. After all, she'd often promised herself, *"No more critter knickknacks!"* This never-kept promise usually came over her during marathon bouts of dusting. But there wasn't a creature alive that didn't nab her heart. She felt pretty sure she owned at least one replica of every animal that set foot on Noah's ark. No real ones, even though she loved animals, but since Toby...well, that was more history.

She blinked. A beam of light came out of nowhere, nearly blinding her, distracting her from her sad reverie and the dream of which she no longer spoke. The light's shimmering brightness even followed her for several footsteps, stopping her in her tracks. *How can* that *be?* After a quick study, she realized that from the other side of the table, another shopper had picked up a snowglobe, held it to the light, and swiveled it to activate the snow, slowly tilting it and causing the beam of light refracting through the orb to follow her. Cassandra continued squinting until the admirer set the globe down and released her—at least momentarily—from its alluring magnetism.

Still, she couldn't walk away. She could only draw nearer the snowglobe that she could now see contained tiny figurines of a black-and-white Border collie, a lanky gray greyhound, and a small reddish mutt, all surrounding a little girl with hair the very color of her own.

Cassandra stood staring at it, hearing her grandpa's words ring in her head. *"I'll tell you what, Betty,"* he used to say, as he winked at Cassandra, *"my Cassie girl,"* which always came out as one endearing word, *"is going to one day become the best veterinarian in the whole state of Minnesota. You mark my words!"* He'd said it often enough that everyone believed it, *especially* his Cassie girl. *"Her natural instincts and trusting nature is* exactly *why all her critters trust* her *the moment they meet her. They sense her kind heart, same as her patients will one day, when their owners bring them to her office."*

But this was now. Clarence Dzwonkowski—dubbed Wonk by a few of the locals who didn't know the *w* in the Polish immigrants' names was pronounced as a *v*—was long gone from this earth. To Cassandra's great grief, she still struggled with the fact that neither his prediction nor her dream, the very deepest desire of her heart, would come true: she would never be a veterinarian. In fact, after Toby's death, coupled with her failed goal, she promised herself she would never again even accept the privilege and honor of caring for one of God's critters. She didn't deserve to. Perhaps that's why the figures in the snowglobe—the way the dogs appeared drawn to the girl, especially that little mutt that looked so much like Toby—tugged at her heart.

When another shopper picked up the globe, again the light zinged Cassandra's eye, causing her a momentary blinding and panicky thought: what if the shopper snapped it out from under her?

"I'm sorry." She spoke in a strangely crisp voice, one unfamiliar to her, as she reached toward the woman and held out her hand, "I was about to buy that."

"I was just *looking*," the woman mumbled as she frowned, passed the snowglobe to Cassandra, and moved on.

So sudden and desperate was Cassandra's need to own the mesmerizing snowglobe that without even looking at the price tag, she decided to buy it. She asked the vendor how much, and the man said that since he'd never seen one quite like it before, he'd have to charge her forty bucks. She withdrew two twenties from her wallet, and that was that. Margret would have elbowed her to remind her to barter him down.

The combination antique and junk dealers located in the outdoor area (where more junk than valuables was sold) were known for their customary bargaining. The "finer" goods of the more "respectable" dealers sold inside the arena, swine barn, or poultry shed, where they were protected from the elements. Even so, the buildings were built in a way and the traffic was such that dirt prevailed, no matter *what* was on display. Years of accumulated grime continued to fall from the rafters like a fine rain. Between endless bouts of dusting their china and other certifiable antiques, the elite inside exhibitors pointed their noses in the air, rearranged their little settings, and held their prices firm. Every year Cassandra snickered to herself how the "respectable" dealers secured the coveted and prominent locations where otherwise, during the county fair, the pigs pooped, the horses pooped, and the chickens with blinking eyelids and cocked heads pooped while gawking at passersby. She ought to know: she'd spent as much time studying the crazed-looking chickens at the fair as the boys would allow before tearing her away to buy them cotton candy, corn dogs, or another ride on the merry-go-round—or worse yet, the Tilt-A-Whirl, which rhymed with hurl, which is what that thing made her want to do.

Today she could keep her own pace and do what *she* wanted. Even though Margret wasn't here, she smiled, glad Ken had insisted she come by herself. *It is a great day, and this snowglobe is amazing,* she thought, smiling back at the girl in the globe, who was smiling at her. *What a find! Talk about making something happen!*

After she put her wallet away, she handed the snowglobe to the dealer and turned to survey the energetic collectors crowd, which sometimes appeared only slightly less crazed than the chickens. She thought about all the stuff people bought, sometimes having no idea what it was for or where they'd put it when they got home. So many strangers, milling around with shopping bags of every type and size… She turned to watch the outdoor vendor finish wrapping her snowglobe in several layers of newspaper and then tape bubble pack around the growing mass. She had to give him this: he was careful, albeit slower than a mudslide.

"These vintage domes are sure heavier than today's plastic ones." He added yet another sheet of bubble pack, which he methodically taped in three places. "It's been a good long while since a Bakelite base came my way. Nearly every inside dealer who saw this one tried to buy it before the grounds opened this morning, so rest assured you're getting your money's worth." He sounded genuinely sad to let it go. "I heard tell they used to make the snow out of bone fragments in some of these real oldies," he said, inspecting the package. Then he added yet one more layer of bubble pack.

After he finally handed it over, Cassandra gingerly situated it in the top of her shopping bag. She felt relieved to have the globe in her possession, yet slightly unnerved by the comment about bone chips.

Whose bones, she wondered.

And why, even though the forty bucks was no skin off *anyone's* nose, did she still feel guilty for having spent so much on one globe?

Guilt. My personal MO. All hail Our Lady of the No Wishing, Wanting, Being—or Having. Nice job, Mom.

Four

Fifteen minutes before noon, Cassandra experienced a sudden wave of exhaustion. Her bouts of wakefulness with Bradley, coupled with her early morning start and her ongoing emotional roller coaster, had taken their toll.

Food. That's what she needed to keep her from sliding further down the slippery slope into negativity. She wanted to be *happy* about her snowglobe, not feel guilty about it. *Why is there always such a tug?* Cassandra's favorite lunch, "Dog, chips, can of pop, $4—even change appreciated," was located across the entire fairgrounds.

Her right arm felt like it was ready to break off. She wondered, seriously wondered, if she might lose a digit or two from the weight of the monster shopping bag dangling from the crook of her now-blue fingertips. She'd found a little something for each of the boys, plus a unique old pocketknife for Ken. With each new addition to her bag, she'd made sure the fragile and expensive snowglobe remained on top.

Now she *really* longed for Margret's presence. Eating alone wouldn't be fun. Cassandra felt a flash of anger at her friend, or maybe it was just hurt feelings. It was hard to tell since the emotions sometimes posed as each other. But the worst part was that being angry at Margret made her feel guilty too! *Get over yourself!*

She hiked the getting-heavier-by-the-minute shopping bag up onto her shoulder and rearranged her purse. *Wait till Mom spies my new critter finds. She'll probably plan a shopping intervention that lands me on Dr.*

Phil. Betty kept her house so clean and clutter free that her children referred to the home they grew up in as Sterileland.

Cassandra wadded four bucks in her left hand, which she also used to plunk her wallet back into her purse. Grandpa Wonky had been fond of saying how much he loved his Lefty. Next came the Big Maneuver: pay for the food, secure both the shopping bag and her purse—why hadn't she thought to wear her fanny pack?—all while carrying the hot dog, chips, and a can of pop without initiating a catastrophe or rendering herself vulnerable to becoming the next victim in the police blotter. She could hear that deafening "Shopper Beware!" announcement again. What was supposed to be a relaxing getaway for this home-day-care provider and busy mother of four had instead morphed into a roller coaster of tired, happy, memory-jarring, and guilt-*guilt*-GUILTY emotions.

Thankfully, just when she arrived at one of the jam-packed outdoor banquet tables, someone cleared out. With a great sigh of relief, she sat down, then plopped her handbag on her lap and secured her shopping bag on the ground between her feet. As soon as she lifted the hot dog to her mouth, something thwacked her so hard on the back of the head that the force nearly knocked her off the bench.

A loud, radical word escaped her lips as she instantly assumed the worst. For all these years, her mother really *had* seen it coming. She'd finally been knocked in the head!

The next thing Cassandra knew, she'd likely be standing in heaven (if she could still enter after using that word) trying to explain to Jesus why she'd been so dumb as to not have believed Betty Kamrowski, who was not only her mother, but the Queen Mother of *all* doom and gloom.

Then again, Cassandra thought, wasn't her very own dumbness the reason she'd never become a veterinarian?

In a sudden flurry of pent-up emotional frustration and anger, Cassandra secured a death grip on the strap of her handbag, stood, whirled on her heels, and said, "Get away from me!"

Rather than confronting a thief about to do her in, she instead found herself yelling straight into a massive designer bag suspended on the back of the stunned woman spinning to face her. As the woman turned, her colossal satchel once again accidentally thwacked Cassandra, this time in the face, causing Cassandra to reel back, plop down, and throw a hand over her nose, which instantly started bleeding.

"Oh! Oh! I am so *sorry*!" The prominent-looking woman—the same woman from whom Cassandra had so rudely snatched the snow-globe—glanced over her shoulder to make sure she wasn't taking any-one *else* out with her twirl. She removed the giant Gucci tote bag from her shoulder and set it on the ground, then knelt in front of Cassandra and stared at the blood dripping between her fingers. "Goodness me! I am *so* sorry! What can I get you? Ice?" Cassandra nodded. "Can some-one bring us some ice, please, and some napkins?

"Here," she said, reaching into her blazer pocket and extracting a neatly folded cotton handkerchief with purple and white lace around the edge. "Use this."

Cassandra's eyes darted from the out-held hanky to the woman's face as a dose of quadruple guilt heated her cheeks. She pinched her nose and spoke through her fingers, blood dripping across her lips down onto her T-shirt as she formed the words. "Thank you, but I'll wait for some paper napkins. I'm afraid I've already been rude enough to you today." *Great. First guilt, now true confessions.*

"I *insist*!" The woman flipped open the hanky and gently pushed it under Cassandra's fingers until she took hold of it. Cassandra winced. "Oh, I'm sorry! Did I hurt you...*again?*"

"*No!*" Cassandra realized her nasal twang sounded angry, so she lowered her voice. "I just hate to ruin your good hanky. I mean it has *lace* on it!" With her young sons, Cassandra couldn't imagine even owning a hanky like that, let alone removing it from a hidden corner in the back of her underwear drawer and offering it to a bleeding stranger who'd now yelled at her—twice.

A tall, striking olive-skinned man maneuvered his way through the crowd with a zip-top bag filled with ice chips. He also carried a bottle of water. Someone else handed her a wad of paper napkins. "Here you go," he said, giving the bag and bottle to the woman, who administered the first aid and introduced herself to Cassandra as Josie. Cassandra watched as Josie held the man's deep brown eyes with hers for a moment, then thanked him. She withdrew the delicate blood-soaked hanky from her nose to replace it with the ice bag, then realized she had no idea what to do with the woman's saturated mess. Her every move seemed to make matters more humiliating. So many more paper napkins were now coming their way that Josie peeled off a couple and held them out as a receptacle. People were pressing in and staring.

"Thank you!" Josie yelled to all the strangers striving to help. "We have *enough* napkins now!"

Leaning toward Cassandra to hand her a two-inch-thick stack of the paper goods, she quietly said, "Seems we've become the center of attention here."

Cassandra moved the ice bag toward the bridge of her throbbing nose, tucked several of the napkins up under it near her nostrils, then pressed it tight to help stop the bleeding. "I am *so* sorry," she said, tilting her head back in hopes of at least slowing the flow. She sounded so nasal to herself, she wondered if she could even be understood. For a moment, her eyes locked with those of the extremely handsome man who'd brought the ice and water. She felt herself blush; she must look quite the sight. Then she looked back at Josie to continue her apology and explanation. "I thought you were..." She made a *tsk*ing sound, closed her eyes, rolled her head back and forth, and let her voice trail off. What was the use? She'd have to explain her entire life to get to the point. "Never mind. Some stories are just too long."

"I'm the one who's sorry," Josie said. "I was so worried about somebody rifling my bag that I twisted the handles together and slung it over my shoulder. I didn't look to see if anyone was behind me. Is it letting up?"

Cassandra pulled the bloody wad of napkins away from her nose, peeked at it from over the bag of ice, refolded it, dabbed, dabbed again, refolded it again, and held it to her nose. "I think so."

"Ladies, do you need more ice?" asked the man who'd supplied the first bag.

"I think I'm going to live." Cassandra felt herself blush again. He had the most penetrating and yet reassuring brown eyes. "I'll let you both get back to your..." she stopped and chuckled, "shopping and chomping, if I haven't ruined your appetites and worn you out by now."

"I'll be on my way, then," he said, before disappearing into the crowd.

Cassandra felt an inexplicable gut-wrenching sadness to see the calming comfort of his brown eyes go, until she realized they were the exact same color as her beloved Toby's.

❧

June 1979

It was the faintest of whimpers, one most people would never have noticed. But Cassie's six-year-old ears and heart were created to not only hear a critter's plea for help, but to pursue it. She drew a deep breath, held it in, and stood still as a statue on the path. Listening.

There it was again, a little to her left!

Slowly, she exhaled while taking a couple of steps in that direction, then she stopped and inhaled again, every cell of her body readied to accomplish one mission: rescue. She held her breath for as long as she could, but aside from a few rowdy birds, the woods an eighth of a mile behind her house were hushed. She emitted a very controlled and silent exhale, this time through the circle she made with her lips. She leaned slightly forward to force all the air from her lungs. Then, a deep inhale. During the last year, she'd learned she could hold her breath longer when breathing through her lips. Many a night she'd drifted to sleep while practicing for such an opportunity as this.

Just when she thought her lungs might burst, she heard the whimper again. It was weaker this time, more like a muffled whine. Yes, she was heading in the right direction. She took a few more careful steps. Each time she repeated this cycle, she had to wait a little longer to hear the sound again. Whatever it was—it sounded like a dog, although she couldn't be sure— was frightened by her presence yet unable to conceal its pain. She needed to gain its trust, approach with caution. After all, there'd been that time with the raccoon. "Some critters can't help but to act mean, my Cassie girl. It's not their fault." Inhale, hold, listen, exhale, step, step...

Then she spotted it! Curled up under the tree. A small coyote? Cassie stared into its eyes, but only for a moment. Grandpa Wonky had taught her that maintaining eye contact with critters often felt threatening to them and could therefore prove to be dangerous.

Her brief glance at its face revealed it was not a coyote. Coyotes have yellow eyes. This fellow's eyes offered deep brown comforting pools of sincerity. They were such wonderful eyes that Cassie's heart throttled in her chest, her cheeks blossomed, and her own eyes welled with tears. She quickly blinked them back so as not to lose her concentration and frighten the dog, possibly causing him more distress. She studied his abdomen, took note of his rapid breaths. The poor thing was scared out of its wits, obviously unable to flee. Guardedly, she let herself sink down Indian style on her crossed legs. From that position, she could spring back up and run, should she need to.

"You're gonna be fine, boy," she said quietly, in her most adult and soothing tone of voice. "Just fine," she said, letting her eyes run over his body, looking for the source of his pain. "You must be so lonesome out here by yourself. But it's okay now. I'm here."

She started humming a quiet tune she'd composed, one that soothed her when her dad got into the drink. The pooch's breathing seemed to slow a little—a good sign—so she kept humming. For both of them, she hummed. He didn't look all that old; just a little gray hair around his dark muzzle. He was rolled into such a tight ball that his bushy tail, matted with cockleburs, curled all the way around his chin. His legs were tucked under him. He looked sort of like her neighbor's German shepherd, but not really. "Some kind of mutt," she heard her Grandpa say in her head. Mutts were her favorite too.

She stopped humming for a moment, exhaled, and leaned slightly toward him, keeping her eyes diverted. As if she'd known his name all along, she said, "You're going to feel better in no time, Toby. You'll see." He emitted a short, low, fainthearted growl. She did not allow herself to jerk back, which might startle him into protective aggression; she simply began humming again, intermittently reassuring him with her gentle words. "You're such a handsome guy, Toby. And so brave. I promise to help you get well. You just have to let me—believe in me. You're okay. We're okay, Toby. We are o-kay." More humming.

Carefully, Cassie set her hand down in front of his nose, palm resting on the ground. Toby turned his head away and stared into the woods. Cassie watched his chest rise and fall. He was much calmer than when she first arrived. She synchronized her breathing with his. Together they waited, staring through the trees as if expecting an angel to appear from among the millions of branches.

At the exact same time, an inexplicable prompting caused them to turn their eyes toward each other. Toby held Cassie's gaze for a moment. Then he cocked his head, looked down at her hand, stretched his neck, sniffed, and began to lick her knuckles. In turn, as lightly as a feather might rock through the calm fall air, she stroked the top of his head with the fingertips of her free hand—each acting as if the angel had indeed appeared, right in front of their eyes.

What else was there to do but reach out and touch it?

Five

The Sunday morning of the Collectors Convention, Margret and Leonard Anderson were attending church. They'd uttered "Lord, hear our prayer" over and over during the service. Through their years of trying to conceive a child, and when the miracle came true, and after Margret miscarried, they'd often uttered those words together in the confines of their home.

After Margret graduated with a degree in business communications, she married Leonard, the college quarterback who was as dreamy and nice as they come. Happily—and as fate would have it (and through Margret's irresistible influence with her daddy)—Leonard, known by all as Leo, accepted a handsome job offer to work for Bambenek Enterprises, the premiere advertising agency in the Midwest.

"For the good of *all* of us," Margret told both Leo and her dad, "and in order to keep my own identity," she told Cassandra, "I will not work in the family business." She accepted a job as an assistant to the vice president at a bank in a neighboring town. "Let's face it," she told Cassandra, "I'm a secretary, but my business card looks great!"

With financial assistance from the wealthy Bambeneks, the newly-weds bought a big house in Wanonishaw, right on the parade route. And in Wanonishaw it didn't get more prestigious than that. Although Cassandra told Margret she was The Woman With Everything, she was never jealous. She was simply happy to have her around and to call her friend.

But now, from Margret's point of view, Cassandra ended up being the one with everything that truly mattered: fertility and a house full of kids. After years of trying, hope, prayers, heartbreaking disappointments, more waiting, and horrendous physical duress, Margret and Leo found themselves unable to bear children. Son after healthy son that Cassandra delivered, baby shower after baby shower that Margret threw for her, the more difficult it became for her to fight a growing chasm of jealously and despair about her own state of barrenness. But if Margret was to continue to be a part of her best friend's life, she needed to spend time with Cassandra's sons, whom she adored, hearing about Cassandra's sons…and, sadly, occasionally coveting them. Sometimes when Auntie Magpie—a tag Ken jokingly used one day when Margret was chatting it up with then-two-year-old Chuck—would baby-sit, it felt difficult to surrender them when Mommy came home. To hold a child, to stick her nose into the whisper-soft hair near the top of a baby's ear, brought out such a fierce longing that at times Margret feared it might consume her. Thankfully, the two women were close enough that they could discuss anything, including this chasm.

Until now.

Margret hadn't told Cassandra the real reason she couldn't go to the Collectors Convention with her today, which was that she and Leo would be traveling to the Mayo Clinic in Rochester, again, to consult with their third fertility expert, bright and early on Monday morning. If all signals were go, they would prepare for another round of in vitro fertilization procedures—something they'd decided to keep to themselves.

Previously, Cassandra had been there to help support Margret through her disappointments, but this time she chose not to tell her best buddy about their plan. The two of them had clung to each other and cried themselves empty after Margret's miscarriage. But it felt different now. If this round of medical science didn't produce a child, Margret didn't think she could bear the weight of Cassandra's sympathy too.

As odd and small-minded as it seemed, Margret found herself wondering what a genteel mother of four boys could *really* understand about the depth of her terrible void, longing, and waning loss of hope, especially when she knew very well that Cassandra would, as usual, spend much of their time at the Collectors Convention talking about her brood, admitting how good it felt to be away from them for a day.

During fits of anger and frustration, Margret would rebel against the church's ritualistic prayer response, "Lord, hear our prayer." She asked Leo, "Do you think God doesn't listen if we don't beg Him to listen? And if He does hear us after we pray, plead, and then *beg*, why doesn't He *answer*?"

"I think God is God," Leo said. That's what Leo always said when he didn't know how else to respond to questions about holy things for which he had no answers. That's also what he said because that's what he said *he* had to rely on: God being God. What else did they have?

"Seriously, Leo," Margret said, bringing up the listening topic again after church as they drove along the great river road on their way to Mayo. They'd decided to take Highway 61 rather than Interstate 90 since the scenery was always so relaxing along the river. Well, they relaxed as best as they could, considering they were likely on their way to engage in a last-ditch attempt to bring a child into their lives. After the miscarriage and dozens of conversations, they'd also decided adoption was not for them. "*Seriously.* Do you think God listens to us if we don't ask Him to? And don't tell me 'God is God,' Leo. I already know that. I just wish I knew *God* better so I could understand why He's put us through all this."

Leo, who never tired of studying the Mighty Mississip, as he called it, slowed the car and pulled off the road into one of the lookout spots they were about to pass by. He maneuvered the vehicle until they faced the river, then shut off the engine. They had plenty of time to get to their destination and check in at the hotel; their appointment wasn't until early the next morning. Today was supposed to be about nothing but relaxing and enjoying the beautiful fall weather and a few early colors. They'd even talked about getting takeout and picnicking along the way. Now they sat, the big question once again between them.

He patted her leg, which was Margret's signal to unbuckle her seat belt and scoot over beside him, a ritual they'd started in their college days. She slid across and rested her head on his familiar shoulder. For quite a while, they sat in silence watching the brown waters flow by, searching the sky for eagles, for which this stretch of highway was famous. One swooped down, scooped something out of the river, and disappeared into a shoreline stand of trees.

"Margret," his voice was low and almost hoarse, as though he were about to cry, "I wish I could be the husband you need right now. I wish I could say to you, 'Margret, without a doubt, God is always listening. He hears our prayers and will eventually, absolutely answer them the way we want. With the help of the gifts God's given the doctors and the great minds He's grown in medical scientists, we will have our baby!' But I can't tell you that because I don't have a *clue* what God is thinking, or doing, or not. As much as I want to give you a child," he said, his tears spilling over his lower lashes, "I cannot make it happen on my own. I am so sorry…"

Margret sniffled, then her slender body broke down in silent sobs. This trial had been so exhausting, scary, and long. It seemed like they were always hanging on a ledge, waiting for *something*, or *some* kind of result. He wrapped his arm around her as together they wept, the powerful waters of the Mighty Mississip seemingly drawing their tears unto itself, as if to carry them downriver.

Six

"What is it, hon?" Ken asked, gently pushing his weeping wife away from him far enough to look her in the eyes. That's when he saw her shiners. "HON!"

"I am so *sorry*!" All she could do was sob. "I've held it together all the way home from the Collectors Convention, but now…" Her tears flowed. As soon as she started crying, it set off the little guys, Howie crying the loudest.

"Were you in a wreck?" Ken asked.

"No. Worse."

"Something worse than a car wreck?" His voice was barely audible.

"Yes." She sobbed a moment longer, then sniffed, grabbed a paper napkin off the table, and gingerly dabbed at her schnoz, as Grandpa Wonky used to call it. Next she wiped Harry's schnoz, then she reached for another napkin to tend to Howie, who needed a big comforting hug too.

Ken, whose heart raced with fear that his wife had been violated in some unspeakable way, wiped Bradley's little face with the bottom of his sweatshirt. Finally, they all settled down.

"Let me turn off the pan of hot water on the stove, then let's start over." When Cassandra had surprised him with her early arrival home, he'd been about to make macaroni and cheese for his and the boys' dinner. Now he'd need to get out another box. Or maybe they'd just order pizza. Or go to the police station, or… But first, he had to find out what happened. "Spill it," he said to her after he plunked Bradley into his highchair and sent Harry and Howie to Chuck's room to play until dinner was ready.

She told him every detail of her day, including the part about the snowglobe's radiating light in her eye and its magnetic tug on her heart. The little girl's hair color, her smile, the way the dogs surrounded her, the fact she hadn't even bartered price... "I spent a wad on this one, Ken."

"Is *that* supposed to be the bad part? Another snowglobe? So what? Honey, what happened to your *face*?"

Although she omitted the part about the ice-bag man's eyes reminding her of Toby, she told him the whole story until she came to the part where he walked away; then she began to tremble. "The seat next to me had opened up, so Josie sat down with me. She said she hoped my nose stopped bleeding soon; she had a rental car to return and a plane to catch, but she didn't want to leave me until she knew I was okay. She reached into her blazer pocket and pulled out a business card. She told me to *please* let her know if I ended up with doctor bills. I refused to go to the first-aid station at the fairgrounds since it was all embarrassing enough. She thought I should get my nose checked, though."

Ken waited for Cassandra to continue. She seemed to need to shore herself up for whatever was coming next.

"I went to put her card in my wallet. My purse was right there in my lap," she said, pointing to her lap to demonstrate. "I tore my handbag *apart*, Ken! No wallet. I looked through my shopping bag, under the table, all over the ground. I thought my head was going to explode, it was throbbing so badly. I checked back near the food line, the lost and found...

"Oh, Ken...somebody nabbed my wallet! I bet they got it right out of my bag the moment after I paid for my lunch. What is *wrong* with me?" She broke down crying again. He wrapped her in his arms and assured Howie, who'd wandered back in and puckered back up, that Mommy was okay; she was just a little upset.

"Thank God that's *all* that happened, Cassie. Between your face and your tears, I was afraid… I dreamed up all kinds of terrible things that might have happened to you. Did you notify the police?"

"That's *not* all that happened, Ken—or is going to." He raised his brows. "After all my frantic running around and coming up empty-handed, my nose started to bleed again, so I went back to the food area, grabbed a handful of napkins, and flagged down a security guard. He paged the police for me. And wouldn't you know…a reporter and a cameraman came rushing over with them! Oh, *Ken*." She now sounded utterly defeated. "The reporter interviewed me and said I'd likely air on the six o'clock news tonight." She nearly wailed the last part. "I just *know* my *mom* will see it!"

"You sound more upset about that than having your wallet ripped off."

"You know very well, Kenneth Higgins, that Bad Betty can deliver a fate worse than pickpockets!"

Indeed, Cassandra's interview appeared as the lead story on the six o'clock news. *"Another victim at the Collectors Convention."* There she stood with a microphone in her face, her eyes already turning black, a crust of dried blood under her nose.

Could I get more adorable? she thought.

Within thirty seconds after the segment concluded, the phone rang. It was Betty. "Haven't I been warning you your whole entire life? Haven't I?"

"Yes, Mom."

After Cassandra hung up and repeated the conversation to Ken, in an attempt to lighten her mood, he said he hoped Betty started warning her they'd one day win the lottery.

"Funny, Ken. Notice how I'm not laughing. But, you know," she said, rubbing the back of her head, "maybe she should."

Naomi knelt down in front of her two-year-old son, Ben. She unbuttoned his sweater and handed it to Cassandra, who was balancing Bradley on her hip and wearing Harry on her right leg like a koala clinging to a eucalyptus tree. Cassandra and Ken had often joked about how they were sure their third son, Harry, was part monkey, although whose family tree actually spawned the monkey was never agreed upon.

"I still can't believe it was *you* on the six o'clock news last night!" Naomi said. "You poor thing. I mean…" She stopped talking long enough to spit-wipe a dried booger off Ben's left cheek. "After getting mugged and robbed, I'm surprised you're up for watching your own kids today, let alone anyone else's."

"I wasn't mugged, Naomi." Naomi was famous for dramatizing. "That's not what the news said, is it?"

"Benjamin! Play *nice* with Howie." Howie, the child most like Cassandra, was shy, gentle, and no match for the aggressive Ben, who had taken to pinching.

"Naomi, they didn't report I was mugged as well as robbed, did they?"

"I guess not. I guess I just assumed, what with your black eyes.

When I phoned you last night about sitting, you didn't say you weren't mugged."

"Guilty by stupidity *and* the sin of omission," Cassandra said. She sighed and set Bradley down, who crawled toward the floor lamp, from which she quickly diverted his attention. Exhausted from a second nearly sleepless night and suffering from the badgering her head had taken, her every move hurt.

"Stupidity?" asked Naomi, looking at her wristwatch, then reaching for the doorknob. She was always running late to work.

"It's all too long a story. I'll save it for another time."

"I'll be praying that you aren't a victim of identity theft too. You know," Naomi said, stopping and turning in the doorway, hand on the doorknob, "now that some unsavory character has your address, maybe you should start locking this door."

"Thanks," Cassandra said as she shut the door behind her. *Give me a few* more *things to worry about, why doncha.*

Maybe feeling lately like I wanted to scream was a premonition. Maybe I should have screamed, just because! Well, one thing is for certain, I surely did "make something happen!" At least the credit-card people were easy to deal with, even though changing the numbers on all our auto-billing will be a pain-o-la.

"Gads! Did I also have a blank check in my wallet?" she asked the room full of preschoolers, none of whom paid any attention to her. She better call the bank too. As she was heading for the phone, the doorbell rang and the door opened. A zing ran through her as she whirled, the image of an unsavory, identity-stealing character still lingering in her head. But it was just Kerri, quickly dropping off four-year-old Megan, the group tattletale, who'd be the only girl among four boys today. When Chuck was home from first grade and Robbie, her part-timer, showed up, it was boys, six to one. Nonetheless, Megan still tried to boss around *all* the boys, and much to Cassandra's dismay, the little girl often succeeded, even when Cassandra herself could not get them under control.

Cassandra sighed and closed the door behind Kerri.

Then she locked it.

Seven

Betty Kamrowski had to agree with Burt the butcher: her daughter *did* look terrible on the television the night before.

"Does she look that bad in person?" he wanted to know. "I hear TV adds ten pounds to you, but I didn't know it could make a whole face look distorted like that."

"I haven't seen her yet." Betty snorted as her nose lifted slightly higher in the air. "And I tell you true, Burt, I had to learn about the incident the same way you did. I nearly fainted in my lounge chair when I realized that horrid-looking face belonged to one of my own flesh and blood, who did *not* find it necessary to call her own mother to tell her about her terrible ordeal. But then, I'm not surprised."

"About the fact she didn't call you, or that the theft happened?" he asked from behind the counter, weighing and cutting her a two-and-a-half-pound pork roast from the six-pound roll. As much as he liked Betty, he was too busy today to get lost in one of her mini-lectures about selling a poor widow more than she needed, and *certainly* more than she could afford, the word *certainly* always firing through her rounded lips like a musket ball. When she protruded her lips like that, they kind of reminded Burt of Donald Trump, something he would *certainly* keep to himself, even though he thought she wore the pouty look quite well.

"Both. That child of mine has always been careless. I mean, how do you end up getting knocked in the back *and* the front of your head, then be surprised when you discover your wallet has disappeared?"

"I was glad to hear on the noon news today that they caught that band of bandits," he said, ripping off a long piece of tape to seal the butcher paper he'd wrapped around her roast. Throughout his forty-four years in the butchering business, Burt had honed this procedure to a fine art. It was like watching the exacting skills of an origami expert create something wonderful out of a hunk of meat, a roll of paper, and freezer tape or string. Everybody talked about it

"Yes, I heard that on my way over here from work. I called Cassandra on my cell phone, but she said they didn't find her wallet and they didn't hold out much hope they would. I'm guessing the woman who *accidentally,*" a word around which Betty drew air quotes, "rammed her bag into Cassandra—when she was coming *and* going—was working with the thieves. I bet the guy who brought the ice was one of them too."

"I don't know what you're talking about. I thought she was mugged."

"That's what everyone thinks. Everyone but Cassandra, that is." Everyone knew that Betty believed that when she believed something, so did—or at least so should—everyone else. "I hope the police asked her for descriptions of those two who supposedly helped her. She insisted on the phone that they were innocent, but that girl is *so* naive. She even talked about the man's kind eyes, which he was probably using to distract her while the head-banging woman lifted her wallet. I don't know why they didn't report on those two in the newscast last night." Burt handed her the roast, which she immediately pumped up and down in her upturned palm a few times, as if considering its weight. "And come to think about it, Cassandra said that woman was not only from out of town, but out of the state. What more proof does she *need*?"

"How'd she know that?"

"She gave Cassandra a business card and told her to call her if she needed any medical attention. Said she'd cover any costs Cassandra might incur. Phooey! Everyone knows anybody can get a business card made with anything on it, even if they make it all up. Why, I could go right down to the printer today and have five hundred cards made up saying I'm a cowgirl from Oklahoma, and nobody would question it. The printer would just take my money, print up the cards, and off I'd go."

Burt cocked his head, stared at Betty a moment, then broke out in a major smile. "Cowgirl from Oklahoma, huh? *I* might question it," he said with a wink. "Although I bet you'd make a darn pretty cowgirl."

Betty blushed. He wasn't flirting with her, was he?

"You know very *well* what I mean, Burt Burt."

Every time Burt heard someone refer to him by his first and last name, he winced. He wondered what on earth his parents had been thinking, sticking him with a name like that. No matter how often they'd tried to explain about the distinguished first name passed down through generations of his mother's family tree and the unfortunate coincidence of her falling in love with someone with that same surname, he would never understand how they could do such a thing to a kid. But since he opened the butcher shop decades ago, it was a rare occasion when someone referred to him by his full name, since around Wanonishaw, Burt was just Burt the butcher, cleaver-wielding origami expert. For that, he was grateful.

"Maybe you should see the doctor tomorrow about your nose, hon," Ken said. "The swelling seems worse instead of better." He lay propped up in bed, watching Cassandra gingerly smooth night cream on her face from a jar she kept in a drawer in the nightstand.

"If my schnoz is broken, it's broken. They wouldn't do anything about it anyway."

"You don't care if people think I'm married to Rocketta Balboa?"

"Very funny." She crawled into bed. "I wish *I* could feel funnier about all of this."

Ken's humor was the thing that had most attracted her to him. They met on a blind date, the fourteenth blind date Margret set her up on. By the time the girls were twenty-five, the already-married Margret was determined to help Cassandra escape her childhood home. She simply had to find a rainbow to override the dark cloud Betty Kamrowski held over her daughter's head, and Ken was not only a rainbow, he was a pot of gold to boot.

"You're too hard on yourself, Cassie. Always have been. Professional pickpockets are good at what they do. It could have happened to anyone, and in fact *did* happen to lots of someones during the event. I'm just glad they caught them."

"It's still so unnerving, though," she said, snuggling up to his side. "I feel so...violated. And careless for leaving my handbag open after I paid for my lunch."

"You called everyone today on the identity-theft list we drew up last night, right?"

"To the best of my knowledge. I called the bank too. I can't remember if I had a blank check in my wallet. I don't think I did, but you know me."

"Yes, beautiful, I know you," he said, his voice lowering a notch as he reached for her. "Things are what they are, hon. Forgive yourself, and let's move on to something more interesting. Like about how intimately I know you."

Forgive myself? Now that, dear husband of mine, is always *the issue for me, isn't it?*

After a few long, careful kisses, during which he tried to avoid bumping her nose, Cassandra said, "I wonder if Josie's wallet disappeared too?" After all, Josie had spent so much time pampering her that she sure hadn't been paying attention to her giant bag.

"Josie?" He backed his head away from hers enough to bring her face into focus. One thing he knew for sure, no sense pursuing anything while she was distracted.

"Josie…I can't remember her last name. You know…the woman whose bag accidentally whacked me in the head, remember?"

"Oh, that's right. Where'd you say she was from?"

"She said she moved a lot and often traveled for her job, but that her permanent residence was currently somewhere around Chicago. I don't think there was an address on her card, just a cell number."

"Was there a Web address?"

"Can't remember that either. Maybe I'll give her a call tomorrow, thank her again for her help, and see if I can get her snail-mail address so I can send her a new hanky. I still feel terrible about that."

"Cassandra, the woman banged you in the head, twice." He pushed her hair back behind her ear to get a closer look at the damage to her nose. "I'd say at the very least, you're even."

"Now you sound like my mother."

"Ouch. I retract my statement," he said, laughing and wrapping his arms around her. "Do you still love me anyway?"

"Of course I do. I still love *her,* don't I?" *Don't I, God? I do still love my mother, right? Even though sometimes her verbal wounds just about do me in?*

Eight

Long after their tender session of lovemaking, Cassandra lay awake wondering if her mother could be right about Josie. Could she be in jail too? Or did she perhaps escape getting caught? Cassandra hated the way she so often succumbed to her mother's seeds of doubt, even still. After all, Ken hadn't assumed the worst about Josie. At least not out loud. Maybe she'd get up extra early tomorrow morning and Google Josie What's-Her-Name just to see what showed up. Josie—"So she *says* that's her name," her mom had quipped—said she was an independent computer-system analyst. Surely she had her own Web page, right? With a picture of herself? That wasn't an FBI's most wanted mug shot, *right*? Surely Cassandra wasn't *that* poor of a judge of character, was she?

Sure, there was that one rabid raccoon Grandpa Wonky shot—right from his wheelchair—before it had a chance to bite her. *"Jeny Kochany, Betty! What's a seven-year-old girl supposed to know about rabies?"* he'd said to his daughter after she lit into Cassandra about how she should know better than to mess with wild animals. And the fiasco with the new girl in junior high school, the one who said she just wanted to check something on Cassandra's math homework paper—then kept it for herself. And there was the—

Stop it, Cassandra! Petty thieves don't carry lace-trimmed handkerchiefs and let you bleed all over them. She hated how little seed planting it seemed to take to undermine her judgment.

Ken draped his arm across her stomach, something he did in his sleep. Gingerly, she picked it up and set it down next to him. She slipped out of bed and into her robe and ratty flip-flops, then padded her way to the laundry room. The whole Collectors drama had been so traumatizing that when she'd arrived home last night, she hadn't even unpacked her shopping bag. She'd just tucked it up on a shelf above the washing machine where the boys wouldn't get at it, entered the kitchen, and fallen into Ken's arms, crying.

Cassandra cinched the belt to her robe again before lifting the heavy bag from the shelf and setting it on the washer. She laid everything out, then felt badly she hadn't even thought to give her family their souvenirs from her crazed day. *No more guilt! I can't take it!* She carefully removed the layers of wrapping from the snowglobe. It was hard to believe she'd only purchased it yesterday morning; it seemed like a year ago she'd put the package in her shopping bag. And yet it was just as hard to believe that up until now she hadn't found a minute to herself to even look at it. The overhead light in the laundry room wasn't bright enough to study the details, so she tiptoed past the bedrooms to their Everything Room, a combination family room and playroom for the kids, including a built-in crafting corner for her and a sliding door to their fenced backyard.

Soon after their second son, Howie, was born, she and Ken decided they needed more living space, and the Everything Room was the result of a late-night discussion while Cassandra breast-fed their new arrival. They'd considered the possibilities and agreed that they both felt a strong sense of belonging and place within their town and their home, and that they loved their large yard and friendly neighborhood too much ever to sell. After a lengthy discussion, they'd hit upon a perfect plan: they'd turn their small family room into another bedroom for "future possibilities" and build a large multifunction room onto the back of the house. Within months, renovations for the Everything Room neared completion, and—what a surprise!—their next "future possibility" was on the way. After Harry's birth, along came Bradley, and next: Ken's vasectomy. "Amen and hallelujah!" she'd told him on the way home from his procedure. And yet, Bradley was growing out of his babyhood so quickly that some days it nearly took her breath away. She had so many "Oh! It's the last time any of our boys will ever..." moments.

Snowglobe carefully in hand, Cassandra sat in Ken's lounge chair and turned on the radiant floor lamp he bought for himself a few Novembers ago. He'd heard it might help combat the doldrums he occasionally experienced during the long, gray Minnesotan winters, which doctors and salespeople—in that order? she wondered—started referring to as Seasonal Affective Disorder, or SAD. She was happy for anything that would keep him from spiraling into whatever ailed her father, a hopefully irrational fear brought on by her mother when Cassandra made the mistake of mentioning Ken's new light to her.

But she reminded herself that Ken's temporary bouts of the blahs were nothing like her father's mental illness. Ken grew up in California, and he simply wasn't used to such long stretches of sunless days, as opposed to Cassandra, who loved the bleakness of Minnesotan winters. She'd told Ken countless times, making him run to look at the changing, breathtaking landscape when God painted both the sky and the snow with that same dusk-driven, creamy wintry blue hue, but only when the atmosphere was just so. She was not a fan of summer. In fact, too much heat made her sick, literally. In her youth on more than one occasion, she'd passed out from the heat. She was smarter now and stayed better hydrated, but still hated the hot, hot weather that brought her husband to life.

"The heat makes me crazy," she told him early in their relationship.

"Too many gray months make me nuts," he responded.

When they discovered the disparity, Ken, a newcomer to the area, laughed and said it was good to know that at least one of them would be mentally sound at all times, an innocent yet unfortunate turn of phrase. Soon after, she felt compelled to tell him about her father's suicide, something she almost never talked about, not even with Margret. According to statistics, depression was a hereditarily linked illness, and she confided that she worried it might one day cripple *her* mind or that of any future children. Since they were getting serious with each other so quickly, this was something she said she thought she should present to him "in the due process of full disclosure."

His response to her dead serious confession? An outburst of riotous laughter. "Oh, my Cassie girl!" It was the first time anyone had used her Grandpa Wonky's term of endearment since his death. Of course Ken had no idea about the connection. The combination of the endearment and his peels of laughter, similar to those her grandpa broke out in during what he called the "too serious times," made her so happy that tears erupted in her eyes.

Ken said, "I'm sorry. I didn't mean to make it seem like I was laughing at your father's death."

"I know. That's not why I'm crying. They're good tears."

"Truly, I appreciate your honesty and *due process,* Cassie, but believe me when I tell you there isn't anyone on this earth not afraid they might inherit something from their cranky aunt or alcoholic uncle, kleptomaniac brother or diaper-wearing grandma."

"But those things don't lead to death. What could be as bad as...," she had to force herself to say it, "suicide?"

He reached for her hand and brushed his lips across her knuckles. "I know your dad's death must have been terrible. Still is terrible. I *know.*" He drew her close to him, felt her heart pounding against his.

"Mental illness isn't funny. Suicide is a terrible tragedy, a horrible loss. Forever a puzzle. But I also know this: no matter what, you have to keep a sense of humor, even about mental illness," he added, reading her thoughts. "In fact, I think the loss of a sense of humor can be a warning sign that we *are* mentally losing it. You are just so darned serious about your full disclosure that I wanted you to know we all have things to disclose. Sometimes the best response to help ward off the life-sapping fear monster is to keep our faith, chins, and hopes up, and to laugh. Keep us a little perspective!"

"So, what are you afraid of, huh? Seriously, Ken. What do you have to laugh about to stay sane?"

"Let's see. Where to begin? I have lots of things in my family that can kill me. Diabetes, for one. Heart disease, for another. Want me to continue?"

"Yes."

"Geesh! You're a morbidly tough crowd."

At that, Cassandra snickered, which felt good to both of them.

He continued, "All right, you asked for it. I have a cousin with hammertoes."

She giggled.

"A brother with an outie belly button, and…wait. I almost forgot that my Uncle Lou has a third nipple!" he said, now on a roll. She started laughing hard. "But I'm not through yet! I drool in my sleep, and I think my mom suffers from an occasional loss of bladder control, which she blames on having us kids."

Cassandra was now holding her side, especially since she'd seen some of those products in her mom's closet, although Bad Betty would never admit to such a thing. "And my *dad*," he said with great dramatic flair, "*he* farts in his sleep and…"

"Enough!" she said. "I can barely breathe. You win. I get your point."

From that day forward, when either of them got to fretting about something, even something as small as the discovery of a cavity during a routine dental exam, the other would say, "Yeah, well I have *big ears* in *my* family."

Or "You think *that's* something to worry about? I have *baldness* on *my* mother's side! And *hangnails!*"

Who knew what they might come up with during their rapid-fire awful-izing, which usually concluded with a grand finale that made them laugh the most: *constipation!* If they happened to be in the Everything Room when the snap-you-out-of-it game began, one of them would go to the radiant lamp and add, "And what about SAD? Did you forget our kids might have SAD in their genes? Thank goodness for the cure!" Cassandra or Ken would part their hands around it with the dramatic flair of an infomercial.

No wonder I love that man to pieces! she thought as, with a smile, she glanced at the snowglobe in her hands, sat in the heat of his lamp, and reflected on the gift of the Sad Game her husband had taught her, which made her just as happy as when Hayley Mills played the Glad Game in her all-time-favorite movie, *Pollyanna*. If only she'd been raised by a mom with the spirit of Pollyanna. As a youth, Cassandra had watched the movie time and again just to keep from drowning in her mother's hopeless sorrow.

But throughout Ken and Cassandra's ten years of marriage, no matter how much laughter they got out of all things terrible, nothing could make her feel better about the fact that she did not have the brains to become a veterinarian. Not even summer school, two bouts of tutoring, and countless hours in the library between her freshman and sophomore high-school years had helped her pass the "all things math and sci-ence" muster. Testing caused her to seize up. In shame and tears, she'd finally gone to her high-school counselor, who encouraged her to change her target away from becoming a veterinarian, a rigorous and difficult four-year college program, followed by several years in vet school. Heeding his advice, she switched to classes "more in keeping with her skills," which moved her toward a two-year vocational pro-gram for childcare. After five years of working in the day-care field, she'd married Ken. After four more years of Cassandra chugging the forty-minute drive to her full-time job, the two of them decided it was time to start their own family. She immediately quit her job to get the house set up for their new addition, Ken's job paying well enough for her to be a stay-at-home mom. In order to subsidize her animal-knickknack habit, but mostly to help assuage her guilt over any spending, Cassan-dra began baby-sitting for her friends' children. And so it still went today.

It's not that Cassandra didn't enjoy and give thanks for a full life filled with much love; she did. But being unable to become a veterinar-ian—to fulfill the desire of her heart, which, according to her beloved Grandpa Wonky, God Himself had given to her—felt not only like a defeat of purpose but like a colossal failure of faith and therefore a direct sin against the Almighty. Couple that with what ultimately happened to Toby—the details of which she had *never* shared with Ken—and she had no doubt that she was too untrustworthy to ever care for another *real* critter. Period. No matter how many times throughout the years she'd gone over it, hoping to talk herself out of the decision, she always came to the same conclusion: undeserving.

∾

In the welcoming silence of her late-night house, and under the brightness of Ken's radiant lamp—what else could explain why the snowglobe felt so incredibly warm to her touch?—Cassandra watched the snow fall over the three dogs who appeared dependent upon the little girl. In real life it was late Monday night in Wanonishaw, but in the globe, time stood still. She stared at the face of the child. What was it about the girl that reminded her so very much of herself at that age? The hair, she supposed. But Cassandra also thought she could see the veterinary dreams in the girl's eyes. In fact, the closer Cassandra studied the girl's face through the gently falling snow, the more the girl appeared to blink back her own tears.

My blackened eyes must be playing tricks on me.

The little girl who would grow up to be the woman for whom no amount of Sad or Glad Games could eradicate the hole in her heart, the longing in her soul, or quiet the disapproving and "so disappointed" comments of Bad Betty. The mother of four curled up in her husband's lounge chair, longing to surround herself and her children with the unconditional love and trust of cats and dogs, rabbits and gerbils, hermit crabs and any other creature Wanonishaw would allow, but who believed herself to be unworthy of their trust. Cassandra could not forgive herself for her failure to achieve her heart's desire, and her shortcomings had surely caused her to lose her last furry friend.

Why does that little mutt dog in this snowglobe have to look so much like Toby? It was uncanny how the snowglobe, which at first made her so happy, was now washing up such piercing and damning emotions. She would never forget the look in Toby's trusting brown eyes as she walked away from the county animal shelter. They'd been together nearly five years! For months she'd kept her eyes peeled, hoping to maybe catch a glimpse of him with his new owner. She longed to give him a nuzzle under his neck, his favorite spot for what she called a tender tickle. When the longing to see him finally grew unbearable, she begged her mom to take her to the shelter to see if she could find out who adopted him. Maybe she could go visit him. Betty, who'd denied her daughter's ongoing pleas for months, finally agreed to take her when she had an errand to run in Millsford, the neighboring town with the shelter. "But if they can't tell you where he went, I don't want to hear any crying, Cassandra, do you hear me?"

It was at the shelter Cassandra learned the hard news that *nobody* had wanted her longtime, beloved, sweet old friend and that he'd been euthanized.

No, she never deserved another pet. The only thing that would have helped pay penance for her terrible failure to Toby's trust in her was to become a veterinarian. That way she could have saved the lives of other animals—achieve her God-given heart's desire. But since she wasn't smart enough to cut *that* muster…she did not deserve the trust of another defenseless critter. No matter how much she longed for it.

"Oh, Toby," she said, feeling the tears beginning to pool in her eyes. "I am so sorry. Oh, Grandpa…*God,*" she quietly uttered as she cradled the snowglobe in her hands, tears streaming down her face. "I am so sorry to have disappointed You! Please forgive me. Please help me get over my failings and disappointments so that I don't pass a sour spirit to my children the way my mom did to me. Please help me get over *myself* so I can just go back to being the joyful child of God You created me to be, the one I used to be. The one Grandpa Wonky believed in."

A sob racked deep in her chest, causing her shoulders, arms, and hands to tremble. Like a lightening bolt, it struck her what that fidgety, dreamlike need to scream was *really* about: she was *drowning* in years of her own shame and guilt, and she was unable to save herself.

At that instant, the uncommon warmth of the snowglobe chilled to her fingers, and the snow began to shift. As if gathering to form a great tornado, with no prompting from Cassandra, the snow began to rotate. She wiped the tears from her eyes and shook her head to clear her vision, but the crazy scene persisted as the temperature of the globe dropped so violently she was afraid her fingertips were frozen to the glass. No matter how frightened she became, Cassandra could not set the snowglobe down. So rapidly did the snow begin to whirl that its bright, whiteout blizzard suddenly blinded her to the dogs and the girl. Dizziness and nausea threatened to overcome her as the snow swirled, swirled, but the centrifugal—or was it magnetic, or both?—force of the storm held her locked in its trance. She wanted to call out to Ken, but as if stuck in that bad dream, her voice would not work. Her heart beat so fast she thought it might erupt.

Just when she felt she might black out, the storm began to subside and the temperature of the globe began to warm again. When the snow stopped swirling, the three dogs and the girl had vanished. She stared in utter shock as the last flakes covered their footprints, until nothing remained in the globe but the landscape and the familiar-yet-startling creamy, wintery blue hue that dusk ushered across the sky and snow, turning it all the same color—but only when the atmosphere was just so.

Nine

Cassandra heard a determined banging on the front door, then the doorbell rang, so she dragged her weary body to open it. "Oh. Hi, Mom," she said, not even making eye contact with her mother. She carried Bradley under her left arm like a sack of potatoes, and a dishtowel hung over her right shoulder. She looked even worse than she had on the television night before last. Her eyes were not only black and blue but also bloodshot. Her nose looked disfigured, and her hair was a mess.

"And you were expecting…?" Betty followed Cassandra into the house. Cassandra locked the door behind them.

"I wasn't expecting anyone. To be honest, I forgot I locked the door."

"It's about time you started taking some precautions!"

After last night's creepy incident with the snowglobe—after which she wasn't able to sleep—Cassandra was hanging on by a thread, one ready to snap. She could feel that yet unleashed scream beginning to crawl up her throat. What was her mother doing here anyway?

"Mom! It's Wanonishaw! There's never anything in the Police Roundup section of the *Bluffs Courier* other than an occasional moving violation by out-of-towners passing through our speed trap."

"There is no need to snap at me, Cassandra. I just came by to see for myself how you're doing."

Cassandra blew a deep exhale through her lips and put Bradley down. He took off crawling straight for that old floor lamp again. She wondered why only one of her four children had taken such a liking to that thing, which had been in exactly the same spot since they'd married and moved in. He'd already knocked it over once. Luckily the bulb hadn't shattered, or the pole hadn't landed on him, knocking him in the head. *Wouldn't that be something to have* two *of us completely out of our minds!* She was going to have to move the rickety old thing, and that was that. Better yet, maybe she'd get rid of it. She was tired of it anyway.

"I'm sorry, Mom. I didn't mean to snap."

Betty removed her hand-knit, cable-stitch sweater and hung it in the front closet. On a better day, Cassandra would have silently laughed at her usual thought, which was that a doomsday Mr. Rogers *lived*! But not the day following last night's inexplicable snowglobe incident, when Cassandra could barely seem to process any thoughts. Earlier, when day-care kid Megan got into it with Harry, who did not feel like being bossed around today, she'd nearly lost it. She'd almost called the girl's mother and told her to come get her domineering daughter—and all the rest of the kids, including her own.

"Come on, Mom. I gotta get back to the Everything Room. The kids are restless today, and I have to keep my eye on them every second."

"I don't know how you can even see out of those eyes. I'll have to tell Burt he was wrong. It wasn't the camera that made your face look so distorted the other night."

"Heaven forbid Burt doesn't weigh in on something he knows nothing about." The statement came out in an uncustomary sarcastic tone, especially for Cassandra.

"Cassandra! What on earth? Burt Burt is a fine, caring person."

I've had it with my mom dumping hot coals on my already smoldering head. Is everybody smarter and nicer than I am? Cassandra whirled on her heels and burned an angry, desperate stare into her mother. "Well so am I, Mom. So am *I*." Hot tears welled in her eyes, which made them sting all the more. She didn't think she had any tears left in her—at least she was hoping she'd cried them all out after last night's...*whatever* that horrifying experience was with that snowglobe. First the feeling dumb for days, then the whacks in the head, then the loss of her wallet, then the thing with the snowglobe...it was all too much.

Cassandra was aware that Betty studied her every move. Her mother could tell something was wrong with her, something bigger than black eyes and a missing wallet. "Have you heard anything more from the police?" Betty asked.

"No. Yes. As you know, they caught the guys, but I don't know any more than I told you earlier, Mom. They said it was possible my wallet might show up in a garbage can, but they doubted it, since nobody else's stolen stuff from the Collectors Convention had been recovered."

"Have you called your credit-card companies?"

The last thing Cassandra needed was a "did you" grilling from Bad Betty. The long rising scream finally erupted through her lips. "*Yes,* Mother! I've done *everything* you've *always* told me to, including finally getting whacked in the head...*and* robbed! Are you HAPPY NOW?!" Cassandra broke out in sobs. Very seldom did she outwardly reveal her exasperation and anger with her mother, and never did she scream at her. This outburst took them both by surprise.

Howie came over to Cassandra and asked her if she was okay. Cassandra scooped him up, hugged him really hard, and pulled herself together. She had to. "Yes, honey, Mommy's fine. She's just tired today, and you know how crabby you and I get when we're tired."

Betty drove toward her home, lips tucked inside her mouth. She'd left without saying a word. She could count on one hand the times her daughter had sassed her, and every time she'd done so, in the deepest part of her, Betty knew she'd had it coming—although she would *certainly* never admit that. But never had Cassandra yelled at her.

Betty hated the way she picked on her very own daughter, who *did* always seem to be trying her hardest to get things right. It's just that from the time she was little, Cassandra was so vulnerable, so trusting, so naive, so...*special*—all the things Betty had never been. Betty had cried many private tears over the possibility that perhaps if she had been as special as Cassandra, maybe Gerald wouldn't have gone to such desperate measures as to take his own life to get away from her.

Ten

Can you watch the kids for a few minutes while I check something on the Internet?" Cassandra asked her husband. Ken very rarely said no to her requests to take over. He was a remarkable father, always ready to help out, including the moment he walked through the door after a long day at work. He nodded his consent. He was surrounded by the boys anyway, Harry already hanging on his leg. Cassandra gave Ken a quick thank-you peck on the cheek and raced directly to the small office space they'd created in a corner of their bedroom. Her heart thumped in her chest. She'd waited all day to look up Josie Brooks, whose card she carried in the pocket of her jeans, a card that contained only a phone number. She'd hoped to get to the computer early this morning before anyone awakened, but no such luck.

After last night's nerve-racking, unbelievable experience with the new snowglobe—an incident worse than two black eyes or a robbery, and perhaps even her scene with her mom earlier today—she had greater concerns than if Josie was a wallet nabber or her mother would ever talk to her again. She needed to find out if she was sane! When Josie picked up the snowglobe before Cassandra said she was going to buy it, had she seen the three dogs and the little girl? Maybe somewhere along the way, Cassandra had picked up the wrong globe, one with nothing in it. *No, I looked into that little girl's face before I bought it!* Or maybe while distracting her with all his wrapping, the vendor pulled a fast one on her and swapped globes. Last night when she first sat down with the snowglobe, maybe she only imagined she saw the dogs and the girl. What else could explain the now-empty globe?

She held her breath as she brought up a browser and Googled "Josie Brooks+system analyst," which was pretty much all the information she could remember. A few pages of references popped up. She scrolled through the first dozen or so, then clicked on www.josiebrooks.com. It seemed most likely to lead to *her* Josie Brooks since the short preview also included a brief reference to computers. When the Web page opened, what it revealed was unclear at best and disconcerting at worst. She had to talk to Margret since she was the one person who would help decide what to do next.

Margret, the one person she would tell about her *flurrious* experience, which was the way Cassandra described the flurry of the whirlwind of snow and the curious disappearance of the figures. Margret wouldn't think she was crazy—and even if she did, she would neither hold it against her nor tell anyone. Not even Ken, whom Cassandra hadn't yet found the guts to tell.

Margret. The one person Cassandra had also been childishly avoiding since the Collectors Convention. If Margret had been with her, maybe *none* of this would have happened.

"Can you stand, Toby? Can you stand up for me?" Cassie asked while getting up off the ground herself. She'd been sitting in the woods in front of her newfound pet for so long that her legs tingled. She felt slightly wobbly but steadied herself. "And by the way," she said, smiling and placing her hands on her hips, "my name is Cassandra, but Grandpa calls me Cassie, so you can too."

Toby wiggled a little, tried to upright himself, then whimpered and lay back down. He stared at the ground as if embarrassed by his own lack of control.

"That's okay," she said, reaching down and patting his head. "Just relax. We'll figure something out." Toby started licking his left front leg, right at the knee joint. Then he turned his head and licked near his hip. Clearly, he was attempting to sooth the points of his pain. Dogs did that. Since he'd repositioned himself, she could see that his knee joint looked swollen, and it was oozing. Sprained? Sometimes dogs licked things until they licked the skin off. He'd obviously been here awhile... Or maybe a snake bite? Bullet wound? Sometimes they heard shots in the woods. Maybe he had hip troubles. Grandpa said some dogs' hips just got crabby when they got older. Toby didn't look that old, though. But worse yet, for the brief time he'd been uncurled and slightly up off the ground, Cassandra was shocked to see how skinny he was.

"I bet you don't weigh much. Since I'm only six, I'm not too strong yet, but maybe I can carry you back to my house. My grandpa can help me figure out what we should do next. You'll really like my Grandpa Wonky." She would have run back to the house and brought Grandpa back with her, but she knew he wouldn't be able to get his wheelchair up the skinny, weedy path she used to enter the woods. Besides, since Toby was wounded—and especially since he wasn't too big—he was vulnerable to the coyotes. She'd heard them howling the last few nights, and dusk would soon be creeping in on them.

She sat down in front of him again and gingerly slid her arms under his neck and hindquarters. Although he emitted another low growl, when she glanced at his face, he looked away, obviously embarrassed for having done so. "Hang on, Toby, you're going for a ride!" She took a deep breath, then on the exhale she used all of her might and carefulness to get to her knees. Toby whimpered, but he didn't try to leap away, for which she was grateful. She one-kneed a foot to the ground ("Alley-oop!"), then the other. She wobbled and Toby whimpered again, but they were up!

She took a deep breath and rearranged her hands and arms to secure better balance, then took another deep breath, started humming, and off they trudged. With every step, she planned and strategized out loud.

"I'll take you straight to the shed so Mom doesn't see you first. You'll like hiding in the shed. I do too, especially when Dad has been drinking. I'll make a bed for you near the rabbit pen. Wait until you see my rabbit! His name is Clipper. He's got amazing eyes too. You can lie on a couple of the old burlap bags I saw back in the corner, unless they're too stinky or scratchy. After we get your bed made, I'll ask Grandpa to come help me with Clipper. When he gets to the shed, I'll show him you! Can you say 'Surprise!'? Grandpa can help us figure out what to do next. How to make Mom let me keep you, at least until you're well enough to…at least until you're well. And you're gonna be," she said, giving him a kiss on top of his head. "You'll see. I promise."

She had to stop several times and catch her breath, one time leaning back against a tree to give her shoulders a break. Sweat dripped down her face and into her eyes, making them sting. She squeezed her eyelids together so hard it gave her a headache, but when she opened them again, she could see well enough to carry on. Toby eventually rested his silky chin in the crook of her arm. "The perfect fit," she told him. It felt like God had invented her bendy elbow just for this sweet fellow's face. Eventually, Toby closed his eyes. She felt his body weight change; he'd drifted off to sleep. "Good boy," she whispered. "That's just what you need. We'll be there in no time. You're safe now."

At last, they arrived home. Home to the shed. Home to Grandpa's help. Home to each other.

Eleven

Betty wrapped her ancient chenille robe around her shiny polyester beige slacks and pilled knit top, then fixed herself a cup of tea. No sugar, no cream, no flavors, no fragile cups and saucers. Just a sturdy mug and good strong black tea. *"Nothing sweet or frilly for Bet."* After all these years since Gerald's death, she could still hear him say those words to the waitress during their one dinner out each year on their anniversary. Gerald always ordered for her. Every year, Harriet, Betty's sister, gave them money for their anniversary. *"It's enough to include dessert too!"* she'd told Gerald after she counted the bills that first year—and it was the same every year thereafter.

"I'm sorry I can't afford to buy you dinner myself," he said, a sorrowful tone in his voice. *"I'm sorry I can't afford to buy you a lot of things. Next year, it'll be different."* But the only thing that grew different each year was the depth of Gerald's depression.

Betty blew on her tea and tried to take a sip; it was still hot enough to burn her tongue. She'd daydreamed for too long and let the water come to a boil before she poured it. She set the mug on her red-and-white-checked oilcloth table cover and stared at the rising steam. It reminded her of the swirls of smoke from the incense they used to burn in her church. She wondered if they still walked around with it; she hadn't attended church since her husband's death. She'd never been very religious to begin with, going more out of the habit and guilt of her Catholic upbringing than anything else. But when one of the parish's worst busybodies found it necessary to tell her Gerald couldn't go to heaven because of his "egregious sin against God," Betty never again stepped through church doors. If that's the way God was, she wanted nothing more to do with Him.

Sad, she thought, how such a small thing as a cup of tea could flood her with so many difficult memories. But she'd been feeling downtrodden since she'd returned from Cassandra's. Without realizing it—because far be it from Betty to let down her guard, admit she was wrong, and become vulnerable—Cassandra had really hit a sore spot. When she'd mentioned all the times her mother had warned her that one day she'd get whacked in the head, Betty almost felt as if she'd spoken—*willed*—the tragedy into being, which is exactly the way her daughter had presented it. Hadn't having one downbeat parent been enough for poor Cassandra? Why did she herself have to be the second?

Bad Betty. Voice of doom. She'd heard the expressions. Gerald hadn't been negative, though. He'd often just been…missing, even when he'd been there. Missing for all of them. Depression was a gnarly beast.

When the boys were younger, he was still more himself, more the Gentleman Gerald as she'd called him when they'd married; but by the time Cassandra, their surprise child, came along, he'd changed. He waffled between closing the world off and occasionally drinking too much—something Betty was grateful he gave up after a run-in with the local police. Although the police incident just happened once, it was an added shame he felt he'd brought on the family. After he quit drinking, a deeper depression seemed to set in. Betty had exhausted herself trying to cheer him up, until one day for her own sanity, she finally gave up trying. She needed to conserve her energy for her job, her kids, and for circumstances that *could* be changed or thwarted, like trying to protect her daughter from *her* own vulnerabilities. The only thing that brought an occasional spark to her husband's eyes was the bright light of their beautiful girl, whose effervescence and love for her critters seemed to touch the life-sustaining core of his heart. But those hopeful responses soon disappeared too. Then one day he was gone. He'd shot himself in the shed with his Remington 870, leaving Betty alone. His life insurance policy didn't pay a cent because of his suicide. How was she to care for three children, all those pets, and a handicapped father who coddled his granddaughter into believing she could become more than the rest of them?

"Well, she didn't," Betty spoke aloud.

She took two large sips of her tea. It was still too hot. She concluded a burning tongue was what she deserved after uttering such a terrible thing about the one person who understood as much as she did what it felt like to fail.

"Margret. It's Cassie."

"Cassie! What's wrong with your voice? Oh! I bet it's your *nose*! I wanted to call you, but we didn't get back from our trip until late, and we've been running ever since. You beat me to it." Margret crossed her fingers, something she always did when she lied. The truth was, since her visit to Mayo, she hadn't yet recuperated enough emotional reserve to go another round of baby talk, especially not with Cassandra, who knew her better than anyone, including Leo. She hadn't even discussed the aftermath of her appointment—a truly mixed bag of information and possibilities—with her mother, who knew nothing about their doctor's visit either. She and Leo swore to each other that this time they would keep it *all* to themselves. "I didn't hear about your robbery at the Collectors Convention until I stopped at Burt's to pick up some pork chops for dinner. Are you okay?" At least that part was the truth.

"I'm not sure. Can you come over tonight? Maybe after nine, after we get the kids down?"

Margret hesitated a moment, deciding whether or not she was up for questions about where they'd been and if they'd enjoyed their time away. She'd been pretty vague with Cassandra when she'd begged out of the Collectors Convention, and she knew by the tone in her friend's voice when she called to tell Cassandra that she wasn't going that her friend was both hurt and miffed—although far be it from Cassandra to express herself. Maybe Cassandra would be so preoccupied with her own recent events that there'd be no follow-up conversation about her absence. Margret hoped that was the case. But since Cassandra knew her so well, if pressed, Margret wasn't sure if she could continue the charade and keep her promise to Leo or not. It would be hard to hide something like this when Cassandra was looking right at her. "Let me make sure Leo doesn't have any plans for us tonight and I'll call you back."

"Okay. Call me as soon as you know. Bye."

Cassandra hung up the phone and stared at the computer monitor. The Web page looked exactly the same as it did before she called Margret: disconcerting. There was no picture of Josie on the page, just a little X in a box where it looked like one was supposed to be. "Josie Brooks…problem solving…creative planning…help your business accomplish its objectives…certified in…" Cassandra had no idea what that all added up to, but it sounded impressive. And like her mom had said when she'd rambled on this afternoon about anybody being able to print anything on a business card, so, too, Cassandra supposed, could they put anything up on a Web site, true or not. She scrolled to the bottom of the page. "This Web site was last updated February 2002." Six years ago. *Great. But I am just going to give her the benefit of the doubt. I am not my mother!*

A few long hours later, dinner was over and the kids were in bed. Ken was parked in front of the television and thankfully Margret arrived.

The women made their way to the office area. "Sit down here," Cassandra instructed, pointing to the computer chair. She got on her hands and knees and retrieved what looked to be a wad of bubble pack from under her side of the bed. She unwrapped the layers, hoping above hope to find a snowglobe with three dogs and a girl inside, but alas, all the heavy globe contained was white snow. Even the blue hue was gone.

"What do you see?" She handed Margret the globe.

Margret looked at the globe, then shot Cassandra a quizzical look. "What do I see?"

"Yes. Describe to me everything you see." Maybe the objects had only become invisible to her.

"I see a snowglobe, a heavy snowglobe," she said, lifting it up and down, "that has nothing in it but snow." She started laughing. "Hey, did the robber get whatever was in here too?"

"This isn't funny, Margret!" Cassandra nearly spat. "Nothing is funny about a broken nose or getting my wallet ripped off or buying a snowglobe that either had nothing in it or was an apparition or that has an evil spell on it, or…maybe I am finally going mental, just like my dad! No, nothing about *any* of this is funny! And if you'd been with me, probably none of this would have happened!" Cassandra couldn't believe what came out of her own mouth.

"Whoa!" Margret set the snowglobe down on the desk, turned, and put her hands on her hips. "A...tell me you're not serious, and B...I have no clue what you're talking about. Evil spells? I hate to be the one to break it to you, but you *do* sound slightly crazy right now. Do you have a concussion or something? Has anyone checked your head, or did the doctor just look at your nose? What is *wrong* with you?"

Tears sprang into Cassandra's eyes. She grabbed Margret's hand and dragged her to the side of the bed where she motioned her to sit, then she sat down next to her and just sobbed. She spoke between bouts of catching her breath, more tears, and wiping her nose. "I don't know. No. Nobody checked my head because I haven't been to the doctor. I just know my nose is broken. I know it the same way I know that when I bought that snowglobe, there were three dogs and little girl inside it. Then this crazy thing happened, and now even the blue hue is gone!" At this, she wailed. She cried so loudly that even though Margret got up and shut the bedroom door, Ken came down the hall to see what was going on.

"Hon! What is it?" he asked, as he began to walk toward her.

"*Go away!* I'll be fine. I just need to cry. Right, Margret?" Cassandra turned her swollen eyes toward her friend, who shrugged at Ken.

"We're fine, but I'll let you know if we're not, okay?"

"Okay," he said, as he shut the door.

"I'm sorry, Margret," Cassandra said through sniffles. "None of this is your fault. I don't know what I'm talking about. Honestly, I *am* out of my head."

"Seriously, Cass, maybe you *should* go see the doctor."

"Is he going to tell me he sees three dogs and a girl inside the snow-globe? Is he?"

"I doubt it…but maybe he can explain why you think you saw them."

"I saw them! I tell you, Margret Anderson, they were *there*."

"Okay. *Okay.* I believe you. Settle down, Cass. Does Ken believe you?"

"He doesn't know about this. You're the only one I've told. But maybe now that you're here, we can find out if Josie can verify…anything."

"Josie?"

"Josie Brooks. Her Web site is right there," she said, leaning over and wiggling the mouse so the screensaver of her family disappeared and the Web site came back into view.

"I give up. Who's Josie Brooks? There's no picture here. Do I know her?"

"Not that I know of."

"How do you know her, then?" Aside from Margret and Leo's college friends, if one of the girls knew someone, usually so did the other. Or at least they'd heard enough about him or her to possess a vague familiarity.

"Let me tell you the whole story. I'll start from the beginning. But I'm gonna give you a quick version since I need you to help me find the courage to call Josie before you go. I'm afraid to hear what she might have to say."

"Hello." The woman's voice sounded tired.

"Hello, Josie? This is Margret Anderson."

"From…?"

"I'm with Cassie Higgins. You don't know me, but she knows you. Well, she doesn't really *know* you, but here she is anyway." Margret held the phone out for Cassandra, who stared at it a moment, then reached for it like it might be the wrong end of a hot curling iron. She could hear Josie's *"Hello. Hello?"* on the other end of the line.

"Josie. This is the woman you met at the fairgrounds." Silence. "At the Collectors Convention? You let me use your wonderful lace hanky when—"

"Oh! *Cassandra!*" Josie cut in. "I was so hoping you'd call. I couldn't believe I didn't get your number before I had to leave for the airport. I thought about it, but once they started your television interview, I had to head out. How *are* you?"

"Relieved. Relieved this is really you."

"I don't understand."

"My mom got me worried that...never mind. I'm just glad to have the chance to tell you I'll be fine."

In the background, Margret spoke loudly, hoping Josie would hear her. "She hasn't been to the doctor. She's not fine at all. That's why she's calling you."

"I'm sorry...is she talking to me?"

"Sort of. Actually, she's trying to send *me* a message to be honest with you."

"So you're not fine, then? Is your nose...your head, going to be okay? You haven't seen a doctor, then?"

"I'm sure my nose and head are fine. Mostly." Cassandra watched Margret pick up the snowglobe, point to it, and then to the phone. "I do have an unrelated question to ask you, though, and it might sound strange."

"Go right ahead. I'll answer, if I'm able."

"Do you remember when you were holding the snowglobe that I asked you to hand over?"

Josie chuckled. "Yes."

"Can you tell me what was *in* that snowglobe?"

She was quiet a moment, then chuckled again. "To be honest, it disappeared before I really had a chance to study it."

"It was something, though, right? It wasn't just an empty globe?"

"I couldn't describe the contents exactly, but I believe it contained a dog or two and a child, which is why I picked it up. I told you I was Christmas shopping, and I have a nephew who's into animals. Why do you ask?"

What could Cassandra say that wouldn't sound crazy? "Something, um, kinda strange happened, and I was just trying to verify something."

"Strange? Like?"

"Oh, never mind. It's possible the guy who sold me the globe swapped it out with another one before he wrapped it. He was talking about how other vendors had been after it that morning and how unusual it was. I bet he got a better offer. I think I'll just chalk it up to that."

"Can't you call him? I would."

"No receipt or name. I don't remember ever seeing the guy there before. Those outdoor people come from all over the United States. They kind of work a circuit. I'd have no way to track him down."

"Think the people who run the show might? Surely they have a listing of who was set up where. Vendors always have to pay a fee, then they get assigned a space, just like at any trade show." She explained that she'd attended plenty of industry trade shows in her career.

"I appreciate your thoughts. In fact, I had them myself, so I phoned the fairgrounds, and they put me in touch with the convention's headquarters. No luck. They only assign the indoor spots and the outdoor spots are first-come, first-served. Yes, they had a list of contact information for outdoor vendors, but they can't make it public record. Besides, there are hundreds of them. I could be calling until doomsday." *Which I feel like I've already entered.*

"Too bad." They shared a brief silence. "So, you got bonked in the head by a careless woman, robbed, and ripped off by one of the vendors. You didn't have a very good day, did you?"

"To say the least. Thanks for your concern and your help, though. I'll let you go now. I'm sorry I interrupted your evening." Cassandra felt weary. Lack of sleep, all the crying, and now, the affirmation that there *had* been something in the globe.

"I still wish you'd go to the doctor, Cassandra. I'd feel better if you did, just to make sure. Shoot me an e-mail after you do, okay? And include your phone number, just so I have it." Josie gave Cassandra her e-mail address, and they said their good-byes.

"So? Spill it," Margret said.

"So, she confirmed what I thought I saw. Dogs and a figure."

"Then the guy must have swapped out the snowglobes."

"Then how do you explain that I saw them after I got *home*? How does *anyone* explain what I watched happen?" Cassandra sat on the bed, the globe once again cradled in her hands. The globe, which felt neither warm nor freezing cold. An empty globe, vacant except for falling…bone fragments?

Good grief!

∞

As Margret drove home, she wondered if Cassandra's decades-old, pent-up emotional torment concerning dogs wasn't somehow short-circuiting the reality of her experience. Her crazy snowglobe story was impossible to believe. Cassandra's talk about the child in the snowglobe having hair the color of her own ignited Margret's memories of the aftermath of Toby's death.

Gert, the ancient German shepherd the Bambeneks owned back when twelve-year-old Cassandra lost Toby, was a safe haven where Cassandra could unload her grief. Margret remembered a particular day. About a month after she learned of Toby's death, Cassandra stopped by to visit her, and Margret hadn't been home when she arrived. According to the conversations Margret had with her mother afterward, Irene tried chatting with Cassandra, but Irene said the poor thing just seemed to have turned inside herself.

Irene finally told Cassandra she could wait in Margret's bedroom, if she liked, and listen to her stereo. Cassandra headed up the stairs with Gert, as always, right on her heels, hobbling in her old-age way. Some forty-five minutes later, when Margret arrived home and walked into her bedroom, Cassandra had fallen asleep with Gert. They lay on the floor, Cassandra spooning Gert, her arm securely wrapped around the dog's chest, her wet cheek buried in Gert's long fur. Margret tiptoed back downstairs to get her mother. Together, they stood in the doorway to the room and wept silent tears for their dear friend. They crept back downstairs and waited for Cassandra to awaken, never mentioning what they'd witnessed. After that incident Cassandra was finally able to resume life with at least a little sense of normalcy.

But two days later, Gert died.

Cassandra stayed away from the Bambeneks' house for nearly two months. She later confessed to Margret that in her worst moments, she wondered if she'd somehow squeezed the life out of Gert when she'd cuddled her so tightly. Or maybe, Cassandra said, tears streaming down her face, she'd poured so much sadness into the old dog that Gert's heart just couldn't take it.

Margret pulled into her driveway, her eyes a blur. She hadn't thought about that incident for a long while, but it still pierced her. She couldn't even imagine what it must have done to Cassandra's heart all these years. But as an adult, surely Cassandra knew better than to hold herself responsible for the deaths of either of those dogs.

Surely.

Twelve

After Margret left, Cassandra sat on the bed, rolling the snowglobe between her hands, first clockwise, then counterclockwise, clockwise, then counterclockwise, trying to re-create the way the snow gathered and rotated on its own, right after…she cried and prayed, asking God to forgive her and to help her heal! This was the first time she remembered what preceded the incident. Surely, she thought, going *insane* isn't an answer to that prayer!

But no matter how she rotated the globe, she could not re-create the way the snow had gathered on its own. She set it down and stared at it, wondering again about the mystery of the bone fragments, if indeed that's what the snow was. How was bone ground, broken, or shattered into such tiny pieces, and who on earth first thought to use it for snow?

And *whose* bones?

A new thought entered her head. It arrived with such clarity and strength that it nearly took her breath away. It was a thought or an answer or a voice with enough power to have been the very Voice of God.

My body was broken for you, and I will wash you whiter than snow.

It was a statement, an answer, a thought—*God's Voice?*—that would haunt her the rest of the week as she puzzled over the recent events.

The next Sunday, just before the pastor of her Lutheran church handed her the communion wafer, he spoke the familiar words, "The body of Christ, broken for you."

The instant the wafer hit her tongue, again, the Voice.

*This is my body, broken for you, and your children, and your father...
and your mother.* Before fainting dead away, she saw a blur of white.

When Cassandra came around, she lay on the church floor with her
head in Ken's lap. She looked up at him until her eyes could focus.

He was not a happy camper. "We are going straight from here to
the doctor's office. It's time you get your head checked, and no arguing."

Slowly, she sat up and looked around. They sat away from the communion rail, back out of sight of the congregants. She must have passed
out. As she reflected on the last thing she heard before she saw the
whirring of snow, her heart started racing, and she thought for a moment
she might black out again—wished she *could* black out again and be
done with this insanity—but she did not. "Where are the kids?"

"They're still either down in the nursery or in Sunday school. I
called your mom, and she's coming to get them. I'm taking you straight
to Urgent Care. *No arguments.*"

"Okay. Did I bang my head again?"

"No. We were kneeling next to each other, remember? When I
noticed your head suddenly fall back, I caught you before you hit the
floor."

"Thank you," she said with a lame smile. "My getting knocked in
the head three times in the same week would have made my mother
way too happy."

Although she was just being funny, the minute the words left her
mouth, the conviction—the ringing words of the Voice—that Christ's
body had been broken for Bad Betty, too, pierced her to the core.

⤬

While they sat in the Urgent Care waiting room, which was mobbed, Ken asked Cassandra the question she dreaded. "What's going on with you and that new snowglobe?"

"What do you mean?" But she knew. She'd obsessed over it during the week, moving it from here to there, holding it in her hands, rotating it, like she couldn't stand to have it out of her sight. It was beginning to feel like a *holy* puzzle of some kind, one she needed to solve. Still, she hadn't divulged the story to Ken, who kept catching her staring at it.

"I mean, Cassandra," he spoke in a tone similar to the one he used with the kids when they tried to avoid fessing up, "tell me what is going on with the empty snowglobe. You haven't been yourself since you came home with that thing. I have to admit, it is the *oddest* of your critter knickknacks. Or is it just the first in your new *invisible* critter collection?" He grinned, but Cassandra didn't crack a smile. He studied her face. "Yes, you might have a slight concussion or something, but there's more. Whatever it is has to do with that snowglobe. I swear, if you don't tell me, I'm tempted to throw it away, just to help you snap out of it."

"No!" She looked around and realized she'd shouted loudly enough for people to turn and stare. She knew she had to tell Ken the whole story. In fact, it would be a relief. In a near whisper, she shared all the details with him, through Josie's verification that she'd seen dogs and a figure. "And I *know* the girl had hair the same color as mine." Repeating every detail brought her right back to a state of anxiety. When she finished speaking, he just stared at her. "How do you explain something like that, Ken? *How?*"

"I have no idea, hon."

"CASSANDRA HIGGINS." Saved by her name, or so she hoped.

Ken stopped her before they stepped into the examination room. "Just so you know, I'm here for you, and we'll get it figured out. But also, just so you know, we're not done with this, Cassandra."

She hoped that didn't mean he was calling a shrink as soon as they got home.

Thirteen

No, Mom. They didn't find anything wrong inside my head," she said into the receiver. It was the first time she'd spoken to her mother since she'd yelled at her—and since the very Voice of God (what else could it have been?) had pricked her conscience about her mother. Cassandra worked extra hard to maintain a tone of niceness. "Yes, my nose is broken, but it's healing fine. No, I don't need to call Josie to give her the bill. Thanks for taking the boys…and I'm sorry it took us so long, but I'm sure when Ken came to pick them up, he explained how mobbed Urgent Care was."

Ken had dropped her off at home before he went to get the boys. They agreed neither of them was up for a Bad Betty conversation, but especially not Cassandra. He also knew if he went to get the boys rather than having Betty drop them off, he'd have control over how long his visit lasted, which was just long enough to gather them into the car.

"Yes, I washed my hands when I got home, Mom. I know those waiting rooms are full of germs. You've taught me well about germs, Mom, and I thank you." Cassandra smiled; this part of the conversation actually struck her as funny. Maybe it was the headache medicine the doctor gave her. The funniest part was that Betty understood the necessity of washing your hands decades before cleanliness became newsworthy enough to headline during flu season. *Cutting-edge Betty. Now there's a thought.* "I'm well on my way to recovery. Yes, I'm doing my usual baby-sitting tomorrow. Thanks for calling, Mom. I hear Ken and the kids pulling into the garage now, so I'll talk to you later. Bye."

Cassandra, who'd run straight into the house and gathered the snowglobe in her hands after Ken dropped her off, quickly put it in the back of her underwear drawer, where it would stay safe from everyone. Including her. She *had* to stop thinking about it.

She was making herself truly crazy. Her head was fine, and her confirmed broken nose was healing. The boys needed her full attention and the assurance that things were getting back to normal, even if Mommy still didn't look like it. Her baby-sitting clients depended on her. The snowglobe was empty of figures, and no amount of staring or shaking it changed a single thing, not even the temperature or the way the snow fell—slowly—the same way snow always fell inside a snowglobe. She hadn't found a hidden trap door in the bottom of the globe—a new thought that excited her while waiting in the doctor's cold office. The only thing different was that she noticed for the first time an odd symbol or insignia in the base of the globe. Maybe someone's initials? Or Celtic art? She'd have to find Ken's book on Celtic artwork. Or a map? A tiny *something* was etched into the bottom of the Bakelite bottom, but not even her magnifying glass could help her make sense of it. Maybe this was a clue to its maker? Or her *flurrious* experience?

She opened her underwear drawer again for one last look, but the kids came thundering down the hall. "No more snowglobe, Cassandra," she reprimanded herself. "Put this thing away and forget about it! It's probably just an accidental scratch anyway. It's time to let go—at least for now."

"Do I need to take that thing away from you so you can let your head rest?" She whirled around at the sound of Ken's voice over her right shoulder. He must have led the pack down the hall. "Cassandra. Look at me. Do I?"

"No. I just thought I saw a..."

"Saw a what? Did something happen with it again?" He started to reach around her for a look.

"It was nothing. Just a scratch in the bottom of the base," she said as she turned to face him, leaned back, and closed the door with her elbow. "And I promise you, Ken, I'm done with it."

"Promise?"

"Promise."

❧

The next morning, right after Ken left for work, Cassandra opened her underwear drawer to take another look at the symbol. *So much for promises.* Where the globe had been, she just found a note. It was from Ken.

> Hon,
>
> Don't worry. I am not throwing your "magical" (I'm winking here) snowglobe away. I'm just hiding it for now so I can help you keep your promise to yourself to just *be* for a while. I thought the temptation might be too difficult to resist, since you do have to get into your underwear drawer every day. Right? I hope so! (I'm winking here too!)
>
> I love you,
> Ken

Cassandra folded the note and tucked it back where she found it. *He knows me way too well.*

❧

Every word of Ken's note was true. He loved his wife. He also knew that try as she might to keep her promise, it would be difficult for her to ignore something right in front of her face. He had her best interest at heart when he retrieved the empty orb—*all* of their best interests.

But mostly, he wanted to spend some time with the mysterious snowglobe himself. There *had* to be an explanation. He doubted Cassandra's far-reaching theory that the vendor had pulled a fast one, especially after he'd seen the globe for the first time. Anyone could tell it was really old. It did look like a Bakelite base he found on the Internet, and the weight of it pointed toward heavy glass for the dome. The vendor seemed to know what he was talking about. But bone fragments for snow? How could anyone tell? That sounded like a Gypsy's "Gotcha!" to him. Until he discovered references on the Internet that some of the first snowglobes *did* use bone fragments for snow, and when he read it, a prickle ran up his spine. No wonder Cassandra was freaked out. What he couldn't find was a reference to the type of bones.

But ever if the vendor *had* swapped out her globe, that didn't explain how she saw the black-and-white Border collie, a gray greyhound, a mutt, and a little girl with hair the color of her own, a detail she'd repeated to him several times, after she got home with it. And if she did, where were they now?

That night after prayers with the boys, Cassandra lay down with Howie for an extra long time. Her distorted face and jittery presence had taken their toll on her sensitive child, and it was time to set him at ease. She spooned around his little body until she felt the deep breaths of his sleep on her arm, where his head rested. Just when she thought she might nod off, the relaxing combination of sensations awakened a dormant memory. In a dreamlike state, she slipped back in time to a few weeks after her Grandpa Wonky died, just a little over a year after her dad had taken his life. She was eleven, lying in her bed with her arms wrapped around Toby, silently weeping into his soft coat, which she faithfully brushed twice a week.

After the death of her dad, Grandpa Wonky kept the spark of normalcy alive in the house, but now…nothing was normal. She missed her grandpa so much that it actually hurt her belly. Her mom shuffled around like a ghost, pale, not eating, working as many hours as she could. Her brothers, four and five years older than Cassandra, stayed away from the house more than usual. They took on odd jobs offered by neighbors to keep them busy and to help with their financial situation. When they *were* around, they fought most of the time, and Cassandra's mom asked them to go outside if they couldn't get along. After her dad's death, time and again, Grandpa Wonky encouraged Betty to cut them some slack, saying he thought the boys were working out their emotions in physical ways. But after *he* died, the boys seemed endlessly determined to have at it, their arguing and shenanigans causing Betty to be at constant odds with them.

Cassandra felt her breath aligning with Toby's. She wondered what it would be like to be dead. She held her breath for a moment, until the thought scared her into a quick exhale. She hugged Toby tighter, just to make sure she *was* still alive.

With her back to the bedroom door, she faced the window. Her drapes were open, and from the glow of the streetlight, she noticed it was snowing. She heard her bedroom door squeak open. Grandpa Wonky was the one who used to tenderly tuck her in at night. Must be one of her brothers looking in on her, to make sure she'd gone to bed. Her mom often worked too late to be home by her bedtime, so she'd taken it upon herself to try to hit the sack by nine.

She squeezed her eyes shut and pretended she was asleep. She heard the door close again, thankful no one entered. But her heartbeat quickened when she realized someone was walking toward her bed with soft, light footsteps. Whoever it was came all the way to the bed and just stood there. Toby lifted his head, then plopped it back down again, his tail thumping once on the covers. Obviously, it wasn't a stranger, or he'd have been barking like a maniac. She felt her pulse in her throat, but still, she did not move. Ever so gently, as if not to awaken her, whoever it was snuggled up next to her. How there was even room on her twin bed for someone else to fit, Cassandra didn't know.

Suddenly, she recognized the scent of her mother. When Betty left the factory, she always smelled faintly of industrial oil. She usually went straight to the bathroom and showered, then took her clothes to the basement.

Nothing could have surprised Cassandra more than this silent visit from her mother; Betty had never been one to cuddle. She didn't know what to make of her mother's presence, but she dared not speak. She forced herself to keep her breath even while her mother nuzzled in. Cassandra felt her mother's breath on her neck, and the palm of her mother's hand land gently on her forehead.

But as quickly and quietly as Betty had arrived, she gingerly stood to leave. Cassandra heard her mother sniff, then whisper, "We'll make it through this, baby girl. We'll make it. We have to be strong. What choice do we have?" A few soft shuffles and the creak of the door let her know her mother was gone.

A grown Cassandra, clinging tightly to Howie, felt hot tears pouring down her cheeks. How could she just now have remembered that moment with her mother? It was one of the few indications that Bad Betty Kamrowski had a heart, a soul...and a weak spot for her daughter. She must, because why else would she have called her baby girl?

Fourteen

Ken noticed that Burt Burt, a happy-go-lucky fellow by nature, was in rare form. Why not? Business was crazy good. Today the usual hearty Thursday customer line snaked all the way from the butcher counter to the door, occasionally doubling back on itself.

"How are you today?" Burt asked each customer when each arrived at the counter. That was one of the things Ken most liked about Burt: he actually meant it when he asked. "Thanks for your patience when business is *booming*!" Clearly, Ken thought, the man harbored a grateful heart.

Burt's shop, the only butcher in town, was always highly trafficked, but when it came to weekend holidays, Burt's was *the* place to shop. When the weather forecast was even halfway decent, it always brought out the grillers. Ken had no idea how many folks honestly cared about Christopher Columbus, but this Columbus Day weekend might be the last three-day weekend for outdoor cooking before they'd have to start wearing warmer clothes to grill. The forecast was premium, with the high expected to be a sunny fifty-seven.

When Ken first moved to Minnesota, he couldn't decide whether the locals were born with antifreeze in their veins or if they'd just become immune to the cold. On those first blustery days of winter, when everyone could see their breath in the air, he'd sported his new down parka, then felt like a geek when he noticed that many of the locals, including his wife, still wore sweatshirts (Minnesotans' version of phase-one winter attire) and Bermuda shorts. "BERMUDAS!" he'd exclaimed to Cassandra, who wore her own pair of Bermudas with knee-high socks. "What's *up* with you people?"

But he never questioned why they bought from Burt's. Once Ken took his first bite of Burt's homemade "Wanoni Bologni," he was hooked. People drove across the river from Wisconsin just for a pound of thick-sliced Wanoni Bologni, which, to the locals, was the *only* way to buy it. Whether you rolled a slice and popped it into your mouth, fried it, or grilled it, Burt's garlicky Wanoni Bologni hit the spot. (If you didn't believe it, all you had to do was read the sign in Burt's window.) Bologna, brats, Italian sausage, Polish sausage, lunchmeat, ribs, roasts, steaks, stew meat, or hot dogs, off to Burt's the masses ventured, but especially on Thursdays.

On Thursdays, "Beat the rush!" day, Burt served what he called "Burt's Durves," his special concoctions of hors d'oeuvres. They could be as simple as cotto salami or imported cheese or both. Might be peppered venison sausage made into "Bitty Burgers" or miniature rye bread topped with ham. Sometimes he slow-cooked a pot of Burt's Famous Brandied Weenies. "ABSOLUTELY ONE PER CUSTOMER!" He served each of his Durves with a side of your choice, either a special mustard (Featured Mustard of the Week! He had a whole shelf devoted to mustards from around the world.) or his homemade killer horseradish that he called Burt's Burn. Hands down, that was Ken's favorite. The mustard and horseradish were served in little pleated paper containers that resembled miniature chef's hats. People either dipped their Durve into the cup or squeezed the contents onto their Durves, depending on the Durve. By special request, you could also get your sauces blended. But the most fun was dreaming up new, creative, and ridiculous ways to order your Durve from Burt. How this riotous practice got started, no one could recall, but it was full-on competition now.

Leo, who loved bantering with Burt any day, said, "I'll take one Durve, blended, straight up, hold the foam." Not to be outdone by his friend, Ken ordered, "A Burt Durve, Wanoni style, and burn me, babe!"

After the guys finished their Durves and made their grilling purchases for the cookout at the Higgins home on Saturday, they walked to their cars together.

"Cassie find out any more about that snowglobe thing?" Leo asked.

"Nope. In fact, I hope she's forgotten about it." Ken felt no need to tell Leo he'd hidden it from her. Thankfully, she hadn't asked him about it either.

"Strange, though, huh?"

"Nah. I figure the vendor just pulled a fast one on her. You know how gullible she can be sometimes." Ken swung his bag into the trunk, closed the lid, and walked around to the driver's-side door. "See you guys Saturday."

"About five, right?"

"That's the way I heard it, but you know the girls. Things can always change, so stay tuned."

After the Higginses added their third child to the brood, they always held the barbeques. Before Harry, they used to take turns, but then Cassandra said it was just easier for them to host since the kids had their toys, their beds, and the childproof Everything Room. "As if," Margret told Cassandra the evening they witnessed Chuck stuffing a piece of peanut butter toast into the DVD player. Cassandra always added, "Besides, everything is so nice at your house. I'd hate for the kids to wreck something."

Each time Margret heard those words, she wanted to shout how she'd trade *all* their orderly niceness, expensive accessories, and her bank vice-presidency job for the chaos of a house filled with children. Instead, she bit her tongue and tried to be thankful for the fact that, yes, she and Leo did have nice things. Thankfulness helped keep her body relaxed, which doctors believed played a key role in the child-conceiving battle.

When at long last it was Betty's turn at the counter, she ordered "One hors d'oeuvre with *no* sauce, thank you." Same as usual. For years, Burt noticed that sometimes she'd wrap the treat in the napkin he handed to her and tuck it into her handbag. She was so thin. He often wondered if that's *all* she ate for her dinner. But then he knew what it was like to have to dine alone; he'd lost his wife five years ago.

"You having a cookout with one of your kids this weekend?" he asked Betty.

Betty tucked her lips inside her mouth. "I'm just looking forward to a nice restful weekend alone. Work's been real busy, which is good in this economy. But at my age, I don't bounce back the way I used to."

"You say that like you're old."

"Well, what do you call sixty?"

"Midlife, because if you're old, then I'm ancient!" At a merry sixty-two, Burt was slightly shorter than Betty, and decidedly rounder.

"What'll you have today?" he asked, wiping his hands down the front of his apron. "I got some real nice veal cutlets on a super-duper special," he said, pointing to the tray.

Betty bent to look in the case and took note of the price per pound. "Even at the sale price, I'm surprised *anyone* can afford your super-duper special!"

"Now Betty, I'm guessing you haven't checked what they're getting for veal down at Center Foods lately, have you? And I'll bet you a dollar to one of Blanchard's dough-nutty donuts you'll get a better tasting slice of veal here."

"I don't doubt that," she said, snagging a quick peak at the growing line of people behind her. "I'll take two Polish sausages."

"Two? Got you a fellow?" He winked at her again.

Betty went crimson. "Burt," she said, almost under her breath. "Honestly, the ridiculous things you say!" It was clear she hoped nobody overheard him. "I'm going to make a couple of meals out of them."

"Like?"

"I'll probably add half of one to some scrambled eggs, then make a hot dish out of the rest."

"What kind of hot dish?" he asked, as he origamied the sausage wrapping. Out of the corner of his eye, he noticed a newcomer to the shop studying his technique, so he gave the package a flourish of extra flips and a hearty palm smack when he was done. He grabbed his big flat pencil from behind his ear, wrote on the package, and told Betty her price.

"Just something simple. Maybe I'll slice it up with some potatoes and cabbage, add a little green pepper. I have to admit, the garlic you put in your sausages makes just about any dish taste good."

"Thank you, ma'am. That's the nicest thing you've ever said to me!" he gushed as he handed her the goods. And *again*, that wink, which he just couldn't seem to keep his eye from doing.

∽

Betty paid up and went on her way, but she couldn't help but wonder if Burt spoke the truth. *Was* that the nicest thing she'd ever said to him? After all these years of buying meat in his shop? After all the times she just knew he added a few extra ounces here and there and never charged her or, on occasion, had even handed her two hors d'oeuvres, one piled atop the other so nobody would notice?

Betty's tongue was healed from the tea burn, but two days ago, she'd accidentally chomped on it. The pain had become a constant reminder that her tongue held power. Cassandra's outburst had tripped some kind of trigger within Betty, who'd oddly found herself obsessing over the sum whole of her life. Whether she was working on the factory line, washing dishes in her kitchen, or leaving Burt's, disturbing thoughts and questions interrupted her peace. Like, when was the last time she'd paid Cassandra a compliment or called her sons rather than waiting for them to call her? They both did well in their jobs; finances weren't tight for them like they were for Betty. Sure, it would cost her long-distance charges, but so what. She could afford a few *calls*. And did she ever pay anyone compliments or cheer them on? If someone said, "Oh, I know Betty Kamrowski! She's…" What would they say? …crabby? quiet? mean?

And if they asked *her* who she was, how would she answer? Would she dare to be honest and answer…lonesome? miserable? guilty? tired?

Was it possible she'd become an old hag of a widow, nothing but a thorn in her children's sides? If so, no wonder she felt lonely and isolated. Who'd want to spend time talking to someone like that? The last time her older son called, he even asked her why she always began a call by making him feel guilty for not calling. The conversation remained its usual cool and distant "How's the weather" and "Tell me about the kids," but it was perfunctory at best, ancient hostilities and misunderstandings bubbling right under the surface. She wondered, in fact, if either of her sons really knew her at all, or did they just know the crusty woman she'd had to become so early on.

She wondered how she let her life slip into such a quiet desperation. Why, she wondered, was she locked on these hapless thoughts?

Then again, who was there to cheer *her* on? Who was in *her* corner? Did anyone have a clue how wrung out she often felt at the end of the day when she dragged herself back to her drab little house? Did Cassandra give a thought to how horrifying it felt for Betty to see her baby girl on the television looking battered, without even a call to her mother? Did Cassandra understand how awful it was to sit home alone on a holiday weekend? Had she refused their invitations so many times that they'd finally tired of inviting her?

Then again, why would *Cassandra have called if all I had to say was "I told you so. Your whole life, I told you you'd get knocked in the head"?* But didn't Cassandra understand? Betty had only repeatedly told her that in an effort to *protect* her, to warn her that she needed to wise up, so that something like this *didn't* happen.

Have my tongue and my thoughts now talked my children and *me into believing I am nothing more than a tiresome shrew?*

Am I?

She purposely ran her sore tongue up against her teeth, as if to punish it.

Twenty-five years. Twenty-five years earlier her husband left her to fend for herself and for their children. A quarter of a century. She thought back to their wedding day. Their young elopement and the bright hope in her heart, the joy that enveloped her as they snuck away. She summoned up the image of her and Gerald dancing their first polka in their living room as a married couple, recalled the sensation of her full cream-colored skirt (hand stitched and embroidered by her mother) swishing around her calves. For a moment her spirits were lifted by the memory of their perfect twirl, but now…

Gerald was gone, and where had his "Bet" gone?

How could so many years have slipped by without her noticing?

During the rest of her seven-block walk home, for the life of her, she could not think of one nice thing she'd ever said to Burt or even acknowledged he'd often given her more than what he'd charged her for. Her cheeks reddened: she did, however, badger him about not *selling* her more than she could afford.

Had she even sent him a card after his wife died? Burt and his wife had sent her one of the few cards she'd received after Gerald's death. She remembered how they'd each written on the card, too, and dropped a hot dish at her door. A person didn't forget such personal and welcome gestures. Under the circumstances of Gerald's death, most people hadn't known *what* to say, how to respond or help. She supposed it felt awkward for people to even comment after a suicide, but…they did nothing. The silence had been nearly unbearable, almost as if the suicide hadn't happened. But everything had changed.

When she got home, she turned on the oven and started to unwrap her package. "Happy Columbus Day, Betty," it read in thick carpenter's pencil on the outside of the paper. As if to pour more hot coals on her head, she discovered four Polish sausages in her package instead of the two she'd ordered and paid for. She gasped.

How could simple Polish sausage, a gift from a kind soul such as Burt Burt, tilt the scales so swiftly that the weight of her brokenness and guilt suddenly—and literally—hunched her spine? With a great gust of an exhale, she moaned as her eyes welled with tears.

Fifteen

Irene watched her daughter hold a potato under the filtered water pouring out of her tall gooseneck faucet. Irene had stopped by Margret's house on her way home from helping her husband at the office, just to say hello.

"Obviously," Margret said, nodding at the giant bag of potatoes on the counter, "I'm taking potato salad to Cassie's this weekend for the cookout. I think I'll make some deviled eggs too. Leo picked up a jar of one of Burt's milder mustards. I thought I'd give that a try in a small batch. What are you and dad up to this weekend?"

"Nothing much. Dad said he wants to do a little more yard winterizing." Irene picked up a chunk of raw potato and popped it into her mouth.

"What kind of winterizing? Do you need us to come over and lend a hand?"

"We might be getting up there in age, dearie," she said, giving her daughter a gentle hip-check, "and I might be helping your dad less with the bookkeeping at work, and he might be preparing for semi-*semi*-retirement, but you betcha we can still plant bulbs and cover rose bushes. And a few other things I shall not mention." She winked at her daughter.

"Mom!" Margret laughed, then said, "Well, why not?"

"Exactly." Irene raised and lowered her eyebrows a few times.

"No matter what else you're doing—or not—if you or Dad decide you need help with ladders or anything, give a holler. I imagine we'll stop by this weekend anyway. You pick anything up at Burt's? Cooking out?"

"Your dad went. He said he's going to surprise me. He's so excited the weather looks like it's going to hold out. 'Still grilling season, Reenie,' he said. And I asked, 'Grilling what?' and he said 'You'll find out come Monday!'"

"Think he picked up enough for four of us? We're having our picnic with Cassie and crew Saturday. Sunday we're planning on just lolling around after church, but Monday sounds like a great day to do more lolling at your house." Margret shook the water off her peeler and cleared her voice.

"Hey, speaking of lolling, have you and Dad given any more thought to what you're going to do with yourselves after he's retired—completely out of the business?"

"It's a subject your dad doesn't want to talk about. He says he'll think about it when the time comes. End of story."

"Sounds like Dad. I just can't imagine him staying idle for long, though."

"Me neither. He's always been a man of excesses, which is why I bet he picked up plenty of extra meat to feed you two on Monday too. When doesn't he? I'll have him get back to you."

"I think I'll peel a few more potatoes then, and make a double batch of deviled eggs. There—you already got your side dishes covered."

Irene watched her daughter scrape the potato peeler over another potato. It pleased her that among all of Margret's expensive, high-tech, ergonomically correct kitchen gadgets, she still used a decades-old peeler, one that used to be hers. She remembered when the transfer—what Margret referred to as an early inheritance—took place.

A couple of years before, Margret was at her house, standing beside *her* while *she* peeled potatoes. As usual, their lively chatter had progressed as swiftly as Irene's hands put the potato through the drill. Irene was aware of her daughter watching her peel and rinse, peel and rinse, then plop the potato into a big saucepan full of water, where it would remain until she started the dicing.

Suddenly Margret said, "Mom, one day when you're gone, I want that potato peeler. It brings back so many memories."

Irene turned off the water and pivoted to face her only child.

"Remember how when I was really little, I used to pull a chair up next to you to help?" Irene smiled and nodded. "I loved watching you peel potatoes, Mom. You were—and continue to be—so efficient at it. And your hands have always been so beautiful."

Irene pulled her hands from beneath the running water and took note of how many age spots they'd sprouted—another soulful reminder of the passing of time. Nonetheless, her fingers still remained long and delicate, just like *her* mother's, right up until her death at age ninety. Sometimes heredity was a wonderful thing.

She went back to peeling, but her daughter continued to stare at her hands while she worked.

"Those hands helped me learn how to do so many things." To Irene's surprise, Margret gently sandwiched the hand in which she held the peeler between her palms, water pouring over them like a sacred baptism. "You were so patient with me, even when I was a brat."

Irene smiled. "Who says you're not *still* a brat?"

"Agreed. Seriously though, Mom, I can't imagine how many cumulative years we must have spent standing here while I talked and you peeled and listened. I am so grateful you're my mom." Margret's voice cracked. "Not everybody gets so lucky."

Irene withdrew her hand from her daughter's clasp, then turned

Margret's palm face up and slapped the peeler into it. "Why should you have to wait until I *die* to get this ratty old thing? Here you go! Anyway, I bought a new one about six months ago. I don't know what possessed me, other than it had this wonderful, cushy, fat, blue handle. It looked like it might be easier on my aging knuckles. I haven't bothered to even take it off the cardboard yet."

Just like that, a piece of family tradition had been passed along. Irene still prayed that one day the peeler would be inherited by a grand-child, but—

"Earth to Mom! Earth to Mom."

Irene blinked. "I'm sorry. Did you say something?"

"Where'd you go?"

"Oh," she said, putting her arm around her daughter's waist and drawing her close, "I was just thinking back on the day I gave you that peeler."

"You want it *back*?" Margret cocked her head and pretended she was going to cry.

"Of course not. I love my new peeler...and I love watching you use this one."

"Good, because you'd have to wrestle me for it." She gave her mom a peck on the cheek. "Besides, I feel close to you every time I use this old thing. Doesn't it just do your heart good to know that every kohlrabi and zucchini I peel reminds me of you?"

Irene chucked her daughter's nose with her damp knuckle. "Once a brat, always a brat."

❧

The scent of garlicky baking sausage wafted up Betty's nose. It smelled the same as her father used to make. He, too, always added fresh chopped garlic to the mix before stuffing the casings. *"And an extra dollop for good health."*

He was such a cheerful soul. Oh, how she missed his positive presence! Even though she often fussed at him for what she perceived to be his bouts of melancholy, dreamy thinking, or not facing up to the reality that life was *hard,* she depended on his happy counterbalance. She didn't realize just how much she leaned on him—*counted* on him to stop her fussing—until he was gone. Then she had to hold herself telescope straight just to keep from toppling over into a pool of utter despair.

For the first time in years, Bad Betty Kamrowski caved in to such an indefinable longing that she sat at her kitchen table and cried. Not even the incense in her church had ever incited such a powerful, deeply rooted longing—but for exactly what, she wasn't sure.

How odd to be thinking about the incense again, she thought. She only knew that for whatever reasons, the combination of Burt's kindness, the negative power in her own tongue, and the familiar and pleasing fragrance of a food from her heritage had made her irreconcilably sad. It was much easier to stay crusty—which kept her vulnerabilities tucked in where they belonged. But now, her innermost private thoughts were turned inside out, straight into a big pile of hurt.

She *missed* hearing her parents' odd and rough mix of their native Kashubian Polish words and their newly discovered English. She longed to once again smell the rich scents rising from their endless pots of soup, to see the red of their homemade *barszcz,* to feel the crunch of her mother's cucumber salad with loads of sour cream, and to imbibe in the heartiness of homemade potato and cheese pierogi—none of which would ever taste or smell the same without her parents there to pass and share them.

When they were alive, she'd constantly reminded her family that they were *Americans* now, so why didn't they stop with their odd Polish behaviors and recipes? Their staunch old-worldliness was embarrassing. But now she realized that the older she'd grown, the more she'd felt drawn to their ethnicities—her ethnicities. She missed hearing the sound of *Jeszcze Polska nie zginela,* the Polish national anthem, scratching through the speakers on her parents' ancient turntable. When she tried to sing it, to her disappointment, she realized she no longer remembered all the words in Polish. She looked around the room, as if to make the turntable and the vinyl record of her youth materialize so that she might hear it again, to make her immigrant grandparents proud that she still remembered.

Whatever happened to the record, the turntable—my memory? Acht. No doubt they, too, were victims of so many deaths. *"Co mam zrobić?,"* she heard her mother say. *"What am I to do?"* They were all gone. To cover the funeral costs of Gerald and her father, which were only a year apart, she'd had to sell so many things. She concluded that a person could not make rational decisions during times of severe grief and that they should not be held responsible. *But you do what you have to do, and that is that.* Betty's mantra.

She folded her fingers, studying them as if they didn't belong to her. Her hands were shaped like her father's. What she wouldn't give to hear them clapping along to the records on the old Victrola. She pictured her mother's strong hands smoothing the brightly colored, distinctively recognizable Kashubian hand-stitched floral patterns on one of her many aprons. She chuckled, recalling her mother striving to translate *her* own mother's frantic native Kashubian tongue, a different dialect than spoken in other areas of Poland, in an attempt to explain *Śmigus-dyngus.* "Grandmother says, *'How could you not look forward to the Monday after*

Easter in Poland?' *Mói bracia* used to awaken me by pouring cold water on my head and by tapping my legs with twigs."

Betty recalled that her little Cassandra, always the sensitive child, asked, *"You have to* hit *somebody to celebrate?"*

"Mother, are you sure you're interpreting that correctly?" Betty asked. It didn't sound fun to her, either. Both she and Cassandra were assured that there was a difference between tapping and hitting. However, Cassandra's brothers also heard the story and decided that *Śmigus-dyngus* was a Polish holiday tradition worth carrying on. But when the twig tapping got a little out of hand, *all* the kids ended up being sent to their rooms by Grandpa Wonky, who was as tolerant as they come. Oh, how they'd all laughed time and again recounting the tale.

Betty realized she was smiling. She decided it was time she allowed herself to embrace the roots from which she came, something she'd spent far too much energy renouncing. *Is this what happens when we age? We get all...soft?* How many times had her old friend Carol, who volunteered at the Polish Cultural Institute in Winona, called and asked her to come visit, to have coffee, to see all the wonderful things in the museum? Betty had always replied, *"Why should I care about a Polish museum?"* Or *"Maybe someday, but not today."* Or her classic, *"I'm just so tired."* Perhaps it was time to connect, to reconnect, with some of those people and pieces from her past.

But just like that, her kindling enthusiasm faded. *So many lost years...*

She slumped so far down in her chair that she finally let her forehead rest in her upturned palms. Within a few seconds, she heard the terrible sound of her own tears tapping onto the oil cloth. She had never felt more hopeless. How, she fretted, would she ever recover from allowing herself to *feel*?

She recalled once asking her dad how he could possibly stay so strong in light of his circumstances. *"Bóg jest ze mną."* God is with me. *"Bóg czuwa nade mną."* God is watching over me. Then he added, *"Niech Cie Bóg błogosławi."* May God bless *you*.

If there *was* a God, and if He hadn't already written her off like He turned Gerald away from heaven, might that God—the God of her father, who'd asked that God to bless her—be her salvation from her own impossible self? She doubted it, but what else could she try?

She vowed right then and there that this weekend, she was going to go to church—even if God struck her dead for doing so. Maybe she'd try one of those big Lutheran churches in a neighboring town. One where she could blend in with the crowd, hopefully go unnoticed. She'd sit way in the back, in case she needed to flee.

Wouldn't it be a shame if God *did* strike her dead before she had a chance to make some amends, maybe open some new doors? One of her hardest rejections came from her grandson Harry. Harry, who clung to *everyone's* legs, had never once tried to grab hold of hers.

Her dear grandsons. She chewed her bottom lip. The thing she said most often to them, the last thing she said recently was, "You boys are so rowdy, you're going to be the death of your mother."

"Oh, *God*!" she cried, the power of her own tongue never feeling more palpable. She lifted her tear-laden face from the table and turned her eyes upward. "I take it back. I certainly don't mean it, not any more than I wished for Cassandra to get injured. I promise, I'll never say anything like that again!"

She gasped. *Look what I accidentally did!* For the first time in decades, she'd prayed. She heard the clock ticking in the background. *Tick, tock, tick, tock.* Her remaining years were ticking away. She couldn't bear to think she'd have to spend the rest of her days this alone and miserable. Surely Gerald's Bet still lived within her somewhere.

But whose Bet was she, now that Gerald was gone?

Is this how his slide into despair began?

In a welcome moment of distraction, she answered her own question. *I'm the Bet who has to check the Polish sausage so it doesn't burn. We do what we have to do, and then we move on.* As she opened the oven door and sniffed, taking in the wonderful garlicky aroma, a funny thought—a true rarity for Betty—struck her. She remembered how the priests used to talk about the "incense of prayer." Wouldn't they be surprised to learn that the essence of Burt's garlicky Polish sausage could render and lift prayers as well? That thought made her laugh—until she cried again, her salty tears sizzling onto the hot pan as she watched the steamy smoke curls rise.

"What have we got here?"

Cassie startled. In the midst of her singing, she hadn't heard her Grandpa Wonky wheeling up behind her and Toby hunkered down just outside the shed.

"Toby, meet my Grandpa Wonky! He's going to help us!"

"Toby, is it? Jak się pan ma, Toby? How do you do?"

"He's hurt, Grandpa. Something's wrong with his leg. It has a sore. I want to make him a bed in the shed, but I don't want anything dirty to touch it. Plus, he can't really walk."

"Where did you find such a fine fellow?" he asked, slowly bending over and moving the back of his hand toward Toby's nose.

"In the woods, curled up under a tree."

"How did you get him here?"

"I carried him."

"All the way from the woods? By yourself?"

Her sweaty dirt-streaked face told of her heroic efforts. "He needed me, Grandpa. I couldn't just leave him there."

"I expect he did, my Cassie girl. I expect he did."

"Your mom's at the grocery store," he said. He knew exactly what Cassie was already thinking and why she was back here behind the shed with Toby, looking over her shoulder. It was a freeing, yet activating bit of knowledge for both of them. In high gear, together, they managed to wash, disinfect, and bandage Toby's leg and make him a bed. They wadded up newspapers for a cushion and laid a threadbare towel over them. He assured Cassie that her instincts about not using a dirty burlap bag were good.

"What can we feed him, Grandpa?"

"Let me think on that. You know we're going to have to tell your mom, don't you? And likely pretty soon. We don't want her to find out when he barks or comes gimping into the backyard. We can't just keep him locked in here all the time."

"I know," she said, her voice forlorn.

"Why don't you go in and wash up? I'll stay here with Toby for a while and make sure he gets something to eat tonight. Let me handle your mother, okay?"

Her big round eyes studied him. She bit her lip and looked back and forth between Toby and her grandpa. "Okay," she finally said. "Toby, you be good for Grandpa. He's the best thing that's happened to you today." She gave Toby a gentle hug and a kiss between his eyes.

"No sir," Grandpa said, reaching for his granddaughter's hand. "Nothing better will ever happen to Toby than the moment he met you. And don't you worry. I'll deal with your mother. If nobody claims him—and you know we'll have to post a sign, right?—he'll be yours forever."

Nothing in the world could be better for his granddaughter's heart than to have someone like Toby to wrap her loving arms around. After all, he likely wouldn't be here for too many more years. Doc hadn't given him much good news during his last visit. Betty was tied up in knots, Gerald was in a world of his own, her brothers were self-absorbed...and that child needed some tender loving. Toby looked like just the guy to deliver it.

Cassie crawled up in his lap. Toby's head popped up. He seemed to be deciding if Cassie needed protecting.

"If he looks too sad or growls—and he can't help it sometimes, Grandpa, but he won't hurt you, I promise—just start humming like this, okay?" She threw her arms around her grandpa's neck and hummed until he joined in. With a sigh, Toby rested his head back on the ground.

Sixteen

Heading into the Columbus Day weekend, Cassandra couldn't seem to settle down. She'd cut out caffeine, gone to bed early, walked the whole parade of kids around the block twice, and bought herself a bottle of stress tablets. She'd read somewhere that vitamin B complex was good for your nerves. Still, her heart raced as if she were waiting for something big to happen, like it might do if she were preparing to give a speech in front of a room of professors. She even noticed herself bouncing her knee.

Even though the snowglobe was hidden, she knew it was out there. Maybe while nobody was looking, it was doing something—or not. She waffled between just asking Ken to give it back, which she knew he would, and knowing it was better just left alone. After all, she obsessed enough about it without having it in front of her. Either way, though, she had this feeling that *what*ever her *whatever* had been all about with that thing, it wasn't over yet.

She needed to focus her energy or channel it or something. The more jittery she remained, so, too, the kids seemed to pick up on those energies. They were nearly bouncing off the walls earlier today.

Now the day-care kids were gone, dinner was over, table cleared and the dishwasher loaded. Ken was outside tilling under the remnants of their small garden plot and tidying up the back porch for the cookout. When she heard the noisy shed door squeak closed, she knew he was done with the tiller and it was time to get Bradley in bed. Plus with the tiller put away, she could safely send at least one of the kids out there to "help" Ken finish up the yard work.

"Harry, I think Daddy needs your help getting ready for Auntie Magpie and Uncle Leo." Without another ounce of coaxing, Harry's two-year-old legs headed him straight for the backyard. "GET YOUR SWEATSHIRT!" she hollered. As soon as Harry was out the door, she put Bradley to bed. Thankfully, he went without a peep. All that fresh air from their walk, she thought.

"CHUCK! HOWIE! Turn that TV off and come help Mommy!" They loved when she needed them, so in a flash, they were at her side. "Chuck, get down on the floor here in front of this cabinet, and scrounge around in the back of it until you see a stack of cookbooks. Bring them out for Mommy, okay?"

"You want me to crawl back into Dead Man's Corner? *No way!*" They called it Dead Man's Corner since as far as anyone was concerned, there could be a dead man way back in the corner of that cabinet and they'd never know it.

"Howie, grab hold of Chuck's leg when he goes in, just in case you have to pull him out, okay? I'll stand by, Spidey." If she ever wanted to prod Chuck, invoking the name of Spider-Man usually helped.

"You should call Harry in to hold his leg," Howie protested.

"But I'm asking you, honey, because you…have more muscles than he does." In a flash, one crawled in and the other was poised for retrieval duty.

After some chaos, out came the stack of books. "Wonderful!" They passed high-fives around, then tried the new knuckle-whapping thing the boys had learned to do while watching the X Games on TV.

Cassandra riffled through the cookbooks. "Here it is. Thank you,

boys! Good work. Just stuff the rest of the cookbooks and Tupper-
ware—and whatever else you dragged out—back in there, okay? And
by the way, you didn't find a dead man, did you?"

Chuck gave her a six-year-old's look of disgust, once again reminding her of her mother.

"Appetizers." The book was vintage fifties, and the woman on the
cover wore an apron and a perky hairdo, and flashed a mouthful of teeth
straight at Cassandra. When Betty brought over the bag of cookbooks,
she'd said, "You're the one who does the entertaining. I sure don't need
these cluttering up my kitchen."

"Where'd you get all these?" Cassandra had asked, pleased about
her mother's gift. "I've never seen them before." The model looked so
happy. Those ladies from the fifties were always smiling, their full skirts
flaring around them like half-open parasols.

"Garage sales. At the time, I used to think I'd do more..." Her
voice had trailed off. "I don't think I paid more than a quarter for any
of them. I tried a couple of recipes." She'd scrunched her face up, just
like Chuck—or vice versa.

"Thanks," Cassandra had said, meaning it. It wasn't like her mom
to come bearing gifts. The gesture felt extra special.

"Just toss them if you don't want them. You got enough clutter in
here anyway." Betty looked around in disgust at the piles of backpacks,
papers, dirty dishes, and snowglobes on the kitchen counter, getting her
gut-punch in.

Cassandra had forgotten about the cookbooks until the other day,
when she'd been searching to see if she could locate where Ken might
have hidden the snowglobe. What better place than Dead Man's Corner? Although she didn't find the globe, she did spy the cookbooks.

"Come to the kitchen table and help Mommy find a recipe for a special treat for our picnic, okay? Something you think Auntie Magpie and Uncle Leo would like."

"Let's make chocolate chip cookies," Howie said. Already, he was heading toward the cabinet with the chocolate chips, preparing to drag a chair over there and climb up to get them. "And let's not burn them this time, okay?"

"What a good memory you have, Howie. All the better to bop you for," she said, smiling and delivering a gentle ding to his head. "We can make cookies tomorrow. Tonight, let's try something different. Look at these wonderful pictures."

"What is *that*?" Howie pointed to an illustration.

Cassandra looked over her son's shoulder, then she pulled up a chair next to him. It appeared to be an old-fashioned shrimp cocktail. *Hmm.* The problem was, she couldn't prepare the shrimp until Saturday, and the boys were ready to help her now—not to mention images of four little boys wielding crystal sherbet cups popped into her mind.

"How about this?" Chuck asked, pointing to what looked like little pizzas.

"Stuffed mushrooms," Cassandra said.

"I hate mushrooms!" Chuck said, frowning and crossing his arms.

"What if they were stuffed with chocolate chip cookie dough?" Cassandra loved throwing her temperamental son a curve ball every now and again.

"Blaaaach. How about we just make the cookies?"

"Yeah, blaaaach," Howie added.

Cassandra flipped through the pages. "Yeah, blaaaach." She closed the book. "How about we just make the cookies?"

There was something calming and comforting about the smell of baking cookies—when baked, not broiled—and she'd noticed her knee was bouncing again, as though powered by a jackhammer.

Ten minutes into the process, she couldn't help but look from one son to the other. They were so engrossed, their faces a smear of cookie dough. The misshapen, mismatched wads of dough on the cookie trays looked like someone flung them there with a wrist rocket. But still, it was absolutely a perfect moment. Perfect. She wondered if her boys would remember the laughter, the mess, and helping Mom in the kitchen as long as she would. She couldn't recall one time from her youth when Betty had asked her to help, a thought that choked her up. *"You'll make a mess. I can do it faster myself."*

When the boys gathered near as she pulled the first tray out of the oven, Harry back with his brothers, she inhaled and said, "Just smell that, boys. I don't know about you, but I think that is exactly what heaven smells like." They all sniffed and snorted and had to agree.

"Do you think Grandpa Gerald smells it too?" Chuck asked, looking her straight in the eye.

Cassandra's breath caught in her throat. "What made you think about Grandpa Gerald?"

"When you went to the doctor's and we were at Grandma's house, I asked her about the picture in her bedroom."

"What did she say?" Cassandra nearly whispered.

"She said, 'That is your Grandpa Gerald.' And I said, 'He's dead, right?' And she said 'yes.'"

"Is that all?"

"No. That's not all she said."

"Well?"

"I asked her if he was in heaven."

"How did she answer?" Cassandra forced her voice to sound casual and steady. She would *never* forget when she accidentally overheard her mother repeat the terrible thing she was told about what happens to the soul of someone who commits suicide. Harry was hanging on her leg, so she bent and picked him up, then settled him on her hip. "Chuck, what did Grandma say?"

"She said, 'You boys need to get out of this bedroom. Who told you you could come in here anyway?'"

Seventeen

Late Saturday afternoon of Columbus Day weekend, Betty's phone rang, a seldom-heard sound that always startled her.

It was Burt.

He wanted to know if Betty had made that hot dish yet. If she had, did she have any left? And if she had some left, maybe she'd like to have him over for dinner that evening. He knew it was last minute, but what the heck. He'd be happy to bring some Durves for them to share before their meal, and if he came over right then, it would still be light outside and nice enough for them to enjoy the Durves on Betty's swell front porch.

With words pouring forth in such a nervous, endless stream that she didn't have time to respond to any of his questions, he said that ever since she'd talked about that hot dish in the shop the other day, he couldn't stop craving a homemade meal he didn't have to make for himself. "And God bless my kids and grandkids" he said, sounding like he meant it, "but sometimes they just about wear me out."

But especially, Burt said, he desired the company of someone to share such a meal with. He said he thought she might enjoy the company as much as he would, and how, after all, it was a holiday weekend and they should do something to celebrate it. Why not together? And did she make the hot dish, and had she eaten it all yet?

"How about it, Betty? What do you say?"

What did she say? What did she *say*? She couldn't even think, much less speak!

What was she *supposed* to say?

She had to think.

The truth was, the hot dish was not only bubbling on the stove right this minute, it was just about done. This afternoon she'd cut up the remaining links, planning to freeze some of it, but then she examined an onion and a few potatoes that needed to be used before they went bad. The next thing she knew, she'd added another can of broth and a little more cabbage and—

She just couldn't believe this. What was Burt thinking? Durves on her front porch? Where neighbors would see?

Her eyes darted around her kitchen. All the cooking utensils were washed and put away; the only thing out of order was the pan on the stove. She'd cleaned the whole house this morning.

Burt had never been to her house. Hardly anyone other than family had. Entertaining wasn't Betty's forte. When you lived on a shoestring, you didn't have much to share. Besides, she hadn't been trained in many social graces, and small talk often eluded her.

Her house was drab.

Burt was short.

But freely and free of charge, he'd given her half the sausage cooking in the hot dish.

"Betty? Are you there?"

"Yes, Burt. I'm here." The tightness in her voice came out as anger rather than the mix of shock, fear, and ineptness she felt.

"I'm sorry, Betty. I didn't mean to offend you. I just thought that…since…maybe…you know, Columbus Day and all…"

Silence.

"Now that I think about it, it was pretty rude to just invite myself over like this. I'm sorry if I've offended you, Betty. Seriously."

Betty simply could not think of anything to say. She swallowed. She stretched the phone cord until she could reach the stove and turn off the burner, as though that might end this conversation.

"I'll let you go then, Betty." Burt's voice sank to a sorrowful note. "I hope you have a nice weekend."

Before she could utter a word, he hung up.

Burt set the receiver in its cradle and shook his head. He sighed and leaned back on the couch. He was tired. Since Thursday, the shop had been crazed. Good crazed, but nonetheless bordering on frenetic. He understood what Betty meant the other day when she said she didn't bounce back the way she used to.

Betty. He hoped she'd come back to the shop, that he hadn't scared her off, not only from him personally, but as a customer.

He shook his head again, trying to recall the last time he'd mustered the courage to ask a woman out on any sort of date. He counted back. *Three years ago Helen Osowski turned me down flat.* In that case, however, he'd been relieved. It had been only a couple of years after his wife's death, and he wasn't ready—nor were his children. Eventually, he realized that sometimes a person had to come to grips with his own loneliness—to make peace with it—before he could try to pawn it off or fill it up with someone else. In the last year, there'd been a couple of widows who frequented the shop, putting a few moves on him, but he'd not been inclined to reciprocate.

But today, with Betty, he'd been more than ready. There was something about the way she always held herself so erect, worked so hard to button up her emotions, took such diligent steps to stretch her dollars—something Burt admired. The way she fired the word *certainly.*

However, more than once, he'd noted the crimson on her neck when he'd teased her. She harbored more feelings than people gave her credit for.

Having himself felt the depths of sorrow after the loss of a spouse, he couldn't imagine living with the aftermath of a loved one's suicide. It was difficult enough knowing what had claimed his wife's life. They could see the cancerous mass on the x-rays. He couldn't even think what it must have been like—might still be like—for *all* the Kamrowski family to have to fight Gerald's hidden demons. And Betty had been so young at the time. All that second-guessing, unanswered questions, maybe even wondering if she might have been able to do something to prevent it.

Once while waiting in the dentist's office, he leafed through a woman's magazine and came across a first-person article about the aftermath of suicide. He'd stopped when he noticed the subject, wondering if the article might give him any insight into the hidden depths of Betty Kamrowski. He'd finished the article at the exact moment they called him in for his exam. He sat in the dentist's chair with his mouth open, thinking about how difficult it must have been for Betty, even before Gerald took his life. While Burt had gently clenched his teeth on the bite wing for his x-rays, he considered the possible secrets and deceptions of a heart. There hadn't been a spark in Gerald's eyes for a long while, and there didn't seem to be a thing anyone could do to cheer him up. Not even Burt's Barbequed Weenies, which had always been Gerald's favorite. Gerald had passed on them the last time he came in, something Burt never forgot, for the very next day, Gerald was dead. He heard that Gerald's mother had suffered from depression, too, although she lived to a ripe old age.

Maybe he'd write Betty a note of apology and have someone drop it at her house with a pound of Wanoni Bologni. At that inane thought, he actually whapped himself in the head. *You've done enough damage. You think lunchmeats can solve everything? Just let this go and see what happens.*

That instant, his phone rang. "Hello?" he said, picking it up before the second ring.

❧

Betty didn't even say hello. She just started yammering. "The hot dish will be ready at five-thirty. I don't like to eat late. We can have a Durve first, but don't bring very many since there's plenty of hot dish. We'll eat the Durves at my kitchen table, if that's all right. It feels like it's cooling down outside." In reality, Betty had no idea what the temperature was. All she knew was that she was not ready to be found sitting on her front porch with a man.

Silence.

What should she make of *that?* Burt was *never* at a loss for words.

"Oh, my," Betty said, her voice suddenly aflutter. "Have I reached…" *Goodness!* She couldn't ask if she'd actually reached Burt. What if she had misdialed and somebody recognized her voice asking for *Burt?*

"Betty…this is Burt! If you were trying to call me, I accept your…invitation. I'll see you at five-thirty. If you weren't trying to call me, well then, I'd say it's not very nice to take one fellow's idea and invite another to partake of it." He burst out in a great laugh.

"Burt Burt! You *certainly* do say the most ridiculous things."

"I'll see you at five-thirty sharp, Betty."

"Good-bye, Burt." Betty hung up and wrung her hands. This was the craziest thing she'd ever done. It wasn't until then that she thought

to thank him for calling. She whispered the words, as practice for saying them when he arrived.

⁓

Burt grabbed his sweatshirt, preparing to hightail it back to his shop. In
a finger snap of nervous excitement, he'd come up with a brilliant brainstorm, but he didn't have much time. For this special occasion, he
would concoct a Dandy Durve! Nothing too fancy or spicy for Betty,
though. Since they were having Polish sausage in their hot dish, he
didn't want to make anything that would detract.

Before he closed his front door, he'd talked himself out of it. This
was Betty. Plain and simple Betty. She wasn't the Dandy Durve type,
and he didn't want to scare her by making her think he was a psycho or
something. That as a singer might write a song for his new love, he'd
created a special Durve for her. No, this was just dinner and a little
shared company.

He hung his sweatshirt back on its peg and stood, thinking, then
went to the kitchen and got out the package of cheese ends he'd brought
home. He used his crinkle cutter to slice them up to hide the fact they
were ends, a trick he'd learned long ago. He grabbed a box of Town
House crackers and splayed the cheese and crackers on a plain white
plate, which he covered with stretch wrap.

At exactly five-thirty, Burt rang Betty's doorbell. When the door
opened, there stood Betty wearing a plain gray dress, but with a colorful apron tied around her waist.

⁓

The look on Burt's face let her know she'd made the right choice,
unearthing the box from beneath her bed and getting out one of her

mother's long-unused aprons. A hand-embroidered apron was a small step out of her doldrums, to be sure, but a first step. She bet the crimson blush she felt heat her neck nearly matched the beautiful red threads in the handiwork. She couldn't help ringing her hands and biting her bottom lip as her eyes darted both ways down the street before she invited him in.

Burt inhaled. "Ya!" he said on the exhale, an expression that betrayed his Minnesotan roots—even though barely anyone in Wanonishaw actually used the word. "It smells *heavenly* in here, Betty!"

"It's just a regular hot dish."

"Here," he said, handing her a plate of Durves. "I brought us some cheese and crackers."

Betty took note of the crinkle-cut edges. *So fancy!* She suddenly felt overcome with the possibility that her hot dish might not live up to Burt's expectations. That the neighbors might have already spied his car out front. That her children might find out he was here.

That her heart would explode right out of her chest and ruin everything.

Part Two

Mid-December 2008

Eighteen

Betty swiped her finger across the small space between replicas of a skunk and a penguin. She looked at the ripple of dust on the end of her finger, then noted the dust-free streak she'd left on the shelf. She'd never understand her daughter's need to tuck so many trinkets—statues, snowglobes, collector's impressions—into every nook and cranny. It seemed to Betty that just keeping up with four sons plus day-care children would be enough, without adding all the extra work of trying to keep dozens of intricate knickknacks dusted. Although, to be honest, *certainly* Cassandra did not care about dust as much as she did.

"I see you found what you were looking for, Mom," Cassandra said, curtness in her voice. Betty, dusty finger held in front of her, hadn't heard Cassandra return from her bathroom run with Harry, whom Cassandra said indicated he might be ready to take a stab at potty training.

"Oh, I wasn't looking for…I mean to say, I was…"

"Mom, we both know what you were doing." Since Cassandra had yelled at her a few months ago, there remained an ongoing tension between them. But being honest with herself, which she was striving to do more, Betty knew the tension had likely existed for decades. Now that Cassandra had grown bolder with her mother, whatever their issues were seemed more flagrant. Betty thought maybe this was a good thing, but she wasn't sure. Maybe a bad relationship was better than one that completely fell apart.

She swallowed. "I'm sorry, Cassandra." She looked straight into her daughter's eyes. "I don't mean to come over and give you the impression

I'm judging you. Looking for dust is just…a habit. I can't seem to help myself. I only stopped by to see how you're doing. I know the boys have been sick…"

Cassandra just stared at her, mouth open.

"Grandma," Chuck said, "come and see our Lego fort!" He grabbed her by the hand and tugged so swiftly that she nearly tumbled forward, and away they went.

The Everything Room was a disaster, toys everywhere. Betty couldn't even chalk the mess up to day care; it was Saturday. She forced herself to focus her eyes on the object of Chuck, Howie, and Harry's pride, all of them pointing and talking at once about the doors and gates on their Lego structure.

Bradley charged into the room. He was all but running already, Ken close on his heels. Betty couldn't believe how much faster he'd gotten since she'd last seen him a couple of weeks ago. He was making a beeline for a large wooden top, just to her left. When he noticed her presence, he puckered up, veered toward the Lego fort, and stumbled into it, crashing it to pieces. The boys started yelling at him. Ken swooped him up to save him from their wrath. He was a good dad, Betty thought, watching Ken's concern. The boys were lucky.

Cassandra was lucky.

"How you doing, Betty?" Ken chirped. "I didn't know you were here! It's nice to see you. And pardon Bradley's rude welcome; he was just surprised. He's hit that weird shy stage." Clearly, Ken had been surprised by her presence too. "Does Cassandra know you're here?"

"Yes. She's in the kitchen. The boys wanted me to see their fort— well, what's left of it," she said, chuckling.

Cassandra walked in carrying a tray with a pitcher of ice water and a stack of plastic cups. "It's too close to dinner to serve juice," she said, nodding at the boys, who were already rebuilding, "but I thought we could at least have something to drink." Betty noticed Ken shoot his wife a curious look.

"I'll get going," Betty said. "I don't want to hold things up. I should have called first, or noticed the time."

"Why don't you join us for dinner?" Ken asked. "We're just having pizza. It should be here any minute, and we always have plenty."

Betty looked at Cassandra, who seemed paralyzed, her tray of water frozen midair. "No, I better get going."

"Oh, come on, Grandma, STAY!" Chuck said. "Mommy, tell Grandma to STAY!"

Cassandra bit her lip. "Why don't you join us, Mom?"

Betty thought for a moment. How would things *ever* get better between them if they kept avoiding each other? "You know, pizza does sound good."

She took her ancient wool crocheted hat off her head, stuffed it into her coat pocket, and shucked her coat off her shoulders.

"Kenneth Higgins." Cassandra turned back the bedspread on the bed. "The next time you pull a stunt like that, so help me, I'm going to…"

"A stunt like what?"

"Don't play innocent with me! First you hide my snowglobe, then you invite my mother to stay for dinner without asking me? I am not one of your kids!" She scurried into bed and drew the covers up over her head.

"In case you haven't noticed, Cassandra," he said, talking to the lump under the covers, "I've returned the snowglobe to your drawer, and you know why I took it. Once, you even *thanked* me for getting it out of your sight for a while! And I thought we *wanted* your mom to spend more time with the boys. When was the last time we were able to get her to eat with us? Am I missing something here?"

"Yes."

"What?"

"Everything. Everything that *matters*."

Not another word was spoken between them that night.

Cassandra knew she was taking something out on Ken that had nothing to do with him, but she just didn't have it in her to talk about it yet. She needed to sort things out. Her mom's apology had thrown her completely off base. It was, to the best of her recollection, a Bad Betty first. Oddly, rather than arriving as music to her ears, she found it hugely unnerving.

Who is *that woman?*

By Monday morning, the curious storm between Cassandra and Ken had passed, mostly because Cassandra apologized for taking her misplaced frustration out on him.

In a festive mood—and in an obvious attempt to maintain calm seas—Ken decided to heat a bowl of syrup in the microwave for the boys (he nearly always included himself in their numbers) for dunking their French toast. It had taken only a few moments of vying over which boy would dunk his fork, or fistful, next before the entire mess was upturned and oozing onto the linoleum. Ken swiped at the spreading mess with a giant pull of paper towels, which dripped all the way across the kitchen to the garbage can. He reprimanded his sons—the older two were drawing faces in the spill. He looked at the clock, then at Cassandra, who appeared in the kitchen squeezing the handles of an eyelash curler still attached to the eyelashes of her right eye.

Her new makeup-on-before-breakfast regimen was only a day old. She didn't usually get it on at all. She felt like it already had turned into another failed attempt to get her life back on track, to get her house in order, to eradicate dust. Breakfast had come and gone, and she was only to the curl-the-lashes part. Since Saturday night, she'd just kept thinking that if she could come up with the right routine and stick with it, she would feel more in control of *something*. Since the rocky experience with the snowglobe, the Voice, and now her mother's apology, she'd started second-guessing *many* elements of her life. If she were only smarter, she could figure all of this out and deal with it!

Her husband had to leave for work soon if he was going to drop Chuck at school, and he seemed to be making a terrible mess worse. Bradley cried in his highchair, and Harry lunged onto her leg, his tacky fingers giving him extra holding power. Howie dragged a wad of French toast through the syrup, and Chuck ran his hands under the kitchen faucet.

Cassandra made one of her Execu-Mom decisions. Without removing her eyelash curler—leaving her looking like she was staring through the crosshairs of a weapon—she unleashed her command.

"NOBODY MOVE!" She opened the lash curler and hurled herself toward the sink, taking Monkey Man for a surprisingly fast ride. "Ken, go get your briefcase." She grabbed the ever-present dishtowel from her shoulder and ran it under warm water, wrung it out, and in a flurry of activity, started wiping hands. When she was done, she gave them order number two. "Now, everyone KEEP OUT of here until I get this mess under control! Chuck, have a nice day," she said, as he slung his backpack over his shoulders. She planted a quick kiss on top of his head and gave his cheeks a love pinch.

"Harry, do not even *think* about getting back on Mommy's leg! You and your brother take Bradley to the Everything Room. And nobody come back in here until I say you can!" Since it was uncommon for her to use such a loud yet low-pitched threatening voice, everyone obeyed. But even after two more rounds of mopping, a hint of tacky syrup remained. She finally had to give up when the doorbell rang, announcing that the day-care kids were arriving. *Great,* she thought. *Just what everyone needs. More kids.*

For the rest of the day, the tacky floor presented an invisible fly-trap. What remained of the ooey-gooey mess collected miscellaneous bits of cereal, dust, and drool. But at last the day-care kids were gone, and her three littlest ones, still recovering from their colds, were miraculously down for naps at the same time. (Well, she could hear Howie talking to a race car, but at least he was resting.) Chuck wasn't home yet because he had an after-school play date.

With Christmas just a little over two weeks away, Cassandra knew she should do a few more Christmas cards or wrap another present or two. Maybe engage in more desperate online shopping. But she once again had that *flurrious* itch and needed to scratch it. So with a few minutes of freedom and the snowglobe back in her drawer, she was ready to have at it.

How time has a way of easing hysteria. Today she trusted herself enough to unveil it again. Still, she set the timer option on her microwave for ten minutes and pushed the start button. When the timer dinged, it meant she'd be done, no ifs, ands, or buts—a promise she made to herself *and* Ken.

As she sat on the corner of the bed and removed the layers of protection, she heard the music from the kids' Alvin and the Chipmunks Christmas carols CD wafting down the hall from the Everything Room. The boys played that CD over and over, singing along, hurling themselves around, and generally acting as wacky as the Chipmunks.

She chuckled. If this snowglobe really *was* magical, perhaps it would now contain a chipmunk, or snowman, or Rudolph, or maybe even a nativity scene. The mall had been filled with Christmas snowglobes, so many that she decided snowglobes must be *in* this holiday season. She'd even seen one almost as big as a basketball that contained a snowglobe within the snowglobe. There seemed no end to the possibilities. But after she finished removing the last round of paper, she discovered what she figured she would: an empty globe, with some snow.

Nearly two and a half months after her flurrious event, rather than freaking out, she felt an odd, curious detachment, yet she wondered if she might possibly be holding something holy. The snowglobe was once again cradled in her hands, filled with possible bone fragments, the ones she'd wondered about aloud—prayed over—that seemed to bring about the Voice. Since she'd blacked out at the church altar, she couldn't separate the snow from the symbolism of Christ's body, broken for both her...and her mom, who had *apologized* for something. Tears welled in her eyes just thinking about it.

"Anything is possible," Grandpa Wonky used to say. She wondered what he'd say about *this*.

Before she completely overwhelmed herself with spiritual meanings that might not really exist—she pondered the events leading up to the experience and decided to try a new approach to the mystery: a clinical one. Not exactly her strength, but she could stage a reenactment of the happenings.

She scurried down the hall to Ken's lounge chair and turned on the sun lamp. She held the globe up to the light's warm glow, staring, but nothing happened. Then she remembered the strange symbol on the bottom of the base.

Feeling the clock ticking, she carried the globe to her craft center, turned it over, and arranged it under her giant pedestal magnifying glass. She loved the alien-looking magnifier Ken had gotten for her one Mother's Day. It had all kinds of armed hinges and clamplike thingies to hold items in place for hands-free work. She mostly used it for beading projects after the kids went to bed. But the kids, well, they used it to study bugs, their fingerprints, boogers, and just about anything else they could fit under it or clamp to it. She quickly wiped a collection of tiny fingerprints and yucky smudges from the magnifying glass, then slowly rotated the globe until she could clearly see the symbol. She began turning the globe clockwise, stopping every fifteen degrees or so to see if that position might reveal…something. But no amount of rearranging could make the etching materialize into something she recognized. It could still be initials, a map, or maybe some Celtic mark.

Feeling the pressure of the timer, she set the globe upright, took quick note of the falling snow—both inside the globe and outside her window—and went to Ken's section of their floor-to-ceiling bookcase. Where was his book on Celtic symbols? She bumped her index finger over each spine to make sure she wasn't missing it, but it was gone. It had vanished as surely as the three dogs and the little girl. Her ten minutes were gone too, for as soon as she stood up, she heard the familiar microwave *ding*.

Quickly, before she had time to break her own promise, she returned the globe to its underwear sanctuary, then went to the kitchen and filled the sink for her mop job. Time to swipe away any residue of the sticky mess before she got permanently stuck there.

Margret first met Ken when he became the "new guy" at Leo's work, and she ultimately set up the blind date that led to Ken and Cassandra's marriage. As soon as Leo told his wife about Ken's great sense of humor, Margret was all ears. After a couple of months of hearing about Ken's straight-shooting style and laid-back demeanor, Margret started asking Leo questions about Ken's work ethic, if he drank too much ("Didn't you say he was Irish?"), and whether or not he seemed honest. She suggested that Leo invite Ken over for dinner, since, after all, what bachelor in a new town wouldn't enjoy a home-cooked meal?

The evening was a huge success. Ken proved to be everything Leo had professed and more. "He's a perfect hottie," Margret told him. "I have just *got* to introduce him to Cassandra!"

Their first date was a double date with Margret and Leo to the stock-car races. At first, it was clear that Ken's deep blue eyes, broad shoulders, wavy hair, and beautiful smile completely intimidated Cassandra.

"He's beyond a hottie; he's smokin'!" Cassandra told Margret and Leo when Ken left to get a cold drink. "And he's got to be way smarter than me—too smart for me, if he's in management at Bambenek's. What were you two thinking?"

But after the races, when they went out for drinks and Ken started telling stories, he soon had Cassandra laughing. Try as she might not to give in, Cassandra warmed to him. Ken wasn't the least bit pretentious, but real and kind. And miracle of miracles, in spite of Betty's warnings about those "slick West Coast types," he was also a gentleman. After only ten months of dating, Cassandra and Ken married. Their first few married years, the couples even vacationed together, before the Higginses started cranking out babies while the Andersons just kept trying.

Now, perhaps, that was about to change, but not in the way Leo and Margret had hoped and prayed. Just this morning, Margret called Leo home from work to tell him her period had started.

First they cried together, then Margret said, "Leo, I'm tired of trying to have a baby. My body has been through so much... *we* have been through so much. I didn't think I'd have the nerve to tell you, but there it is. Admitting this feels like giving up on a family, and I feel like I'm failing you by wanting to quit. I know how much it means to you, how much a child would mean to you. To me. To our parents." At that, tears welled again. "But I just have this feeling it's time to let go of a baby so we can get back to *living*."

"You could never disappoint me, Margret. Not since the day I first set eyes on you have you disappointed me. Frustrated me? Surprised me? Horrified and defied me?" he said, pulling her closer. "Blessed and gratified me—in uncountable ways? Yes." He laughed and gave her a squeeze. "But disappoint me? Never."

"Do you think it's time to let go of our dream? Or have you had any second thoughts about adoption?" She studied him hard, as if trying to read the secret corners of his soul. The doctor had said that if this procedure didn't work, he had one more idea they might try, but it sounded experimental, and he didn't seem hopeful.

"I think," Leo said, a level and earnest tone in his voice, "if we decide to call it quits right now, with God's help, we'll be able to make peace with our decision and move on. As for adoption, unless *you've* had a change of heart, I think we've examined ourselves as much as humanly possible, and no, I haven't changed my mind. Have you?"

She shook her head. Although they knew people who had adopted, flying to far reaches of the world to meet their new sons and daughters, it didn't feel right for them.

"I'll tell you what. We'll schedule a trip to somewhere exotic and try to remember—although I bet it won't be that difficult—what it felt like to make love when we wanted to, just *because* we wanted to." A sexy crooked grin spread across his face.

"Seriously? Would you really be okay with that?"

"Hel-LO, Margret!"

"I'm talking about quitting trying to have a baby, Dingbat. I know you'd be just fine with the rest of it. I hope I would too. Truthfully, I can barely remember our love life without so many restrictions, efforts, and so much stress."

"I understand. Believe me, I understand."

"At least for now, let's keep this decision to ourselves, okay?"

"You're not even going to tell your folks—or Cassandra?"

"No. I know everyone will support our decision, but I'd see the heartbreak in their eyes, and right now, I've got enough heartache of my own. I just want us to have time to heal together, to *really* feel like we've moved on."

With Leo out, Ken decided to spend his lunch hour engaging in a little more online research. The last thing Ken wanted was to get Cassandra crazed about the snowglobe again. But wouldn't it be a wonderful Christmas gift if he could add some kind of insight to her…whatever?

As a bottom-line man, he couldn't dismiss the strange incident. There had to be a logical explanation—or at least a concrete clue to the mystery. One thing he felt sure of: his wife had experienced *something* with that snowglobe. It was completely out of character, supported by her inability to lie straight-faced, for her to have made the story up.

Months ago, he had lined out the things he presumed to be true: she had purchased a snowglobe; the woman in Chicago verified it had something in it; she brought it home and said she *saw* the figures in it, but now they weren't there. So before Ken had returned the snowglobe to her drawer, he carefully examined it and noticed what looked like a symbol or insignia of some kind. He'd actually set the globe on a flatbed scanner and scanned the odd etching, enlarged the image to several different sizes, and printed out copies. They were now splayed next to him on his desk, along with a couple of pages of notes and his book of Celtic symbols. In front of him, the cursor on his computer monitor blinked in the empty box of a search engine.

If the symbol was recognizable, it eluded him. Just when he thought he'd deciphered something within it—say, the outline of a triquetra—he'd change his mind. It appeared to be layered between something else, or had initials or another symbol etched over it, so he couldn't be sure it *was* the trinity symbol. In his best moments, he thought he was on the trail of an identifying breakthrough; then he'd conclude it was just as likely a child had picked up a sharp object and simply scribbled on the globe bottom. He knew artists often created their own mark, so maybe the symbol meant nothing other than "I made this."

Nonetheless, when the mood, the time, and the opportunity struck, he was at it again, searching for a new angle.

But for now, enough with the mystery. Lunchtime was over. Back to work. Back to reality. Back to challenges with tangible answers.

Nineteen

W hat do you think, Margret?" Ken asked. "Do you think Cassandra would be happy if Santa brought her a puppy for Christmas? I know Christmas is only nine days away, and it would be a crunch to get everything in place, but I'm stoked about the idea!"

Even though Ken knew Leo had headed to the YMCA for a pickup game of handball, when this brainstorm struck him on his way home, he turned straight into the Andersons' driveway. He was beside himself with enthusiasm. It was genius: why not replace the missing dogs in the snowglobe with a real puppy? After all these years of Cassandra's objections and excuses, maybe it was time to just jump in. Her reasons for having a critter-free house just caused sadness to surround her eyes, and Ken couldn't see how her reasons were valid. Maybe, he told Margret, the entire snowglobe incident—whether real or just a brain hiccup— was a sign that it was time for her to have a *real* dog again. One that didn't need to be dusted.

Margret and Leo's German shorthaired pointer, Macy, moved from beneath Ken's hands over to Margret, who rubbed behind her silky ears. Macy did a one-eighty and presented her backside, her favorite place to be scratched. She was a great pet, an alpha dog, and a tireless retriever. Over the years, Leo had taught Ken how to hunt with her. He'd even taken him to a gun auction and helped Ken find the perfect fowl-hunting weapon: an old Browning A5. When he came home with it, Cassandra told him he was almost a *real* Minnesotan now. "All you need is a little more blaze orange and camouflage in your closet and a gun chest where we can lock up the weapons from the kids. Once a hunter gets his first gun, he usually has to have another." Ken added something about a hunting dog, too, but she'd just given him that look. She was right about the gun, though. It wasn't two months before he purchased another.

Another Minnesotan outdoorsman trait Ken had learned was how to appropriately appreciate Macy's retrieving prowess, which didn't happen until he hunted with another group of guys from work. Their dogs were pretty much worthless on all obedience and retrieving counts. It helped him better understand Cassandra's knowledgeable comments about people having the right dog for the right job.

Even though he was excited about getting the puppy for Cassandra, in his heart of hearts, he hoped it might turn out to be a good retriever too.

"I don't know about this puppy thing, Ken," Margret said. "You've talked with Cassie countless times before. What's different now? She'll probably just say the same thing she always does, which is 'I get my dog fix from Macy, Minie, and Moe, and that's enough.'"

Minie and Moe were the Bambeneks' Jack Russell terriers. Carl and Irene's first brother-and-sister duo, Enie and Menie, passed away in the same year, and the Bambeneks said they'd never again own dogs the same age since the loss was too great. Six months after the death of Menie, the Bambeneks went back to the same breeder to pick up Minie, but once they got there and saw how attached she was to Moe, they couldn't resist. Moe turned out to be a little dickens, but he was a much-loved dickens, and the Higgins boys' favorite.

"What's different," Ken said emphatically, "is that this time I wouldn't try to talk her into anything. Santa Claus, the sly guy, would finally put an end to the matter and simply bring a puppy down the chimney—wagging tail, puppy breath, and all. Once she saw how happy it made the boys, she couldn't resist!"

"The *boys*, huh?" Margret asked with a lifted brow. He gave her a sheepish grin, a look of obvious confession to at least a part of his motives. Her eyebrows crinkled. "I don't know, Ken. Cassie and her 'no animals' thing has deep, tangled roots. I'm not sure if this would be a wise move or not—especially in light of that crazy snowglobe thing. It might just put her over the edge."

Macy turned in a tight circle until at last, with a great sigh, she thunked down between them onto the floor.

"I figure it this way," Ken said. "Even Bradley's old enough now to hold his own with a puppy. Sure, Macy occasionally knocks him over when we come for a visit, but babies are like giant rubber balls." Macy's ears perked in his direction at the mention of her name. "And the truth is, whatever buried grief Cassie keeps tucked inside herself, maybe this would finally help her let it out. Maybe if she saw the boys with a puppy, *she* could finally let go of whatever holds her hostage."

Margret didn't seem convinced. "If Momma ain't happy, ain't nobody happy. Ever heard that expression?"

"Yeah, but who says she won't be? Maybe it's time to help Cassie move past those old wounds. Force the issue, if you will. Maybe she'd discover that the only place those wounds still exist is in her mind and that her mind is ready to be over it. Maybe the snowglobe thing was the catalyst! We both know from the way she is with our kids—not to mention the ones she baby-sits—that she's a terrific caregiver. And from everything I've heard, she has a special and pure gift, *especially* with dogs. I know she has this hang-up, but—"

"Ken," Margret said, jumping into his sentence, "what you weren't there to see was the severe piercing—the depth—of her wound. Not even I could convince her that what happened to Toby wasn't her fault. And I could talk her into anything.

"Did you know she didn't leave her house for days after she found out about Toby's fate?" He shook his head. "I thought that when she had to give Toby away, I'd seen the worst of her grief. It was awful, Ken. She packed up his bowls, his favorite toys, the ratty blanket he used for a bed…then she packed her *own* blanket, too, so he could 'smell the smell of me and not be afraid,' she said when we dropped him off with that entire box of stuff." Margret stopped a moment and swallowed. "After all these years, just remembering the look on Cassie's face as we left the county animal shelter breaks my heart. Cassie cried uncontrollably all the way home, and Betty looked at her in the rearview mirror and told her to buck up. She said life was hard but that she'd get over it. Can you imagine, Ken? Imagine dropping off one of your *children,* having to give one of *them* away! That's how it felt to Cassie."

"Some days I'd like to give one or two of them away, especially when Monkey Boy nearly rips my leg out of its socket," he said with a chuckle, thinking he would lighten the mood.

"Don't even say such a thing!" she snapped.

He realized his mistake. He was talking to Margret. Margret, who had spent her entire married life trying to conceive a child. He apologized.

But Margret said she was the one who was sorry; she knew how much he loved his children, and she knew he was just kidding. "I'm sorry I overreacted. It's been a strange day, and I guess I was just due for an outburst."

They both smiled, which eased the tension. Then they sat in silence for a moment while Margret took a few deep, cleansing, think-time breaths.

"Ken, I think you're right. It's time for Cassie to heal, and if getting the whole thing out in the open with a visit from Santa leads in that direction, so be it. But I'm going to share something with you, something I bet Cassie's not told you. Maybe it will help you truly understand what you're dealing with here."

Ken leaned back in his chair. For inexplicable reasons, his heart started racing. Whatever he was about to hear, he didn't think he would like it.

"Like I said, I thought I'd seen the worst of Cassie's hurt when Betty made her give Toby to the pound. But after Cass found out he'd been euthanized, she refused to eat a bite of her next six meals. She covered her plates of food with foil and put them in the fridge. She said she was testing how long she could go without eating, should another dog ever show up on her doorstep. With all her heart she believed that Toby would still be alive if she'd thought to tell her mom he could share *her* food. 'I've been so selfish!' she wailed to me over and over. 'Why didn't I *share*?' Of course that wasn't a viable long-term option; she was a growing girl herself. But she couldn't see it at the time. No matter how gruff she acted, Betty wouldn't have allowed Cassie to starve herself. But there was no convincing Cassie otherwise.

"Toby was the last of her endless, beloved stream of critters. From one-legged birds to crippled opossums—and even a goldfish she rescued from a carnival vendor." She stopped and smiled. "You should have seen her begging that tattooed roadie to give her that sick fish. It was high-larious!" Her smile quickly faded. "But Toby was her favorite. He slept with her, sat with her, walked with her.... All she knew was that he'd depended on her, and she thought she let him down. It was like a haunting...or... To be honest, I believe she suffered from post-traumatic stress disorder. She said she couldn't stop imagining his scared eyes when they came toward him with the needle to kill him, or the loving and trusting look on his face when she'd dropped him off. She was inconsolable and incapable of seeing it any way other than that she'd killed him herself, Ken. Only time seemed to help her move forward.

"When she realized she'd never become a vet either, something switched off inside her and that was that. She believed God was punishing her. Ken, she believed—and as far as I know still does—that she had not only let Toby down, but God too. Maybe if Grandpa Wonky had been around, he could have helped her heal and gain a little perspective. Maybe he would have stopped Betty from making her give Toby away in the first place! I don't know, but the closest she lets herself get to her critter-nurturing side is her endless collectibles, as you well know. Sometimes I wonder if she thinks that if she accumulates enough of them, they might fill that hole in her heart, one that's been there more than twenty years."

Ken stared at his hands. He hated even trying to imagine his wife's sorrow. She was only a *girl* when she lost Toby. A girl who needed rescuing herself.

He pictured Cassandra nursing their sons, the gentle way she kissed the tips of their toes, mended their broken hearts, tirelessly spoke and affirmed her love for them. To think she *ever* believed she could be responsible for the death of *anything*... He imagined her, a blooming woman with a vision for a career to use her gifts for helping the entire animal kingdom, when the final nail hit the coffin of her dreams. He thought about all the times she said she was "too dumb" to do this or that. "Cass, you're the smartest person I know," he'd tell her. "Your intuition is incredible!" But his words never seemed to carry any weight.

All these years later, she was still punishing herself and believing in her failures—and dragging around the ills of Bad Betty, a woman who seemed lost to *her* own misery.

"Margret, I hear what you're saying about Cass's sensitivities, and believe me, it breaks my heart. But I also believe that sometimes we just have to let go of our losses and find a new way to live."

Ken was surprised when Margret's eyes sprang forth with tears and she lunged toward him and locked him in a powerful bear hug.

"Is this something that should worry me?" Leo stood in the doorway to the kitchen, grinning, his hands on his hips.

Margret let out a yelp.

Ken had been jolted by Leo's voice, too, and jumped. "Man...way to take a few years off my life."

Margret caught her breath, went over and gave Leo a hello kiss. "I thought you were playing handball."

"The courts were filled, and they had a long waiting list. Some kind of tournament. I didn't feel like waiting, and neither did Roscoe."

"Good," she said. "We can eat early then. I was just about to brown some pork chops when Ken rang the doorbell."

"I'll let you get to it, then," Ken said. "Thanks for the insight, Margret. She can fill you in, Leo. Let me know tomorrow if you want to weigh in on this idea. I'm not going to do anything about it right this minute anyway." He started to leave, then turned. "You know, I couldn't do it without you guys anyway. We'd need some place to leave the little bugger until Christmas morning. Let me know if you're up for that kind of adventure!"

❧

"We baby-sitting on Christmas Eve?" Leo asked after Ken left.

"No, but this will shock you: Ken's thinking about surprising Cassie for Christmas—with a puppy. He wanted to know what I thought about it."

"Hmm. Wonder why he didn't mention it to me."

"Probably because you don't know about Cass's whole history with animals."

"History with animals? They've never had any pets, have they?"

"No, that's just it. But you know what, Leonard Anderson? Never mind all that. I can explain it later. First we've got something to celebrate," she said, heading for the fridge and the bottle of champagne. For years, she'd barely had a sip of wine, what with all the "maybe I'm pregnant" and "I'm trying to get pregnant" precautions. It would feel good to relax and simply let the bubbly liquid tickle her throat. To lift her glass to the future, whatever it might hold. She was anxious to model her newfound freedom to Leo. To remember or relearn—or maybe to learn for the first time—that what they had in each other was enough.

"So, what's with the champagne cooler?" he asked as he pulled out a kitchen chair.

"Wait till I get us all set up, okay? But trust me, it's worth waiting for."

"In that case," he said, rising from his chair, "I'm gonna go change clothes. I'll be back in a minute."

Margret got out their Waterford champagne glasses. Since some of the ice had melted in the cooler while she and Ken were talking, she added another layer of ice chips from the dispenser in the door of their new stainless-steel fridge. They'd switched to stainless appliances, which just arrived yesterday morning, deciding their marble countertops were deserving of them and agreeing that sometimes HGTV and decorating fads *were* the way to go. She remembered when she'd called Cassandra to come check them out. Cassandra had arrived with her two younger children in tow. Chuck was out with Daddy, and Howie was off to what Cassandra had described as an oddly declared one-on-one evening with

Grandma Betty. That left just Monkey Man and Bradley who were, of course, in need of the most attention. As it turned out, Bradley was just tall enough to stand on his tippy toes and push both the ice lever and the water lever, something they didn't realize until he was drenched.

"I used to think I wanted a fridge with these dispensers," Cassandra had said. "Big mistake, eh?"

"You betcha." They'd laughed the entire time they patted Bradley down with paper towels in futile attempts to dry him off.

As Margret listened to the crunching ice fall into the champagne cooler, she smiled. *Longstanding friendships. Auntie Magpie and Uncle Leo. Something else to toast.* She set the champagne on the table next to the cooler; she'd let Leo open it. Since he wasn't back yet, she quickly cut a few slices of Havarti cheese and dumped a handful of crackers in a bowl. Not as good as Burt's Durves, but it would do.

Leo entered the kitchen wearing his favorite jeans and a sweatshirt that brought out the gray in his eyes.

"You're just as handsome as the day I met you," she said, walking up to him and giving him a light kiss on the lips.

"Really?" He studied her face. "So, what are we celebrating?"

"When you get the bottle open, the glasses poured, and you're ready to make a toast, I'll tell you."

With haste, he accomplished the task. They lifted their glasses in the air.

"So?"

"So, we're celebrating our new beginning." She clinked her glass against his. "We're celebrating *life*! It's time." She smiled, then pressed her lips to the glass and tilted it, allowing the effervescence to tickle her nose before letting it slide down her throat. It tasted wonderful.

He looked perplexed. He took a wary sip and swallowed.

"Nice champagne," he said, turning the bottle around to read the label. "But I'm confused. I mean, I'm happy if you're happy—and you're glowing, so I think you are. But I'm confused as to *why* you're happy."

"Take another drink of your champagne before it gets warm, Leo. Just enjoy the moment and don't try to analyze it. Let's just be in it. Let's just relax into the knowledge that today a normal woman—who has not felt that way for a very long time—and a normal man are preparing to make love *when* they want to, *because* they want to, and *how* they want to."

"I'll drink to that," he said. He clinked her glass again, waggled his eyebrows, and downed a second sip. Then he clinked her glass again.

"What's that clink for?" she asked.

"More of the same."

"Amen." She heard every word he didn't speak and felt exactly the same way.

They nibbled on crackers and cheese and enjoyed a few more sips of champagne.

"Leo, I know there'll be times when I'll likely revisit our decision, when I might even question *this* moment." She picked up her glass and moved around to his side of the table, then sat on his lap. "But right now, I'm so glad to have you for my husband, this house for our shelter…a stainless-steel fridge that spews ice chips," she said, smiling. "I'm grateful we have parents close by who love us and dear friends who are always happy to share *their* kids with us. I just want to mark the moment with a celebration I won't forget. I want to be able to remember it when a gloomy whispering cloud rolls by and tries to lure me into chasing it again."

He looked into her eyes, then bit the inside of his cheek, a sign she recognized meant he had something on his mind.

"What, Leo? What are you thinking?" she asked.

"You don't want to know," he said, shaking his head. "I don't want to spoil our moment."

She set her glass down, placed her hands on his cheeks, leaned her forehead against his, and said, "Yes, I do want to know what you're thinking. Our moment is *our* moment."

He sighed. "When I walked through that door and saw you and Ken in that hug, I—"

"You what?"

Tears filled his eyes. "I thought..." He swallowed, hard. "I wondered if it ever crossed your mind to wish you'd married someone else. I mean, we both know I have a problem with counts. We've never even been sure what—or even if—your body has an issue." He rested his cheek against her chest. "Maybe you'd have children by now if you'd married someone else."

Margret lifted his chin. "Leo, *please* tell me you didn't think Ken and I were—"

"Heavens, no! I know you both too well for that. It's just that seeing you in another man's arms brought something into focus for me, something that scared me."

"Stop!" She put her hand over his mouth. "I love you. I want to be only with you. Children or no children. To have and to hold, till death do us part, I am yours and you are mine, Sir Dingbat. We have each other, Leo. You and me and God will be enough. We're healthy, young, financially secure, and we have all this love to give. We'll find another place to pour it. God will lead us, and we'll follow. But for now," she said, turning and picking up her glass, "all we have to do is to celebrate and enjoy the reality of *us*."

Twenty

Betty stuck a mini-marshmallow in the middle of the chocolate chip cookie and used a half stick of beef jerky, Burt's special homemade, to serve as the handle of her edible pinwheel replica. To make it look more realistic, she sliced the cookie into eight pie-shaped sections, then pulled them slightly apart.

"There. That's better!" She hid the plate containing the pinwheel in the cabinet. She decided she'd bring it out if things weren't going well with three-year-old Howie. This would be her first attempt at a one-on-one, which she hoped to establish on an ongoing basis with each of the children, rotating one child a week. But first she had to survive Howie.

She knew Cassandra's boys weren't all that crazy about her, but they gushed when Ken's folks came into town. It's not like she was jealous, exactly. (Okay, maybe she was.) But she wanted to make things better between her and the boys, so try she would.

Since their Columbus Day hot-dish date, she and Burt had been spending more time together. Once she'd witnessed how much Burt's grandchildren adored him, and especially how much fun he had with *them*—even when she thought Burt acted a little too goofy for a grown man—her heart longed to experience a greater openness with her grandsons. She felt robbed of that with her own children.

When Cassandra dropped Howie off, she'd acted as uptight as a momma bear dropping her cub into the mouth of a mountain lion. If Cassandra didn't keep her nails so short, Betty felt sure she would have held her claws out in front of her and swiped the air a few times before she left, just to remind Betty that she'd have to deal with Momma Bear if Betty harmed her cub in any way.

"Just remember that he's a tender-hearted boy, Mom. He's easily wounded by harsh words, and it takes him a long time to get over it." Cassandra had grown increasingly bold with Betty. It irked Betty to think her daughter didn't trust her with her own grandchildren, especially this one, who was clearly the most like her daughter. But she understood why now, and that was a start.

Since the day Cassandra had lashed out at her, reminding her mother that she, like Burt, was a good person, Betty longed to affirm her love for Cassandra, to help her daughter understand that she'd *always* known her daughter was an especially good person, a vulnerable one, which is why she was so protective of her, albeit in backhanded ways. But words had never been Betty's best commodity.

For the sake of all of them, the best way she could imagine to start chipping away at the iceberg of their relationship was with the children. She'd been, uncommonly, all ears lately, tuning in to conversations between people talking about how much easier grandparenting was than parenting, and how they wished they could have been grandparents *first.*

Like Burt had said—and then two days later, the pastor—God was indeed a God of second chances. If so, maybe Betty could make up for some of the harshness of her past, and she would begin with her grandsons. She hoped her pinwheel cookie, Burt's Dessert Durving creation for his grandchildren, was as good a tactic as any, since what else did she have at the moment? But she decided not to start her one-on-one visit with it and tucked it away in the cabinet.

The cookie emergency moment surfaced not long after Howie

arrived. He sat on the floor, still wearing his coat, staring at a television set that wasn't on, his backpack on the floor next to him. Sadly, he'd slipped into this trancelike state the moment Cassandra closed the door behind her. He looked like a scared and lost little puppy. Being the second child out of four, and a child whose home was often invaded by day-care kids, he was likely never alone. Why hadn't she thought of that before she'd selected him to launch her new program? All she'd thought was that the quietest child would be the easiest.

She shored herself up. "Howie. Come with Grandma."

Although he didn't move his head, she noticed him staring at her reflection in the television. She stood behind him with her hands on her hips. They studied each other in this odd way for a while, Howie's eyes as big as saucers. Betty shifted her gaze from his eyes to her reflection in the television.

No wonder he was afraid to move! Her stance, her expression—she looked nothing short of the Wicked Witch. Or even worse: she looked like Bad Betty Kamrowski, living up to her reputation.

She dropped her hands from her hips and watched herself until she was satisfied she'd relaxed her posture—well, in a stiff sort of way—and pasted on a satisfactory smile. Howie didn't take his eyes off her.

"Howie, Grandma Betty has a surprise for you in the kitchen," she said, forcing an unnatural and uncommon lilt into her voice. "Want to come see what it is?"

More staring.

"Well, then I guess I'll have to eat that chocolate chip cookie all by myself."

He looked away from her for a moment, then his eyes came back to hers, as if checking to see if she was still there.

"I'll tell you what. I'm going to put the cookie on the kitchen table and pour us each a glass of Kool-Aid."

Since the moment she'd purchased a packet of the grape-flavored drink, she wondered if it was a mistake. Did today's kids even like the stuff? While she'd waited for the bagger to finish loading up her groceries, she noticed nearly every mother in the checkout lines around her purchasing multipacks of those little bags of juice. She'd seen the kids sucking on them at Cassandra's and thought, *How wasteful.* She'd asked her checker how much a box of the juice bags cost, and when she heard the amount, she gasped. How could anyone afford them? "That is ridiculously high!" she'd said. The clerk frowned, then didn't make eye contact with her again.

Maybe she'd had the same look on her face when she first asked Howie to come into the kitchen. Interesting how the face acted when you weren't paying attention to it.

What a fascinating thought. She couldn't wait to share this with Burt, who would likely bust out in his big jolly laugh, even though she wouldn't mean it to be funny. He'd laugh so hard and his laughter would be so contagious, she'd be unable to keep herself from joining in. She loved the way he helped her not take herself so seriously.

In the beginning, she'd tried to stifle her response to his peculiar bouts of guffawing; it didn't make sense to laugh at something she didn't believe to be funny. But after she couldn't keep herself from giggling once, she realized how good she felt afterward. She felt...uplifted. More at ease. Her sharing about faces and their actions might end up just like last week's misadventure when she'd asked him, in all seriousness, "How do you stay so patient with people who come into the shop and are so demanding?" She had no idea what was so funny about her question, but deep inside herself, something busted loose, and she began laughing at the happy sound of *his* laughter.

"You should see your face!" he'd said, at the height of her laughter. His eyes were just twinkling. "I knew the real Bet was in there somewhere."

The real Bet. Oh! He called me Bet!

Suddenly she realized that while she'd been reliving that wonderful moment with Burt, she'd walked into the kitchen, set the plate with the cookie on the table, pulled up a chair, sat down—and so had Howie. It was like magic. Here she was seated at the kitchen table, unconsciously smiling, with a smiling Howie who couldn't take his eyes off her cookie creation.

"Well? What do you think it is?"

"A windmill! I have a real one of those. Mommy bought it for me. It's in my room. When the wind blows, we're gonna take it outside."

"What color is it?"

"Green."

"Is green your favorite color?"

"Mm-hmm."

"Me too. Burt says I... Oh!" she suddenly said, causing Howie to lurch, put his hands in his lap, and stare at them. She was so surprised to find herself talking out loud about Burt—and to one of Cassandra's children, for goodness sake—that it momentarily undid her. "I'm sorry, Howie. Grandma didn't mean to startle you."

He glanced up at her, and she reminded herself to smile.

"I know Burt Durve," he said, a dead serious expression on his face.

"You do?" *Burt Durve. Won't he just love hearing that?* His likely reaction made her smile.

"He sells weenies."

"You are exactly right, Howie! What a smart boy you are."

Cautiously, as if testing the waters of trust, Howie flashed her a half smile.

Betty's eyes widened. If she didn't know better, she'd think she'd time traveled. When Howie unleashed that wary half smile, he looked *exactly* like his mom at that age. *How vulnerable she was. It's so easy to see that now… I fear I was too blinded by my own sorrows to realize it then.*

She watched Howie's smile dissolve when he noticed the change in her face. The dark cloud of her thoughts had obviously affected her appearance, and she forced herself to smile again. Although Howie's face didn't return to its brighter beam, he did seem to relax. She realized Howie seemed to respond emotionally to her every gesture and look. *What power we hold,* she thought. *Why is it so easy to see with Howie? Did I completely miss it with his mother? Jeny Kochany, Betty, indeed. No wonder Dad so often reminded me to lighten up.*

Then a thunderbolt of a thought hit her. *Yes, Cassandra was vulnerable. Vulnerable to every look on my face and my every word and warning. She was, and still is, as vulnerable as Howie—and as I was after my husband's death.*

Tears sprang to her eyes, and then into Howie's a moment later. She blinked. She blinked away her tears and her quivering lip. She tried to blink away the image that had haunted her for years and which surfaced at the most unlikely times: the terrible discovery of her husband's lifeless body.

She rose from the table and said, through a forced upbeat voice, "Grandma forgot the napkins." She turned her back to Howie, leaned on the kitchen counter until she cleared her head, grabbed a few napkins, wiped her face, and blew her nose. She tossed the soiled paper in the garbage and brought two napkins back with her, wearing the brightest smile she could muster under the circumstances.

"I say we should eat this thing!" She pointed at the cookie. "What do you say, Howie?"

"Uh-huh. We can share, okay? Mommy says it's good to share."

Betty swallowed, then swallowed again. She took a drink of her Kool-Aid and said, "Your mommy is very smart, Howie."

"I know." He blew on the windmill cookie, as if he might cause the chocolate chip blades to churn.

Betty thought they had turned, for suddenly, she felt the unmistakable fresh winds of second chances blowing her way.

Together, they devoured their windmill until every last crumb of cookie and sliver of the beef jerky was gone. While eating, they had a bit of awkward discussion as to why Grandma didn't have any Christmas decorations up.

"Because, well…I don't know. I think I have a little tree in a closet somewhere. I guess I should get it out!" And so she did. They put her foot-tall tree on an end table. It looked pretty pitiful, really.

Howie suggested they make some ornaments out of tinfoil, "the way Mommy does it." Betty was glad she'd picked up a thin roll at the Dollar Tree the last time she'd gone there for some canned goods. Then they played Chutes and Ladders, a game Howie unloaded from his backpack. She wondered if Burt played that game with his grandchildren.

Burt. There she was thinking about him again.

Chutes and ladders. *Feels like my life right now.*

Twenty-One

Burt glanced at the clock on the shop wall. It was two flank steaks past four pork chops. "Ten after four already. Where does time go?" For the first time in eight years, he wondered what on earth he'd been thinking when he'd had the clock special ordered. Clearly, he hadn't. "Sometimes you're two ounces short of a pound of sense."

"Talking to yourself again, Burt?"

"Who else is going to tell me what I already know?"

Ken burst out laughing, causing Burt to do the same. When the two heartiest laughers in Wanonishaw erupted together, it was loud, and Naomi, the day-care mom Cassandra described as a drama queen, slammed her hands over her son Ben's ears when they entered the shop.

"What's so funny?" she asked Burt as she grabbed for a number, although Ken was the only person ahead of her. Customers knew to be safe rather than sorry and grab a number, as the crowd could swell, and people were always in such a hurry that they feigned not noticing they weren't next. However, if Betty Kamrowski was in the shop, everyone knew you could count on her to set the perpetrator straight.

"What's so funny?" Burt asked, repeating her question as he extended a large knife toward Ken, who plucked the slice of Braunswager from the end of it. "*We* are!" More laughs from the men.

"Off work early, Ken?" Naomi asked, nodding toward the clock.

"Yes, just claiming a little comp time. I had to put in a few hours over the weekend."

"Poor Cassandra," Naomi said.

"Poor Cassandra? Poor *Cassandra*? Burt Burt. How is it that the little women get to stay home eating Milanos all day while the kids entertain each other, and we macho men don't get a bit of sympathy for all the hours and after hours we have to put in?"

Naomi drew in a deep breath. "Little women? Eating Milanos?" Her cheeks flushed and her jaw tightened. "I think you have forgotten, Ken Higgins, that I go to work, too, and that I pay your wife to watch my son"—she pulled Ben toward her, as if to prove he really existed—"for the excellent care she gives to him. And if I pay her, that means *she's* working. And—"

"Naomi," Ken said, holding his hands up in a gesture of surrender, "remember when Burt said we were *funny*? I was just pulling your chain." He shrugged toward Burt. "I guess I just sounded rude instead. My sincere apologies. I meant no harm. I can only blame it on the Braunswager."

He smiled at Burt, who enjoyed watching someone else squirm for a change. Burt's quirky sense of humor had landed him in his own share of trouble over the years, especially with Betty. But at long last even Betty was catching on to it, or lightening up herself.

Naomi smiled, looking a little sheepish. "Blame it on the Braunswager. Sounds like a good book title."

"What'll you have today, Ken—aside from the heap of trouble you got yourself into?" Burt said, smiling at Naomi.

"Go ahead and take care of Naomi. Hard-working ladies first, Burt. I'm in no hurry."

"Thanks," she said. "And I won't let Cassandra know you weren't in a hurry to get home." Burt caught her exaggerated wink.

After she left, Ken admitted he really hadn't come in for any meat, but that he'd take a half-pound of sliced turkey, shaved real thin, to help pay for the free Braunswager. What he really wanted was information.

"I'll tell you what I know," Burt said, grabbing the hunk of turkey breast, maneuvering it into the slicer, and giving it a slap, as though forcing the bird to submit to its demise.

"First, the question I am about to ask is just between you and me, Burt."

Although everyone understood that Burt possessed a wealth of knowledge about nearly every Wanonishawian, he was a man of his word, which he gave to Ken, modeled by picking up the end of his giant ball of string and acting like he was trussing his lips together.

"Know anyone with puppies they need to give away?"

"Hmm. Pups." Burt assumed his usual Burt-slices-lunchmeat stance (left foot about eight inches in front of the right, slight bend in the knees to save the back) and hit his rhythm with the machine, the turkey slices falling off in neat little folds. "Can't say as I do. Santa doing a little shopping for the boys?"

"How would a guy like me, living here in Wanonishaw, Minnesota, know what Santa's up to at the North Pole, Burt?"

"Good point."

Ken watched Burt work his magic and concluded that Burt got the meat weighed, origamied, and tied faster than Santa could lay a finger aside his nose, let alone get up the chimney.

"But in case Santa did want to get the family a pup," Ken said, wiping his hands on a napkin, "and needed a little help finding one, I'm sure he'd appreciate it if you let me know. And remember, this is top secret. Especially from *any* other family members, if you get my drift." He raised his left eyebrow.

Burt cocked his head and gave Ken a sly smile. "Yes, I get your drift. Loud and clear, Sir Elf. No family member, not even of the in-law variety, shall be privy to your secret."

Burt knew there'd been talk about him and Betty. You didn't live in a small town like Wanonishaw and keep a secret. He'd been seen knocking on Betty's door on many occasions, and the report got back to him at the shop. He had no secrets. But he also knew Betty wasn't talking about the two of them yet, so therefore in her mind, it wasn't public knowledge, whatever their unspoken "it" was.

"Have you noticed my mom smiling more?" Cassandra asked Ken one evening while they prepared dinner. They usually had the boys set the table, but they were otherwise occupied, giving Cassandra and Ken a rare chance to visit before bedtime.

"Yup."

"What do you make of these one-on-one visits she's had with Howie and Chuck?"

"Nice," Ken said, plunking the plates on the table.

"Nice…that's all you have to say? You don't find it curious?"

"I find it nice, don't you? The boys seem to think so, too."

"Ken!"

"What else do you want me to say, Cassie?" He got the butter out of the fridge.

"What do you think gives with her?"

"You wouldn't believe me if I told you."

"Try me."

"Okay, but I *will* say 'I told you so!' when I'm proven correct." He leaned on the counter and faced her.

"Fine."

"Burt."

"Burt what? What about Burt?"

"Burt gives."

"What do you mean Burt gives? Burt gives what?"

"You asked me what gives with your mom's new…smiling, and I'm telling you, it's Burt."

"You can't be serious!"

"Dead."

"Why would you say such a thing?"

"Because I'm starting to believe the gossip, and Burt didn't deny it."

"Oh my gosh, Ken! You didn't ask him about it, did you?"

Ken sucked in his cheeks. He seemed to be contemplating something. "Of course I didn't ask him, but I'm putting two and two together and coming up with the love bug."

"Right. Bad Betty and the love bug. Now there's an oxymoron, if I ever heard one."

"Do you think it's not possible for your mom to find love again?"

She pursed her lips and furrowed her brow. "That's a trick question. If I say it isn't, you'll ask me where my faith is. If I say it is, you'll say, *Told you so!*"

"Exactly. So maybe you shouldn't answer me. How about you just think about the possibility."

"Mom—tell Harry to get *out* of my *bed*!" Chuck stood with his arms folded across his chest, a look of disgust on his face. Betty's look of disgust.

Love bug. Right. Cassandra shook her head.

"Tell him Dad said he better behave," Ken said, "or I'll come in there and blow raspberries on his belly." The boys loved it when Ken wrestled them to the floor, lifted their shirts, put his lips to their skin, and blew loud motorboat sounds on their tummies. He'd broken up many a fight distracting them with that so-called threat, which the boys always took as a promise, quit their roughhousing, and lined up to receive.

Chuck took off down the hall screaming, "DAD SAID..."

"So *are* you going to think about the possibility of Burt and Betty?" Ken asked, returning his attention to his wife. "Kind of has a nice ring to it, Burt and Betty. Betty and Burt. You know that old love bug can do wondrous things for just about anybody." He walked up behind her and nibbled her neck.

"I think," she said, turning to give him a kiss, "that I'd rather think about you."

"GROSS!" Chuck said when he returned to the kitchen to yell again about Harry. "Yuck! *No* kissing." He disappeared back down the hall.

Yes, like grandmother, like grandson, Cassandra thought. She could almost hear her mom saying the same thing to Burt.

Twenty-Two

Only one week left until Christmas, and Cassandra was just about strung out. The two oldest boys had suffered the stomach flu, and now Bradley wasn't sleeping well and Harry said his belly hurt. Hers did too.

"Please, God. *Please!*" The only upside was that the day-care kids had stayed home with it too. She wondered who'd given it to whom, but in the end it really didn't matter. It was stomach-flu season. She'd no sooner finished that thought than she felt a familiar wave of nausea and dizziness. She wanted to phone Ken and tell him to get home right away, but there was no time; to the bathroom she raced.

"Harry, can you go get Mommy the phone, please?" she said from the bathroom floor, where Harry had followed her. "Bring me the one in the kitchen." Even though the bedroom phone would be easier for her two-year-old to reach, she didn't want him loose in her bedroom, which was off limits to the boys.

"I can't."

"Why?"

"I no climb on the counter. No *no* NO!"

She couldn't help but smile, hearing her own words wash back over her. He did a pretty good imitation. "This time Mommy says it's okay to get up there, Monkey Man, because Mommy needs the phone. And I know you can climb up on Bradley's highchair and reach it."

"No cimebing!"

Cassandra drew a deep breath. "Harry, you're right. No climbing.

Please get me—" She lurched back up to the toilet bowl and retched. When she was done, Harry still stood, straight as a post, his eyes wide. Cassandra hoped this unusual use of the toilet didn't interfere with his potty training, which was hit or miss to begin with. "Harry, go into Mommy and Daddy's bedroom and bring me the phone. You don't have to climb to reach that one. It's on the table next to Mommy's bed."

"Say pease."

"Please," she said, holding back both a groan and a smile. Harry disappeared. She listened to his little footsteps padding down the hall, then she heard her bedroom door open. "Get the phone, Harry!"

"'Kay!" A man of his word, he soon came back, phone in hand.

"You're a good boy, Harry." She dialed Ken's number. His secretary answered and told her Ken wasn't there. He was on his way home, sick with the stomach flu.

By the time Ken arrived home, Bradley had erupted with diarrhea. It took every ounce of strength Cassandra owned to get through his diaper change without losing it. The one bright spot, she thought, was that at least the flu would go away. Other times she'd been upchucking, it meant another baby.

"Cassie," Ken said, "after Chuck gets home from school and your mom gets off work, we need to have her come get Chuck and Howie. Or maybe Chuck could go to a friend's house and she could pick him up from there, then swing by and get Howie, or vice versa. We've got our hands full just taking care of ourselves and the baby."

Suddenly Howie appeared and piped up. "I wanna go to Grandma Betty's."

Well now, Cassandra thought, *that's a first.* Ken's raised eyebrows let her know he agreed.

"Mom never was much for playing nursemaid, Ken. I don't know if she'd be up for two of them, especially so soon after they've been sick." She looked at her wristwatch; her mom should be getting home about now. "I'd hate for her to catch it, then blame it on us. I'd never hear the end of it."

"But they're over it, Cass. We can't send Brad. We can barely deal with him ourselves right now. And if Harry said his stomach hurts, it's just a matter of time."

"Am I going to Grandma's?" Howie asked, his backpack already in his hand, Chutes and Ladders sticking out the top.

Cassandra felt dizzy again. No, she could not take care of four boys and neither could Ken. She dialed her mom's number. A man's voice answered. "Oh, I'm sorry, I have the wrong number," she said, then hung up and redialed.

Again, a man's voice answered, and this time he said, "Betty Kamrowski's residence."

Cassandra was too stunned to speak.

"Cassandra?"

"Yes. Who is this?"

"Burt. Burt Burt. I'm here at your mom's, taking care of her. She had that awful flu real bad last night."

Cassandra could barely think. Why would Burt the butcher take care of her mother while she had the stomach flu? Had her mom called Burt? Who was running the butcher shop?

As if Burt had overheard her thoughts, he said, "The shop closes at noon on Monday. I drove by your mom's and saw her car out front, which was unusual. She's not usually home from work so early, so I thought I'd stop and see if she was okay—which she wasn't. She'd been up all night with that flu. She's feeling a little better, but I've stayed to make sure she got some liquids in her. It's real easy to get dehydrated from that flu, especially when you get older."

Cassandra couldn't respond. She was too busy trying to process everything he'd said and fighting a wave of nausea. He'd spoken with such familiarity about her mom's job and the time she usually got home.

"You still there, Cassandra?"

"Yes. Tell Mom I hope she feels better soon. Good-bye, Burt. BURT!" she hollered into the receiver, hoping he hadn't hung up yet.

"Yes?"

"Thank you."

"Oh, I'm not really doing anything. Just keeping her company and making her a few cups of weak tea with a dollop of honey. My mom used to say that did the trick, and it still does—Bet's got more color back in her face now."

Bet? The last person she remembered calling her mother Bet was her dad. And Burt was making her a cup of weak tea with honey? No doubt Betty had something to say about that. She liked her tea strong and plain. Period.

Burt had no idea what he was in for, poor sap.

"Is your mom coming to get the boys?" Ken yelled from the master bathroom.

"No!" she responded from the hall bath.

"Why?"

"She's just getting over the flu. And guess who was at her house?"

"Who?"

"Burt!"

"Told you."

"Flu bug. Love bug. Maybe Mom can't tell the difference," she said, her stomach rolling again.

"You have to leave now, Burt," Betty demanded more than said.

"I was just going to get you another cup of—"

"No, you have to go. Right now, Burt. I'll be fine."

Burt studied her face, smiled, then retrieved his coat from the hall tree. "You're embarrassed, aren't you?"

"About what?"

"About the fact that your daughter called and I answered the phone."

"Don't be silly," she said. But the truth was, when Burt headed for the phone so she didn't have to get up off the couch, she wanted to throttle him.

"Silly? Do you see me smiling?" he asked, a dead-serious look frozen on his face, one that didn't come naturally to him. "Does this," he pointed to his frowning eyebrows, "look like a silly face to you?"

Betty couldn't help but smile. How did he *do* that to her? "I see. Serious. You are serious."

"So," he said, relaxing his expression, "now that we are serious and honest, you were embarrassed your daughter caught me here, weren't you?"

All of this was so new, so foreign to her. All the attention he paid to her, the kindnesses he put forth. The laughter he brought into her life. Why couldn't she just relax and enjoy it, and devil-may-care *who* knew about it? But she couldn't, and now her daughter knew she was seeing Burt.

"Yes. I am embarrassed."

"Why?" he asked tenderly, hanging his coat back up and sitting next to her on the couch.

"I don't know how to do this, Burt. I don't know how to…date."

"Well, by golly! Is that what we're doing? Dating?"

She blushed, like she'd jumped to some kind of assumptive conclusion. "Oh, I didn't mean to imply—"

He silenced her by grabbing her hand, a first. He rested his other hand on top of hers, as though clamping it so she couldn't withdraw. She was too stunned to try.

"Betty, we are both adults. We are both widowed. We are old enough to do what we want. Tell me if I'm wrong, but I think what we both want, for now, is exactly what we have: the good company of each other. To be here for each other. Nothing we're doing is inappropriate. We're not hiding—at least I hope we're not. Call it dating, call it going steady, call it seeing each other, or call it anything else you or the busybodies around town can dream up. Personally, I call it wonderful. Let's just enjoy it. We've both been around long enough to know that life is fragile and unpredictable. We need to grab hold of bits of happiness where and when we can. This right here," he said, lifting her hand, "is one of the happiest bits I've nabbed in quite some time!"

Betty had weathered some terrible losses in her life, but never had she felt so low—about herself. At least when Gerald took his life, her father had been there to comfort her. He'd sat in his wheelchair and opened wide his arms. Betty knelt in front of him and rested her head in his lap while he stroked her head. Then he put his hands under her arms and pulled her to

him, holding her tight while she cried. "You couldn't have done anything, Betty. Nobody could have stopped him."

Then, after her father died, she never believed she could feel more alone and miserable—nor would she feel comforted again. The only thing that got her through the losses was necessity: she had to take care of her children. She had to put one foot in front of the other, get to work, and carry on.

But this heartache... Today was the day she had to separate her twelve-year-old daughter from the one thing she held most dear: her dog. Betty knew her youngest child would rather saw off her own arm and feed it to her dog than watch him go hungry. But they simply could not afford to keep him.

Betty already had enough trouble stretching their meals. Now, winter was coming. Their garden would be done for. Toby was due for a rabies shot. The boys were still both going through growth spurts, which meant never-ending bigger clothes and shoes. The last pair of boots she'd bought her second son had nearly left them hungry, but what was she to do? A child had to wear boots in the Minnesota winters. She'd cut back on her own food portions in order to give her children their growing shares, but she had to stay strong enough to work. They could not afford for her to take ill. It was already embarrassing enough that some do-gooders in town occasionally dropped off a few groceries now and again when nobody was home. They never even included a note. Did everyone know she was destitute?

There was no choice, nobody to turn to, no one else to do the hard thing. If she showed Cassandra an ounce of sympathy, neither one of them would get through it.

Betty lay awake nearly all night, shoring herself up. Toby needed a family who could afford to feed him, and the county animal shelter, even though it was a long way away, was the best place for him to find such a family.

She knew it wasn't a no-kill facility, but surely somebody would adopt him, even though he was older than many dogs.

Every time Betty pictured what was sure to be her daughter's wrenching tears, she cried anew, but she didn't want her daughter to have to endure this same terrible, hopeless exhaustion. "No crying." She had to make that clear to her Cassandra. "Crying won't do you any good," she would say. "He's just a dog."

It would be better for Cassandra to hate her mother than for her to starve herself.

Twenty-Three

Long after her family was asleep and the urgency of her illness had subsided, Cassandra still found herself wide awake. She was deadly tired but unable to relax enough to doze off. She couldn't stop thinking about her mom and Burt. The idea that a man was in her mom's house was startling enough, but that she'd allowed him into Sterileland after she'd been sick? It was too much to take in.

Sure, she'd heard the talk—the morsels people felt compelled to share with her. But she just couldn't believe it or picture it or, she finally realized, even allow it as a possibility. And that was the thing that made her feel the smallest: she realized that she did not believe Betty could attract the love of another man. Worse yet, she didn't believe her mom *deserved* the love of another man, not after what she'd allowed her dad to do.

No! I cannot think such a terrible thing ever again! She'd read enough about depression to understand that her dad was lost to his illness. She hated it when she was blindsided by waves of ridiculous, false thoughts about his suicide. In the deepest parts of her head and her heart, she *knew* nobody could have stopped him. Yet this hateful darkness that rose up within her—a darkness that closely resembled how she felt about herself for letting Toby die—sometimes got the best of her.

Blaming herself for the death of Toby was just as ridiculous as blaming Betty for her dad's suicide, she knew. But sometimes it was all mixed up in her head. Still there must have been a way to save Toby. She should have found someone to give him to when her mother said he had to go. And had she given her all to her studies in high school, or had she just let her desire to become a vet slip through her fingers?

Of *course* she'd tried. She studied night and day. Her counselor knew veterinary school was out of her scholastic reach.

Why wasn't it enough that she tended to children, whom she adored? *Why?*

Because God had given her special gifts with animals, God planted her heart's desire, and her Grandpa Wonky believed in her. Toby, Gert, Grandpa Wonky, God…she let them all down.

Her thoughts and emotions crashed around in her head, at utter odds with each other. Misplaced blame after a suicide. Her mother's apology. The aftermath of poverty. Misconceptions. Her beloved Toby. The beauty of her sons. Burt and Betty. An empty snowglobe. Like good fighting evil, taking turns biting each other, then shining a bright and colorful light on the truth, offering mercy—but around the corner, just out of her reach.

She thought of her mom again. Betty was a woman before she was a mother, and a girl before that. Betty was a woman who had borne three children, which meant she had been a woman in every sense of the word.

A woman. Her mother was a woman with a man in her home on that very day. A woman who'd been alone for twenty-five years, who worked hard, who smiled more often lately…who spent one-on-one time with her grandkids. A woman who apologized for something. What had changed? It might be a positive change and maybe had something to do with Burt. But could, or should, Cassandra trust it?

Finally weariness won and she nodded off.

That night she dreamed that the entire earth was black, charred, and barren. Then it started snowing. It snowed until everything turned sparkling white again. When the snow stopped, she couldn't help but to step out into it. There, among the sparkles, she found the fresh, varied footprints of three different dogs. She smiled and began to follow their trail, knowing she would soon find them. When she awakened, she felt utterly peaceful.

"Mommy, I sick!" Harry called from outside her bedroom door.

✲

"Oh, I almost forgot," Leo said to Ken while passing by his desk. "I stopped by Burt's last night for some veal cutlets. Burt said he needed to talk to you. I'm assuming this has to do with the..." Leo looked around to see if anyone was within earshot, "secret-Santa duties. He said he was hesitant to phone your house. For a number of reasons. Ah, the complicated lives we lead when we're privy to secrets and dating a guy's mother-in-law, eh?" Leo smiled.

"You got that right. Did he give you any clues as to whether or not he had a line on a you-know-what?" The secret talk seemed ridiculous, but in small towns, one had to guard his words if he didn't want everyone else to know about his business within the hour. Heaven forbid this conversation should get back to Cassandra or perhaps Chuck.

"Of course not. As far as Burt knows, I'm not supposed to know anything."

"Oh, right. You got a minute, Leo?"

Leo looked at his wristwatch. "About two of them, I'd say."

Ken motioned to his extra chair, and Leo took a seat.

"Have you and Margret thought anymore about this brainstorm of mine? Don't hold back, since I might be about to trip the trigger, and I'd hate to shoot myself in the foot."

"You know, Margret has her reasons for questioning your idea.

Maybe worrying about it is more accurate. If it backfires, it could be disastrous. She shared the whole story with me. Man, you're treading on some tricky and tender ground. But she also said she'd like to see Cassie free from her torment and that perhaps forcing the issue with a dog was the best place to start. Just dive in, help her face her…whatever it is. Of course if it *does* backfire, worst-case scenario, you could give the pup away."

Ken grabbed his head and shook it. "I don't want to even think about that tangled web, which would grow to include four very disheartened boys."

"Me either, but we're getting a little ahead of ourselves here with the speculations. First, talk to Burt."

"If I do go ahead with this, are you guys okay watching a pup till Christmas morning?"

"Sure."

"Great, thanks. I'll probably have to work late again tonight. I better give Burt a call."

Leo checked his watch again, then stood. "I got a meeting to get to."

"I'll keep you posted." As soon as Leo was gone, Ken looked up Burt's number. It took Burt six rings to answer. "Burt, it's Ken Higgins. Leo tells me you wanted to talk to me. Are you alone in the shop?"

"Are you daft? It's *Thursday*! *Durve* Day. And it's the *holidays*. I am swamped and I'm moving faster than a six-wheeled unicycle." Sometimes Burt's analogies made no sense, but people always got his drift, proven by the ripple of chuckles Ken heard in the background. "But I do have some info for you. No time—and especially not a *good* time— to pass it on right now. But you ought to get that info sooner rather than later, so give me a call tonight, okay?"

"Gotcha. Will do."

"Next!" Ken heard Burt holler before he hung up.

Durve Day, and Ken had to work late. He had shopping to do, decisions to make, and Christmas was racing right at them. If Burt *did* have a solid lead on an obtainable pup, he'd have a ton of details to organize, like dog food, a vet, toys, a dog pen, collars, shots, ground rules for the boys. The sudden rush of the reality of everything a dog needed, coupled with how little time he'd have to pull it off—not to mention the fact his wife might pummel him for making the worst assumption of their married life—momentarily overwhelmed him. Maybe this *was* a crazy endeavor. Who in his right mind got a puppy in the winter? Most puppies didn't like the cold, which made house training even more difficult. Maybe he should just pull the plug and buy his wife a nice sweater. Then the memory of puppy breath surfaced. If puppy breath couldn't heal Cassandra's heart, what could?

Ken heard Margret's voice again, raising a good point: *was* he doing this only for himself? That was the beauty of good friends: they were honest and helped you question your assumptions. He tapped his pen on his desk and searched his motives. Sure, he'd like a dog, and so would the boys. Yes, dogs took a lot of work and responsibility, and Cassandra was the one who'd be home with it all day. But in his heart of hearts, he believed that the only way Cassandra could move through her emotional gridlock was if someone, some*thing*, plunged her into it. If the love and presence of another dog could help Cassandra finally understand the truth and far-spreading damage of what had happened so very long ago, maybe she could forgive herself *and* Betty. Maybe she could dive back into enjoying something she loved so very much. It would be extraordinary and worth all the risk. How could she watch her sons with a puppy and not feel her own heart opening up?

It was time Cassandra stopped robbing herself.

After the family finished dinner, Cassandra asked Ken to take Chuck and Bradley with him while he did his errands. Ken couldn't refuse and returned with the boys at eight o'clock sharp. Perfect. Bedtime. He'd definitely get some points for that. He told Cassandra that Daddy now had his own surprise to work on, and he didn't want any questions asked when he returned. He drove a few blocks from home, pulled over, and got out his cell.

"Burt. Ken. Tell me what you know."

"Ken, my boy, you couldn't live long enough for all of that."

Ken laughed. "Right. Then let's stick to puppies."

"I just heard from Elmer Radke today that the Manford Animal Rescue and Shelter has to get rid of a bunch of dogs. Now, I don't know if they got any pups out there or not, but it might be worth checking out. You know, sometimes a dog who's a bit older can be good too. Folks move or die, and their nice, house-trained—and sometimes even pure-bred—pets end up in places like that."

"I haven't seen anything in the papers about them. I'm glad you reminded me about that place. I forgot there even was a shelter in Kilburn or I'd have *started* there. They should do more advertising."

"Never chide yourself for starting with the best source for almost anything, my boy." Burt laughed. "Elmer knows the couple who started and run that place. It's pretty much a one-couple show, but it's a shame, really. There's some kind of terrible illness in the family and—"

"Listen, Burt, I hate to cut you off, but I'm talking on borrowed time here." Ken had turned off his engine when he pulled over, so he was freezing, and it sounded like Burt was in his windup for a big story. Ken knew if he could get back home soon, Cassandra would appreciate his help getting the kids down, read that one last story, listen to their prayers, make that one final trip to the bathroom. He turned over the engine, taking note that it was starting to snow. "Sorry I missed Durve Day. What'd ya serve?"

"I outdid myself. I made those little meatballs. But today, I stirred a can of cherry pie filling in with them after they were done. Thought that would add a touch of holiday color and sweetness, plus it made its own dip. They went over real big. Even Betty liked them," he said, then laughed, and kept laughing as the two of them hung up.

Twenty-Four

Ken tried phoning the animal shelter ten consecutive times during his Friday lunch hour. He even added them to the speed dial on his cell. *Busy, busy, busy.* He wished he'd just driven out there. He looked in the Yellow Pages and noticed the ad said they closed at five, so he couldn't go after work either. With a huge sigh of disgust, he noticed they were only open Monday through Friday, so he couldn't even sneak out to the shelter the next day. What kind of hours were those?

It was December 19, and he was running out of time. *Come on, God, I could use a little help!*

He'd watched a news spot on television the previous night about how many people got pets for their kids' Christmas gifts and how often they didn't work out because the owners didn't think ahead. Yet the pet shops were doing a stellar business, this year's favorite breed being the beagle. The reporter said that whatever dog won Best in Show at the Westminster Kennel Club Dog Show was always the fad dog of the season. He went on to say that people needed to understand that beagles were energetic dogs that required a lot of exercise. They were *hounds.*

Ken wondered how many people were tying up the animal-shelter phone lines inquiring about beagles and how long it would be before news got out that they needed to downsize their inventory.

As a kid, Ken remembered, his parents taught him the hard lesson of how euthanizing their sick dog *was* the kindest thing to do for it, so he understood there was a time and a place for the procedure. But he wondered if any healthy animals might have to be put down in this shelter if they weren't placed in homes. He hated to think about it, but he only needed one puppy.

All weekend he stewed. He was distracted, second-guessing himself and scanning the newspapers for free-dog-to-good-home ads or new litters of mongrel pups—although what used to be called a mutt was now a mongrel with a new name, like CockaPoo Lab'Aire. Most came with big price tags too. He worked hard to resist the urge to cave in and go to a pet store. He was unusually crabby, something Cassandra did not appreciate.

"Christmas season with four boys is rough enough, Ken, without *your* wheels falling off the cart." He was usually the one who held steady. "I'm hanging on by a thread here. What gives?"

He apologized numerous times and blamed his foul mood on too many hours on the job, which wasn't entirely untrue.

On his way to work Monday morning, his first phone call to the shelter connected. Due to the early hour, he'd expected an answering machine, but instead Sheryl Manford, one of the owners, answered. She was coughing and sounded tired.

"Hello," Ken said. "I heard you needed to…place a bunch of your dogs, and I'm in the market for a puppy. Might you have any?"

"Who is this?"

"Ken. Ken Higgins."

"Who told you about our situation?" She sounded uneasy.

"Someone who has only your best interest in mind." He was perplexed by her question. Maybe if he'd listened to the rest of Burt's story…

"Who'd you say you were with?"

"I'm not with anyone. All I want to know is if you have any puppies."

She sighed. "Everyone wants a puppy for Christmas. We have all these sweet, *sweet* dogs who are so loving and need homes, and everyone wants a puppy." She sounded utterly defeated.

Burt's words played in Ken's head, *housebroken* being the first that came to mind. "Might you have any smaller dogs, not too up there in years? We have four boys, the oldest is six."

"Do you own a dog now, or have you owned one before?"

"Several of them, when I was growing up, and so did my wife, who was very good with all types of animals."

"Do you have any dogs or cats *now*?"

"Not yet."

"Have the children been exposed to dogs?"

"Most of our closest friends own a dog or two, and the kids do very well with them. Look, I can assure you we are responsible parents—my wife even runs a day care—and that a dog would be much loved and well cared for here."

"You have four children under seven, and you take children into your home?"

Ken whapped himself in the forehead. This wasn't going well. Time to cut to the chase.

"Look. From what I understand, you have a bunch of dogs you need to place in homes, and I got the impression you're working under a tight timeline. If one of your dogs feels like the right match for us, I'd be happy to supply as many references as you like."

She didn't respond right away, but she began coughing. By the time she finally caught her breath and spoke, Ken had pulled into the parking lot of his office building.

"I have forms you need to fill out for preadoption approval. I don't let the dogs go to just anyone; you and your wife will have to prove your family is qualified. If you choose a dog that's due for any shots or vet visits, you'll need to sign a contract committing to such—and that includes any spaying or neutering, which is mandatory, if it hasn't taken place already. Most of the animals here have been through enough in their lives; we want to make sure we're not setting them up for more trouble. Due to timing and our circumstances, I suppose I could expedite the preapproval process for you. Assuming your application proves acceptable and if you like one of the dogs, we *both* need to agree you're making a good match." He heard her footsteps; a round of barking ensued. He pictured her walking along rows of cages, surveying the possibilities, studying the hopeful faces. Toby's demise tugged at his heart. No wonder Cassandra had been traumatized, picturing so many terrible scenarios. "I could make a couple of recommendations for your circumstances, *if* you're willing to go with a dog older than a puppy. And please don't ask me if I have any beagles. I don't."

"Deal—on both counts! What time can I come take a look? I usually don't get off till five, but my work is finally slowing down now for the holiday, so I think I can manage to be there by, say…four-thirty latest. Would that be okay?"

"I'll see you then."

"Thank you!"

"Don't thank me yet. This might not work out."

"I have high hopes." He hung up. After he heard the click, he said aloud, "It just *has* to work out, in more ways than one."

"Talking to yourself again?" Leo joked, passing by Ken's office.

"Of course." Ken gave him the report. He told Leo he'd give him a call from his cell if Santa would be dropping anything off. They engaged in a little lively banter about the price of temporary boarding. Leo assured Ken he'd have their garage set up with Macy's old cage, just in case.

Ken called Cassandra to tell her that Santa was doing a little Christmas shopping on his way home and that she should go ahead and feed the kids. "If I have trouble finding what I'm looking for, I might be pretty late."

If he did find what he wanted, he'd have additional shopping to do and a new family member to drop at Margret and Leo's, and—enjoy what could possibly be the last few days of his marriage before his wife ran off with the kids, claiming he never really knew her at all.

Cassandra opened her underwear drawer to put away her clean clothes, pushing the snowglobe package farther back into its corner to make room. The Christmas season was crazy enough without adding more flurrious crazies to it. She closed the drawer, then picked up the silver-plated hand mirror on the top of her dresser. Irene had given it to her the Christmas Cassandra was sixteen.

The Christmas season always ignited childhood memories for Cassandra. She sat on the bed, mirror in hand, and began thinking back. As a youngster, Cassandra loved it when Irene had allowed the girls to play beauty salon with her hair, something Betty had no time or mind for. Betty always kept her hair cropped short, taking the scissors to it herself when her simple hairdo needed a trim. They had no money for "the frivolities of a beauty appointment," she said, whenever Cassandra saw her, scissors in hand, heading to the bathroom. As Cassandra grew into a teen, she found herself embarrassed by her mother's oddities, which grew odder the longer her Grandpa Wonky was gone.

Irene visited the salon every week, had her nails done and sometimes even her toenails—something Betty told Cassandra she would *never* understand. "Why anyone would want to fiddle with another person's toes or have someone fiddle with theirs is beyond me." Irene kept her thick, blond, wavy locks lightened, and she owned the most wonderful gold-engraved compact Cassandra had ever seen. She relished watching Irene get out that extravagant accessory and powder her nose. She loved the way Irene's brightly polished nails extended around the rim of the mirror and the way she held her lips so close to it while daintily stroking the lipstick downward on the fullest parts, then swiping sideways toward the corners. As far as Cassandra was concerned, Irene was the essence of womanhood.

But Irene wasn't uptight about herself. Only two days after a salon visit one week, she let the girls part her locks straight down the middle in their declared contest to out*do* each other. Irene laughed until she cried when they held the hand mirror in front of her. Cassandra had made a ponytail and braid on her side of Irene's head, and Margret created a high-flying, as her mother called it, French twist on the other. Irene still kept the old Polaroid picture of the experience in one of the Bambeneks' dozens of photo albums. (Cassandra's older boys loved flipping through the albums, trying to come to grips with the fact that the young woman in so many of the pictures was actually their mommy.)

When Carl had first looked through the viewfinder to take that split-personality picture of his wife, he claimed he'd never seen her look more unusual. The girls talked him into letting them do his hair too. Margret, who was handy with all hair implements, wet her half, combed it straight forward, then slanted it toward his ear, like lopsided bangs. Cassandra combed her side straight back, then felt so sorry for him that she returned her half to his natural style. When he looked in the mirror, he laughed and thanked both girls. He kissed Cassandra on the cheek, same as he did Margret. Like the brandy in the closet, she never forgot that great kindness, the tender gift he'd bestowed upon her—as if *she* were his very own beloved daughter too.

So many ties and memories bound them all together.

Cassandra remembered the Christmas morning after Gert's death, when Margret called to tell her they finally had a new puppy and invited her to come right over. Cassandra hadn't been to their house since the old dog died. But after they got the new puppy, she couldn't stay away. That year, the tradition of having Cassandra over on Christmas morning began. After she'd open her meager gifts from her mom and brothers (socks, underwear, maybe a pad of paper and a pencil), she could barely wait for the phone to ring so she could escape her dreary household and run over to the Bambeneks', still wearing her pajamas and a robe, knowing the Bambeneks would still be in their bedclothes too. Their house would be sparkling from floor to ceiling with lights and ribbons, and they always had a wonderful gift for her, too; but it was their company she most loved.

The Christmas morning visit to the Bambeneks was still on everyone's agenda, complete with pajamas and robes for all, even Ken. It was one of the highlights of Christmas Day for the entire Higgins family, especially their older two boys, who adored Poppa Carl and Grandmomma Irene as much as Cassandra did.

Cassandra wished she could feel as excited about spending time with her own mother this holiday season. *Wishing doesn't make it so, Cassandra.* Would Betty's negative voice ever stop ringing in her head? But she seemed to be changing, and just yesterday, Ken laughed and said, "Maybe Burt's lacing your mother's Durves with happy juice and teaching *her* the Glad Game!"

She wondered how Margret would respond if she asked if Betty could join them for Christmas morning this year. *She'd probably place her palm against my forehead to see if I had a fever.*

Still, Cassandra felt kind of bad for her mom, whom she knew was disappointed again this year because neither of her brothers and their families were flying in for Christmas. Though from the sound of things, they'd been in communication more often with Betty lately. She knew Carl and Irene wouldn't care; they'd often asked Betty to join them.

Cassandra laughed out loud, picturing her mother heading out of the house in her pajamas.

Like that *would ever happen!*

Irene held the cordless phone in the crook of her neck as she stirred the spaghetti sauce. Her posture and cooking purpose—tonight's dinner—mirrored her daughter's, she imagined, who was on the other end of the line. They were finalizing their Christmas plans. Margret would pass along the details to Cassandra as soon as she hung up with her mother, then later, Irene would call Cassandra to reinforce the invitation.

"Think we should invite Burt and Betty?" Irene asked, a devilish tone in her voice.

"Over Cassandra's dead body. Last I heard, Cassie was still…I believe the word she used was 'squirming,' just thinking about the two of them together. She hasn't yet actually witnessed the happy couple."

"I have to admit, everyone in town seems rather surprised."

"I think it's wonderful."

Irene and Margret went back to chatting about the Christmas-dinner details, Irene grateful to note the obvious uplift in her daughter's spirit. When she'd first noticed it, she suspected Margret might be pregnant, since the last time she seemed this happy, the doctor had just confirmed her pregnancy. But during a casual conversation with her mother, Margret carried on about a new brand of champagne she and Leo had recently discovered, and Irene knew pregnancy wasn't the explanation for the change in her daughter's demeanor.

Leo seemed more relaxed too. She'd noticed the two of them holding hands more often, the way they used to when Margret first brought him home from college. One thing Irene was certain of—whatever the reason for the newfound lilt in her daughter's voice, she was happy for it. When the time was right, she knew Margret would fill her in.

She hadn't counted on, however, how excited she'd let herself become thinking Leo and Margret *might* be expecting again, nor how crestfallen she was when she realized that wasn't the case. Yes, she and Carl longed for a grandchild, but more than that, she'd spent years praying her daughter could experience the same joy she brought to their lives. Even during Margret's youth, during her wildest and worst of days, she'd given their lives a dimension of love they didn't know existed.

With Carl starting to bow out of his work, her quitting her part-time bookkeeping responsibilities, and Leo groomed to take over the entire business soon, Irene had allowed herself to imagine that Margret and Leo would be blessed with a child and she and Carl could fill their retired years with baby-sitting. She'd caught herself lingering on advertisements for baby furniture and reading articles about today's safety concerns for tots. She'd fantasized about bringing baby pictures to her bridge groups or to the nursing home where she volunteered. Nearly every time Cassandra dropped by so her kids could visit the Bambeneks, Irene would catch her daughter studying her when she had one of the boys on her lap. She knew how much Margret desired to make them grandparents. In private moments, she grieved for all of them.

For now, they'd just go ahead and firm up their Christmas plans, celebrate the holidays, and enjoy one another's company. Like other years, they would all attend Christmas Eve services together, then come back to the Bambenek house afterward for hors d'oeuvres.

After Margret hung up, Irene bemoaned how quickly the holidays, which she loved, would be over, the decorations down, and everything all too quickly back to normal. The older she got, the faster time flew.

Cassandra looked at her display of Christmas snowglobes, each with at least one critter in it. Every year she'd added one Christmas globe, and sometimes two or more. But this year she'd stayed away from buying one, no matter how many she saw. New snowglobes felt dangerous; maybe her flurrious experience had finally cured her. Her biggest dilemma was whether or not she should bring out her empty globe and line it up with the holiday ones. Just for a joke. Just to help her get to the point where she could maybe laugh about it, look at the thing, not freak out, or get drawn back into its mystery. Deciding to give it a whirl, she unwrapped the snowglobe and set it in the kitchen windowsill above the sink, right between her favorite reindeer globe and the panda elf.

"Mom, there's nothing in that one," Chuck said the first time he spotted it. He stood next to her, pointing at it while she peeled potatoes.

"I know, honey."

"Why?"

"Because I like it that way." She thought about how strange, yet how *kind* of funny, that sounded.

"Why?" Howie now asked the unanswerable question. He'd come over to get a better look at whatever it was Chuck pointed at.

Cassandra thought a moment. "Why do *you* think Mommy might

like an empty globe?" She hoped their answers would bring her a good dose of humor and perspective about the whole incident. *And a child shall lead them,* she thought.

"Because you're a silly mommy," Howie said. Then he giggled.

"Right." She bopped him gently on the head with her forearm.

"I think you like it because…" Chuck rolled his eyes upward and the tip of his tongue slipped out of his mouth, as it always did when he was concentrating on making up a whopper. "Because it leaves room for the Christmas monster to sleep in when he comes in the middle of the night—right after he crawls out from under Howie's bed!" He turned and jabbed his brother in the ribs.

Howie yelped. "Does not! Does it, Mommy?"

"Of course it doesn't, Howie. Your brother is just being mean." She gave Chuck her dead-eye look, which meant he needed to stop it right then. "Right, Chuck? You were just about to apologize for telling your brother a scary story, weren't you?" He looked like he was thinking about it. "And don't forget that Santa is watching you."

"Sorry," he said, though he didn't sound much like he meant it. Cassandra decided to let it go this time. Other days she might have made him repeat it until it sounded "for real," but the kids were so wired for the holidays that she decided to save her do-over command for something more important.

"Chuck does tell good stories, though," she said. Why not affirm his imagination? Maybe he'd become a novelist one day, and she didn't want to stifle his creativity. "How about you think of another reason I might like this empty snowglobe, Chuck?"

"Hmm. Maybe you like it that way because whatever is in there is invisible to everyone but you."

"What do you think Mommy sees in there that you can't?" She

rinsed the potato she just peeled, plopping it on the counter and starting on the next.

"Dogs."

Cassandra gasped, whirled and stared at him. "Why did you say
that?" Her heart pounded. She'd never talked about the dogs in front of
the boys!

"Because," he said, the tone in his voice indicating she was daft for
asking such a dumb question, "you *always* buy things with dogs."

Then off he ran, Howie hot on his trail, each of them on to the next
thing—leaving their mommy alone to catch her breath and gather her
senses. To consider why Chuck thought it was obvious that the empty
globe, sitting there between reindeer and a panda, contained invisible
dogs.

To finish the potatoes.

No matter what might be happening in an otherworldly *realm, here
in my* real *world—we're having potatoes tonight.*

But as she prepped for dinner, she was haunted by a thought: why
could the line between those two realms—what was before her eyes, and
what had disappeared before her eyes—still so easily blur? Was her reality *that* fragile that the imagination of a six-year-old could slam-dunk
her back into her own uncertainty about the incident?

"Potatoes!" she said aloud. "Right here in my hand. Focus, Cassandra, focus."

Twenty-Five

"Why a Monday night, Burt? I don't think that will work out for me. I worked all day, you know."

"Yes, Betty, I know." Burt tilted and nodded his head, smiling and using his I-am-so-patient-with-you voice. It was the look he always gave her when he knew she was making excuses. "I had to work all day too, and so did my daughter."

Betty felt her cheeks redden, a phenomenon she was getting used to since she'd started hanging around Burt. She hated the way she kept putting her foot in her mouth, realizing that sometimes she sounded just plain selfish. Maybe she was selfish. Of *course* everyone else had to work too. In fact, she doubted anyone in Wanonishaw, especially any-one Burt's age, put in the kind of long, grueling hours *he* did. These few days before Christmas, he always opened the shop an hour earlier and closed an hour later, even on Monday, his usual half day. He worked through lunch and never had a chance to sit down and catch his breath. He never lost his patience either, which she knew she'd do if she had to wait on some of his demanding customers. She wondered lately if she wasn't one of them.

She put in eight long hours at the factory, but she sat at a machine all day and got her half-hour lunch and two short breaks to boot. If she physically compared her work to what Burt tackled, she'd lose, hands down. And yet he never complained, aside from every once in a while when he mentioned that his legs didn't hold up as well as they used to— more of an observation, really. As infectious as Burt's positive nature was, equal to it was the amount of times she realized how whiny *she* must sound by comparison.

She couldn't imagine what his children must be saying about their dad dating the likes of Betty Kamrowski. She'd been at his house a few times when his grandkids popped in for a surprise visit, which they did regularly. For the most part she just kept quiet and smiled at them. No need to give anyone a reason to say, "Yup, that's Bad Betty." Maybe *that's* why Burt's daughter Patty had invited her over for Christmas cookies and punch tonight, just to check her out.

Patty was a beautician. No, these days they were called stylists, Betty reminded herself. She reached up and felt the short, uneven line of her cropped hair. For the first time, she wished she was a bit more—exotic. And as for who'd worked hard today, thinking about it, she couldn't imagine someone more in demand the week of Christmas than a stylist! Earlier, when she passed by the Beauty Barn, they'd been mobbed.

"Betty, are you listening to me?" Burt grabbed her elbow, bringing her back to reality. "You look fine. I know it's last minute, but Patty will be so glad you accepted her offer. She said to tell you she was sorry she didn't think about it sooner."

Betty stared at him.

"I'll tell you what, I'll come back and pick you up at seven. That way you won't arrive alone, and you'll have a little time to put your feet up, catch your breath, and get ready to party. Plus, that will give me time to get home and whip up a few Durves to go with the cookies, in case someone didn't have time to eat a proper dinner."

Party? I don't know how to party. "How many people are going to *be* there? I thought just Patty's family and you and me."

"No, Rebecca and Bob and their spouses and kids are coming too.

This cookie night is kind of a tradition. With this much family, you gotta jump in and entertain when you can!"

She reached for her hair again.

"I'll be back at seven sharp!" he said, as he turned to leave. Then he whirled back to face her. "And Betty, you look *wonderful*—as always." He winked before he turned and left.

After the door closed behind Burt, Betty went to the couch and plopped down. Before Burt had surprised her with his visit, she'd been sitting at her kitchen table staring at the gifts she'd lined up. She'd spent the whole of Sunday afternoon at the mall, a place she never frequented. This year, she decided it was time to give her grandsons actual presents—packages they could unwrap and play with instead of the usual envelope she gave each, with a couple of dollars in it.

She'd stood in the toy aisles of two different stores and watched moms shopping with their kids, taking note of what the kids wanted Santa to bring them. She felt like the lamest grandmother of all time: what decent grandparent was so clueless? Most of the time, the kids pointed to gifts that were electronic and too expensive. In the beginning, their choices nearly sent her home. But she stayed long enough at a third store, one more in keeping with her budget, to notice Carry, a young woman who worked with her, someone she felt okay talking to. It looked like Carry was shopping alone. She had a list in her hand and went straight to the building blocks, then to the books. Betty positioned herself until Carry couldn't help but notice her.

"Hey, Betty. Another last-minute shopper, too, huh?"

"Yes. With working…well, you know how it is, what with the hours we put in. Christmas has always been such a bother." Betty felt good having a knowing comrade beside her.

"Oh, Christmas isn't a bother for me," Carry chirped. "I *love* Christmas!" She nearly bowled Betty over with her volume and enthusiasm. "And I especially love last-minute shopping in throngs of people. I find it energizing. All the Christmas carols are playing, my husband is babysitting, finding things on markdown—it's the best." She smiled as Betty inched closer to check out what was in her cart. "So, are you shopping for your grandsons, or do *you* still play with toys?" Carry unleashed a happy laugh. "Just kidding."

"Yes. Well. I usually give them money, but this year I thought I'd get them each a little something to unwrap."

"Lucky boys!"

"I hope so," Betty said, a note of defeat in her voice.

"You can't go wrong with these." The young mother held up each of her carted items. "Kids love 'em, it doesn't matter if they're boys or girls." She looked at her watch, then said she had to get going. The minute she walked away, Betty duplicated each of the items Carry had in her cart: one box of blocks and three books, two of them having something to do with Dora, whoever that was. She thought she remembered hearing one or two of the boys mention Dora.

Now that Burt was gone (but soon to return), she went back to the kitchen to put her shopping finds away. How was it that Burt could show up and undo her world like this? In the wake of his absence, she decided her whole *life* was off kilter.

But then, maybe it already has been for far too long and I just haven't noticed until lately. Until Burt. Maybe it's finally slipping back into place.

She went to the bathroom, washed her face with soap and water, then smeared on a little Albolene Cream, which she used as a moisturizer rather than cleanser. Her mother had convinced her that nothing really cleansed the face better than a good washing. On very rare occasions, the most makeup Betty ever wore was a touch of pink lipstick, which she finally found in the medicine cabinet behind her jar of Vicks VapoRub. She felt impractical, applying lipstick for the sake of another woman she really didn't even know. *Beautifying for a beautifier. I've really lost it.* She almost wiped the lipstick off, but then decided it was so light, nobody would notice anyway.

Next she retrieved an old shoebox from the top shelf in her bedroom closet and opened the lid. Why Betty hung on to all her mother's old barrettes, she couldn't say, other than that they'd been such a defining part of Delores's appearance. Her mom always wore her hair parted in the middle, a barrette on each side to keep her straight shoulder-length hair from swinging across her round face. Sometimes she'd make a couple of braids, bring them to the top of her head, and secure the ends of them with more barrettes. Betty rifled through the colorful array, holding up first one then another. Her hair was too short and too gray. She was too old. Her face was too thin, more like her father's. She'd look ridiculous.

What possessed her to get the box of barrettes out anyway? Maybe the smell of the lipstick reminded Betty of her mom. Delores used to plant a big red kiss on Betty's cheek, stand back and have a look at her lip prints, then declare to her little Betty that maybe *now* she would remember she was loved. Even as a child, Betty seemed prone to forgetting. If she *did* forget, all she had to do was to look in the mirror, her *matka* said. The thought of getting caught with her mother's lipstick all over her face was horrifying, so she'd run right in and wash it off.

What she wouldn't give to find that declaration of love on her cheek right now. Her eyes teared. She blinked, shored herself up, and put the barrettes back in the closet. Good grief, she was getting downright sappy.

It hit her that since Burt was making Durves, she should probably bring something too. She wasn't very well versed in social graces, but at least she knew that much. But what to bring on such short notice? She rifled her cabinets and her refrigerator. She could only come up with an unopened box of Ritz crackers and couldn't decide whether or not that was better than nothing, but she stuck them in a grocery bag and set them by the front door. Just as she was straightening up, the doorbell rang. She looked out her window. What was Burt doing here already?

"I'm sorry to be so early," he said when she opened the door, "but I have to stop at the store and pick up some crackers for my ham salad. Your house is on the way. I forgot I took my last box into the store last Durve day. You ready?"

His eyes suddenly locked on her lips. Betty flung her hand over her mouth. He reached up, grabbed her hand and moved it away from her face.

"You look lovely with lipstick, Betty. It brings out the beautiful flecks of bologna color in your eyes." Betty's eyes widened. "Of course you look fine without lipstick, too, and so do your eyes. *Oofda!* You know what I mean."

She looked down at his hand, which still held hers. When her hand started trembling, he held on tighter.

"Betty, you don't need to be nervous about eating a few cookies with my kids and their spouses, and you've already met most of the grandkids." He gazed down at their hands, then noticed the brown bag containing the crackers. "And you don't need to bring anything, but what a perfect pair, we are! We're like crackers and spread together, aren't we?"

She didn't respond. The way he read her was unnerving.

"You also don't need to be quiet when we get there. You don't need to feel embarrassed about being my girl, and you don't need to wear lipstick or not wear lipstick unless it suits you. In fact, the only thing you need to do is just be yourself. Just be the Betty I'm attracted to. The Bet who has survived so much, works so hard, and is ready to just kick back and enjoy a house filled with laughter and the Christmas spirit. And maybe brag about how good my ham salad is." He gave her an up-close and personal wink. Just before he gave her a little peck on her pink quivering lips.

Betty's throat tightened, and she felt tears welling again. Just be herself? Just be *herself*? She was so busy thinking about that, the kiss didn't register.

Never in a million years could she have believed, for one millimeter of a second, that being herself would ever be enough. Or that she could attract another man, a good man! A fine, sweet man. A dear man who was holding her hand and who... *had just kissed her!*

A man who was too good for Bad Betty Kamrowski.

At that thought, she broke down and cried. Burt wrapped his arms around her and didn't let go until she stopped.

Twenty-Six

Ken was looking for a large animal-shelter sign along the road and a bunch of kennels and drove right past the driveway the first time. Just a small, hand-painted wooden marker, its weathered paint more missing than present, was hammered to a post, indicating where he missed the turn. He was glad he was able to leave work at 2:30; he might never have found the place after dark.

The long driveway up to the Manford Animal Rescue and Shelter lay so that the snow blew straight across it. Although the sun was shining, the wind was fiercely gusting. Ken slowly plowed the minivan through the snowdrifts while waffling between excitement and feeling nauseated. *Am I doing the right thing?* He hoped the drifts didn't get any deeper since the driveway posed a steep uphill grade. Then again, maybe getting stuck would be the best thing that could happen.

He was halfway up the hill and had yet to see anything but trees. *Let me know. Give me a sign. Let me know. Give me a sign.* He was still repeating his nervous, silent prayer, one that had become his mantra, when he spotted an old farmhouse nestled inside a thick circle of pine trees.

Once he pulled up beside the house, he wondered where he should park. A tall thin man appeared next to his van and knocked on the window. He wore a dark knit cap pulled down to his eyebrows. With one gloved hand, he clutched his insulated camouflage jacket—Minnesota's standard fashion statement, Ken thought—tight around his neck; with the other he motioned for Ken to drive toward the large barn. Ken pulled up near the sliding barn door and waited until the man, stooping forward into the wind, caught up with him.

"Shut it down right here." Ken did as he was told, grabbed his hat, pulled it down on his head, and exited the car. *Let me know. Give me a sign.*

"Hi, Ken Higgins," he said, extending his bare hand.

"Craig Manford," the man said in a deep gruff voice, nodding his head but ignoring Ken's outreach. Ken grabbed his gloves out of his pocket and tugged them on.

Craig slid open the barn door, motioned for Ken to step inside, then closed the door behind them. Ken was grateful; the wind howled even more here up at the top of the ridge. It felt twice as strong as it did down in the Wanonishaw valley. They stood in a small entryway surrounded by doors. Craig opened the door to his right, and the men stepped into a small office. He flipped on the light.

The sound of barking dogs, muffled very little by the wall of the small office, was tremendous. Although it was a cacophony of sound, Ken picked out batteries of high-pitched yipping, bountiful barks, and a few deep thunderous *woof-woofs*. The chilly air was laced with the odor of dog feces, but it wasn't too bad. His eyes quickly scanned his surroundings. A large, tidy, gray metal desk with an older-style black phone sitting in the middle of it. One padded metal office chair behind it and two in front, none matching. Four side-by-side metal filing cabinets, each a different height and color, most with a small amount of rust near the bottom. A wall calendar. Several framed documents hanging on the wall surrounding the calendar, and a few yellowed newspaper clips pinned on a cork board. A small, metal, vintage floor space heater, already turned on. That was pretty much it.

Craig shucked off his gloves, tossed them on the desk, and lifted the bottom of his jacket to retrieve a key ring from his pocket. It was attached to his belt loop by the kind of heavy chain a biker might use to secure his wallet.

"I was gonna have you fill out the qualification paperwork first, but since it's so late, no sense taking us both through all of that if you don't find what you're looking for." The guy was all business. "Sheryl gave me your rundown."

He led Ken out of the office, through the entryway, then toward another door. He unlocked a double set of locks, then unzipped his jacket, reached inside a breast pocket, and withdrew a small spiral notepad. He flipped through it, doubling back when he found the page he was looking for. Even though Craig wore a turtleneck and a ratty sweatshirt under his jacket, Ken could tell he was skinnier than a man his size ought to be. Craig zipped his coat back up.

"We'll start at the back with Gomer and work our way forward. Although Sheryl and me have a few ideas, if one catches your eye on the way through and I don't point it out, on the return, you just stop me. But not until we're on our way back."

Yes sir! Ken thought.

Craig walked surprisingly fast, making it difficult for Ken to keep up with him while looking at each dog in the kennels on both sides of him. He only managed to see about half of them. Aside from a couple of dogs that barely raised their eyebrows when he passed, most were either jumping up on the chain-link or standing, nose to gate, barking, their ears flapping up and down as their heads bounced with each bark. Some wagged their tails; a couple seemed like they might like to eat him alive. Ken paused in front of a friendly looking fellow that reminded him of one of his childhood dogs.

To be heard over all the barking, Craig, who was several steps ahead of him, yelled back, "Keep walking. That one's no good with kids!" The energy it took to yell seemed to knock some of the wind out of him, and he slowed his pace. By the time Ken caught up with Craig, he was bent over, hands to knees. He just stood there a few seconds before uprighting himself. Ken must have looked concerned.

"Don't worry," Craig said. "I'm not dead…at least not yet."

Ken couldn't tell if he was smiling or grimacing when he said it.

Gomer turned out to be a shaggy, deaf giant. Ken didn't know if he liked the look in Gomer's eyes or not since he couldn't see them through a heavy mop of bangs. When Craig, obviously very fond of the ancient mass, called out Gomer's name, he did so in a completely different tone of voice than the gruff one he had used with Ken. There was only one word to describe it: tender. Ken's impression of Craig Manford began to shift, and he could tell Craig was disappointed when Ken shook his head. But all Ken could picture was Bradley's head and feet sticking out from under a huge mass of fur while he screamed at Gomer to get off, without the dog's hearing a word.

"This here is Suzy-Q. She's a sweetie pie, ain't ya girl?" Craig stuck his fingertips through the chain-link and scratched her nose. "Due to weak kidneys, she's got a little bladder-control problem, but other than that we believe she'd make a fine friend for a pack of kids."

Ken shook his head again. With two still in diapers (Harry had been more miss than hit lately with the potty training, so Cassandra gave up on it for a while), they didn't need a *dog* with a potty problem.

Craig sighed and his shoulders slumped as he studied his list. From the way his eyes scanned the page after Ken's pass on his first two recommendations, he was clearly mentally checking off several other possibilities. "Too bad you didn't come last week. We had a two-month-old

Lab mix and a two-year-old schnauzer. With Christmas and all, we been pretty busy."

Then Craig came to one that made him nod. "Let's have a look at Dozer." They crossed the aisle and stopped in front of a chocolate Lab. "Full-blood. Housebroken. Loves kids. Only three years old."

"Any issues?"

"Sometimes."

"Such as?"

"You got a fenced-in yard?"

"Yes."

"How tall's the fence?"

"About four feet." This time Craig shook his head.

Ken hated that he sounded so...fussy. All these wagging tails attached to all these wagging bodies, each just looking for someone to love and give it a new home. From the looks of several of the dogs, to let them live out their remaining years in a little comfort—like Toby must have been, waiting for Cassandra to come back, right up until... If ever he understood his wife's haunting, it was now.

"How'd you come by all of them?" Ken asked, rousing himself from further gloom.

"Too big a question. Too little time," Craig said, looking at his watch. "If you do find a dog, we've got ourselves some paperwork, including an adoption contract. Plus, I gotta take my meds and check on my wife soon. Let's just say you dream up as many possible scenarios as you can about how a dog might end up here—you'll still be a few dozen short. People drop them off. They wander in. We rescued a bunch from another shelter. People die and nobody wants their dogs. Over twenty years, lots of ways." He paused and swallowed. "Too old.

Too bad. Too mean. Too red, black, brown, white, or hairy. Too not a beagle." He hesitated, burned a look into Ken, then added, "Or people get pets for Christmas presents, then decide they made a mistake."

Ken raised his eyebrows.

"I'm sorry," Craig shook his head. "That was a lousy thing to say. I don't even know you."

Ken nodded an acceptance of his apology as Craig continued.

"I'm sure you're a perfectly responsible guy. After all, you drove up here in a minivan." This time there was no doubt he smiled. It was a weak smile, but nonetheless a smile. "It's just that the wife and me have poured our hearts, souls, and every scrap of money we've come by into these critters. Man, making the right match is so rewarding." The word *critters* vibrated Ken's heartstring. "But many of 'em we got right now ain't adoption material. Just the same, we love 'em." His eyes swept around the place. "Now the wife and me are both sick. *Real* sick—which, by the way, is the reason I couldn't shake your hand. Doc says to steer clear of as many germs as I can while I'm undergoing treatment, but…" His voice trailed off as he looked from end-to-end of the barn, the kennels a giant habitat of germs.

"I lost my day job about ten months ago; this place has been my wife's full-time mission. She used to take most all of them out for a walk every day. Now we've got no health insurance and not much time to clear the decks. We've got the whole place—property, house, *and* the whole rescue center—up for sale. I'm afraid circumstances beyond our control have left us—well, *me*—a little ill-tempered. No need to take it out on you, though."

"Any offers?"

"We had one, but they're not interested in the dogs. They just want the property and the buildings."

"How many acres you got?"

"Sixteen. Used to have more, but we sold most of it off to subsidize our dog habit." One corner of his mouth lifted in a halfhearted grin.

"You gonna take the offer?"

He bit his bottom lip. "We're not even sure if it's still on the table. When we turned it down, we were still idealistic about the notion that somebody would come along, fall in love with the place—especially the dogs—and bail us and the dogs out. But now we're running out of time. Aw, man, I'm sorry to be bending your ear like this. I guess I just needed to unload, which was inappropriate. Again, my apologies."

"Go ahead and talk if you need to," Ken said, not knowing how else to respond. "Maybe it'll help you vent to talk to somebody who's not involved."

"Not involved, huh? That's pretty funny coming from a guy who's here to shop!" He laughed and his face brightened for a moment. It was the first time Ken saw what Craig must have looked like before he got sick.

"Well, you know what I mean," Ken said. "I don't know why, but it's sometimes easier to talk to strangers about heavy stuff—especially when those closest to us are *part* of the heavy stuff." *How very true, in both our cases.* He gave Craig a halfhearted smile. He was starting to like the guy.

"Since we're being honest, now it's my turn to dump. To tell you the truth, the dog is actually for my wife." He poured out everything he knew about Cassandra and her critters. He started with her natural gift to draw animals, the way she cared for them, her lost dreams to be a vet, her unhealed heartache over Toby, and how it had kept her from owning another dog. Who better to hear it than this guy—one who might lend him some insight as to whether or not he was making a good decision. By the time he was done with Cassandra's history, sans the inexplicable snowglobe saga, he'd rendered Craig temporarily speechless.

A giant gust of wind rattled the outer barn doors, and an even deeper chill swept through the barn. It crossed Ken's mind that the heating bill must be astronomical, just to keep it above freezing.

Craig finally opened his mouth, but nothing came out. He swallowed, laced his fingers, stared at his white knuckles, then looked up at Ken. "Here's the worst part for us...we have to get rid of our own dogs too." He stopped, swallowed again, and blinked back an obvious pooling of tears. "We're gonna move in with Sheryl's cousin. Those two are real close. Her cousin's a registered nurse, which we figure will come in handy, but she rents a two-bedroom duplex, and she has allergies. And at this point..." His voice was barely audible, and he seemed to have shrunk in on himself. "Let me just say that I understand the pain your wife has lived with, having to get rid of a dog she loves and no control over what will happen to it. We can't afford to keep our dogs, even if we did have the room. I doubt we'll be able to care for them much longer, not in the way they deserve."

"And nobody will take them?"

"I haven't had the heart to show our dogs. Might have to, I guess—although I'd hate to see them separated. They're pretty good buddies. Besides, like I said, most people only seem to want puppies and the latest winning or fad dogs."

"No family members?"

"We've only got one daughter, but she's in terrible financial trouble too. Plus, she lives in Arkansas. Some days we both feel like we already got one foot each in the grave. But to think that we might have to put *all* the dogs down"—again, his eyes scanned the kennels—"*including* our own..." He appeared too defeated to even cry. "There ain't another shelter around that don't euthanize after a certain period of time. That's why we started with our operation here. I guess I can understand why they have to do it—especially *now*. Eventually, you run out of space and resources, but the dogs just keep coming in. We've been blessed to either have one adopted or die from old age just when a new one showed up. God's been good that way.

"Maybe putting them down *is* a better option than watching them become unhealthy, stuck in a cage their whole lives, or letting them go with somebody you're afraid won't treat them right. But as of this moment, we just can't live with that as a possibility for our own dogs, who are family members to us. They're our *friends*. They've brought us so much peace in the middle of heartache." He closed his eyes. "We just keep praying."

"How many dogs you got?"

"Three."

Even though the sun was still shining, another wild wintery blast rattled a few loose barn boards, forcing a fine dusting of drifting snow under a small gap in the back door. The dogs, many who had finally settled down, piped up again.

"What kind of dogs do you have?" Ken asked.

"Well, we got Mutt…a red-headed mix of some kind. Who knows how many breeds he's got in him. I hear they have a DNA test to find these things out now, but who cares? He's one of the most loyal dogs we've ever had—and that's saying something. Then we got Sarah. She's a Border collie worth her weight in gold."

Ken suddenly heard his wife's voice, and his heart began to race. A prickle ran up his arms. *A Border collie, a lanky gray greyhound, and a reddish mutt.* He'd heard Cassandra repeat it enough times that it had branded his brain.

"We had a vandal here once, guy who walked in and turned all the dogs loose. That's why we've got all these keys now," he said, patting his pants pocket. "Sarah nearly worked herself to death, trying to corral those dogs back toward the barn. I've never seen a dog with better instincts. She once—"

"What's your other dog?" Ken cut him off. "If you tell me you have a greyhound—"

"Come on, man. You saw her in the window on your way in?"

Ken felt like he was going to faint. "No, I did not see your"—his words slowed—"greyhound in the window. *Please* don't tell me it's gray."

"Grady is indeed gray. That's why we named her Grady. Original, right...hey, you all right? You're as white as a ghost."

"I need to sit down," Ken said, already walking toward the office. "Right now."

No matter how much he tried to fight it, every step he took brought him closer to the same startling conclusion: his search was over. How on earth they'd take on three dogs—ones he hadn't even set eyes on—he had no idea. The only thing he knew for sure was that they were meant for Cassandra, and she would know it too.

When they passed into the entryway between the kennel and the office, Craig closed the kennel door behind them, and a woman entered through the barn door. A bright, blinding flurry of snow swirled in the door with her, twirling around Ken like a mini-tornado. He stood there, as if frozen in its vortex, until the woman closed the door. Breathless, he staggered into the shelter office, sat down, and buried his face in his hands.

"I don't believe this," he said, in a voice not much louder than a whisper. For a very long time, that was *all* he could say.

Twenty-Seven

At Patty's request, Burt hadn't mentioned to Betty that the Christmas cookies and punch night was also when they did their family gift exchange. They'd all drawn names months ago. Of course Betty was not expected to come with a gift, but Patty didn't want her to feel completely left out. Prompted by one customer, certainly not the first, nosily inquiring about her dad's new "friend," Patty wondered if her dad might like to bring Betty along. After she'd called him with the late afternoon invite for Betty, she grabbed one of her shop's gift certificates before she left for home. A benefit of owning the Beauty Barn was that her time and services were hers to give as she saw fit. Every month she donated a style and blow-dry to the women's shelter in a neighboring town, instructing them to pick the woman who most needed a little pampering. From the little she knew about Betty, her downtrodden spirit seemed almost as needy as the women's in the shelter. "One Free Trim, Wash, and Set," she printed on the certificate, using the language Betty might best understand. "Style and blow-dry" might leave her wondering.

As far as Patty was concerned, there could be no better gift for Betty. Since she was a little girl, Patty always noticed everyone's hair, including Betty's obvious severe self-cut.

Her first memory of her classmate's mother was the day of the suicide. She and Cassandra were in the middle of an exam; Patty looked out the classroom window and noticed a crying woman walking toward the school door. Unbeknown to her at the time, Betty was coming to get Cassandra out of class before she learned of the tragedy from someone else. It was remarkable, the image of Betty Kamrowski crying and walking, taking such small steps, as though she didn't really want to arrive at the school door, and it stuck with Patty all these years.

The night of Mr. Kamrowski's suicide, Patty remembered asking her dad if *he* was ever sad, since that's all any adult would say about why Mr. Kamrowski had done such a terrible thing. Burt told her that, yes, sometimes he felt sad. He was sad about Mr. Kamrowski. But he wrapped his arms around her and assured her that he was never that sad because he had too many wonderful things in his life to make him happy, like her. For a long time, Patty wondered if Mr. Kamrowski didn't think his own children were wonderful, too, but when she matured, she learned about the ravages of clinical depression and then understood.

Twenty-five years later, Patty waited for Betty to show up at her house with her dad. Her *Dad*. She didn't really know Betty or Cassandra. What she did know came mostly through the unreliable grapevine and her father, who was always saying something about *Betty this,* and *Betty that*. She knew one thing—her dad had strong feelings for Betty.

When her dad and Betty finally arrived, he was his usual jovial self, acting as though he brought women to meet the family every day. Aside from brief introductions, he ushered Betty into the kitchen like one of the family. But Betty was clearly a nervous wreck. She looked like Burt was holding her up—which didn't take much. Patty wondered if the woman even weighed a hundred pounds.

"Bet and I brought some special Durves and crackers," Burt said, lining them up on the counter.

Bet?

"Well, your father actually…" Betty spoke so quietly, she could barely be heard.

"Nonsense!" Burt said. "We did it together."

As the evening progressed, Patty noticed that her dad seemed to be aware of Betty's every breath, and especially her insecurities. No wonder, though. The Burts were a loud and raucous group, likely pretty overwhelming for someone like Betty. The more Patty observed her father and Betty together, the happier she became that she brought the gift certificate for a haircut. Betty surely did need one. People were always so happy when she donated gift certificates for silent auction fund-raisers. Everybody loved going to the Beauty Barn, and bidding was usually quite aggressive, some even paying more than face value.

But suddenly it struck her that Betty might be humiliated by the gesture, as if Patty thought she *needed* fixing. The certificate might feel like a slap in the face. She hoped her dad didn't think so, but it was too late, the package was under the tree. The gift exchange had started, and her dad was already reaching for the package with Betty's name on it.

"What have you got there, Bet?" He winked at Patty, clearly grateful for his daughter's thoughtfulness.

"Let me see," Betty said, after a half-dozen apologies that they shouldn't have done this, since after all, she'd brought nothing in exchange. Betty was obviously *already* embarrassed. She opened the box and the envelope. At Burt's coaxing, she pulled the gift certificate out and read it aloud. "One free trim, wash, and set." Her cheeks turned crimson and she tucked in her lips as her hand flew up to her neckline. Burt immediately grabbed her hand and settled it on his knee.

"Why Patty, what a lovely gift," Burt said. "How thoughtful, sweetie! You know my daughter owns the Beauty Barn, right, Betty?"

"Yes. Yes, I do."

"She does *wonders* with a head of hair." He rolled his head around as living proof. "Not that you need it!" he exclaimed, after looking into

Betty's eyes, then glancing at his daughter—who worried she had the same expression. "But you sure will enjoy it. She gives the best scalp massage in town."

Patty wanted to kiss her dad. No wonder she loved him so much— no wonder Betty was attracted to him. He didn't miss a trick, always the peacemaker, that man.

Nonetheless, the evening still felt complicated. Patty didn't know what to do with the mixed emotions that flared within her when she saw her dad holding Betty's hand. Betty did not look very comfortable either. She seemed aware that the relationship might be difficult for them, which Patty decided was very respectful.

Before Betty and her dad had arrived, she implored her siblings to try to be accepting. "After all," she said, talking to herself as much as anyone, "Mom's been gone five years. Why would we want Dad to be all alone for the rest of his life?"

Twenty-Eight

Ken rolled over and looked at the clock again. Five a.m., Christmas morning. It felt like he'd been awake for days. He thought surely at least Chuck would be up by now. He also thought he might explode if he couldn't give Cassandra her Christmas gift soon. Maybe he should just wake her up and give it to her now. But she'd been up so late last night, finishing the wrapping.

Three excruciatingly long days had passed since he went to the shelter and learned about the three dogs. Before he'd left the Manfords that evening, he and Craig agreed that Ken should announce the gifts to Cassandra *without* the dogs in tow, just in case. Ken took a bunch of pictures of them with his cell phone. While Cassandra had been in the basement doing secret Santa wrapping, he uploaded them to the computer, then printed them out and fashioned a gift card announcing their upcoming arrival. Another sheet of paper bore a photo of the empty snowglobe. He'd only purchased a few necessary dog-care items, but in a wave of self-doubt, he'd left them in his trunk, just in case.

Leaving the dogs also enabled Craig and Sheryl to adjust to their upcoming separation from their pets, whom they weren't quite ready to relinquish yet. If all went as planned, Cassandra and the boys would meet the dogs out at the shelter the next day. They'd make a visit or two, however long it took, getting acquainted and making sure the dogs would be okay with the boys. Craig said they'd taken the dogs to the nursing home for patient visits, but the three canines hadn't spent much time around small children.

Ken rolled over and stared at his sleeping wife. She lay on her back, hands tucked up under her chin. She looked so peaceful. Surely she would understand the implications of his finding the same three dogs that had disappeared from the globe. Then he envisioned three dogs galloping through the house, four boys hot on their trail, Cassandra trying to catch up with them as they ran roughshod over beds and couches.

He rolled over to face the clock again, turning himself away from the waves of a potential impending disaster. But just as quickly, he felt Cassandra would know that the experience with the globe was a premonition. What else could explain it?

"Ken," a sleepy voice said, "are you okay? Or are you just excited about Santa? How long have you been tossing and turning?"

"Sorry, hon. I thought you were asleep. To tell you the truth, I *am* excited about Santa. The boys are such fun ages... But I'm also especially grateful to God this year. We have so many blessings, Cass."

She spooned him and put her arm around him. He laced his fingers with hers, then kissed her palm. "Merry Christmas, Cass. I hope this is your best Christmas ever."

"I'm sure it will be. Thank goodness I found that train for Chuck, or we'd have a whole day of pouting."

"I think Santa left you a big surprise under the tree," he said, his heart racing.

"Really?" She kissed the back of his neck. "Is it bigger than a breadbox?"

"Two-thirds of it is."

"It comes in parts?"

"Parts...and hearts."

"Maybe I should go look now, before the boys start tearing the place apart. Parts and hearts. Hmm...must be a necklace and earrings."

"Nope, you are way off base. Believe me, you will never guess, not in a bazillion years. It's the Glad Game, supersized and gone wild. I *do* think you should open it now before the boys get up. Let's go!"

He tossed back the covers, and she groaned and shivered before grabbing her robe.

At 5:45, when Howie walked into the Everything Room, the first thing he noticed was not the little train encircling the Christmas tree's base. It was his mommy and daddy. They sat on the couch together, and Daddy had his arm around Mommy, who was crying. She held a piece of paper in each hand. With shuffling steps, Howie crawled up on the couch and snuggled up beside her.

"Don't cry, Mommy. Why are you so sad?"

"Oh, honey, Mommy's not sad. She is glad. She is glad, glad, GLAD." She wiped her nose on the sleeve of her robe before reaching for her son.

"Then why are you crying?"

"These are happy tears, sweetie." She leaned over and kissed Daddy again. "Santa has brought me—our whole family—the most wonderful gift!"

"Where is it?"

"Where's what?" Chuck asked, standing in the doorway, wiping his eyes.

"Santa brought a gift for our whole family!" Howie yelled.

"Duh…look under the tree." Chuck pointed.

Off the couch, Howie scrambled toward the train. Cassandra started to say something, but Ken grabbed her arm. "Maybe we should just let them all wake up and enjoy their presents first. Harry and Bradley aren't even up yet."

"You're right. We'll have plenty of time, especially since we won't even meet the dogs until tomorrow. Maybe we shouldn't even tell them until we're on the way out there."

"Nah, we can tell them later, before we go to the Bambeneks," Ken said, finally allowing himself to relax.

"I can't wait for Carl and Irene to find out. I can't think of anyone who will be happier for me! Oh, Ken, they've been through it with me, to be sure. I've been through it with myself. But you're exactly right: I have no doubt those dogs are for us. Whatever fears and self-doubt I've been carrying around melted straight away when I saw the pictures. Nothing will ever change my mind about that—or explain such a mysterious…miracle. *Thank you*, Ken. Honestly, I just can't believe it." She looked at the pictures of the dogs and the empty snowglobe again. "It is a *miracle*. A Border collie, a lanky gray greyhound, and a reddish mutt. And look!" she said, lifting a lock of her hair.

"The color of your own," he whispered into her ear. They put their foreheads together and laughed.

Ken spoke again. "Just so you're aware, Leo and Margret already know about the dogs. I hope you're not disappointed. When I first started looking for a puppy, I needed their help, in case Santa needed a place to keep the pup until Christmas morning. And after I met with Craig, I had to give them a report. However, I made them promise you could be the one to tell Carl and Irene. I hope Margret kept her word."

"We'll see; you know how close they are. But even if Carl and Irene do know, they'll *still* be so excited for me. I can't wait to show everyone the pictures. Have Leo and Margret seen the pictures?"

"No."

"Good!"

"What about your mom, Cass? I bet she'll be happy for you too."

"Mom. I forgot she was coming to the Bambeneks today. I just couldn't believe it when she said yes. Honestly, my entire world is on tilt right now." Cassandra sat back on the couch, a slight shadow crossing her face.

"Three dogs, Betty at the Bambeneks... *two* Christmas miracles. Maybe we'll get three miracles," Ken said, giving her a playful nudge. "Maybe she'll even wear pajamas."

"As if."

Ken pointed to the picture of the empty snowglobe, then to the dogs. "Anything is possible, Cass. Anything."

"Yes, Ken, anything is possible—anything but my mom wearing pajamas out of her house," Cassandra quietly said when Betty arrived at the Bambeneks, carrying an armload of packages and dressed in her Sunday finest. And wearing... *lipstick?* It felt good to watch the boys rush her mom, who appeared hesitant and... vulnerable. She had to give her credit: after all the years of saying no to the invitation, it took some courage to finally say yes.

Although Cassandra had told her mom that Burt was invited too, Betty declined, saying he and his family had all-day plans. Cassandra was actually relieved. She didn't think this would be the best event for all of them to be together for the first time. Too much going on— although she bet Burt would have worn *his* pajamas.

"Can we tell them now?" Chuck asked Cassandra the moment Betty was seated. *"Please?"*

"Go right ahead," Cassandra said.

"Everyone," Chuck said, using his loudest ringmaster voice, "we have an announcement to make!" He motioned for Harry and Howie to stand on each side of him, yanking them around until he was satisfied with their alignment.

Cassandra got up and whispered in Chuck's ear, "Don't forget to say it the way we practiced."

He threw her his dagger look. "I *know*."

"Ready?" Chuck said in his loudest voice. He paused, waiting to make sure everyone was looking at them. "We're finally adding some *girls* to our family!"

Irene launched up out of her chair like she had a spring in her backside. "Cassie, that's wonderful! And did he say girls—as in plural? Are you pregnant with twins?"

Betty sat frozen in her chair, mouth agape.

"Go ahead, Chuck," Ken said. "Tell them the rest."

"And another boy, too!"

Before anyone else had a chance to react, Howie giggled and burst out, "Santa brought us three dogs for Christmas. Two girls and one boy. We get to meet them tomorrow!"

"Howie. *I* was supposed to tell!" Chuck stomped off to a corner.

"Here, Harry," Cassandra said. "Go show everyone the pictures."

Chuck came running back and grabbed two of them out of Harry's hand. He gave one to Howie. "We *all* get to show the pictures."

The rest of the morning was laced with flying wrapping paper—the boys especially loving Betty's gifts—snacks, many tears, and much excitement about the dogs. Cassandra doubted she'd ever have a merrier Christmas morning than this, and part of that had to do with her mother's presence. Betty remained curiously quiet, though, likely overwhelmed by all the activity. Cassandra was dying to know what Betty was thinking—although she'd bet good money that her mother was thinking if Cassandra couldn't find time to dust now, how would she find time to care for three dogs.

Between bouts of feeling ecstatic and mind-boggled by all that had happened, she found herself wondering the same thing.

What in the world were they in for?

Not until Betty safely closed her front door behind her and took off her coat did she allow the rush of emotions to consume her and tears to spill forth. "At last. At *last*! My baby girl has her dogs back!" Sobs racked her body until her tears were spent.

Redeemed. That's what she felt like. Redemption was one of Burt's favorite words; this was the first time she understood its power. Who could imagine that three dogs could deliver such…grace.

She couldn't stop thinking about something else Burt said a few nights ago, before they'd left for Patty's party. He'd mentioned how much she had *survived*. In all these years, she'd never thought about herself as a survivor, but rather a failure. She'd simply done what she had to do to get by. She'd dealt with Gerald's depression, although sometimes not well. She'd shored herself up after his death, albeit in lifeless ways. She'd managed to keep three children clothed and fed, and soldiered on after the death of her beloved father, while fighting guilt and frustration.

But *yes*. She had *survived*. It was time to see herself through the eyes of Burt Burt, a man who soothed her weaknesses, accepted her foibles, and who reminded her with his sweet kisses that she was still a woman.

She was a survivor. *I am a survivor.* She felt strength pouring into her, just trying the words on for size.

Since that day in the butcher shop when she and Burt had bantered about business cards, for reasons unbeknown to her, she thought about what different people could declare themselves to be. What *would* her cards say? Bad Betty Kamrowski? Maybe she should have cards printed up that simply said "Survivor," just to remind herself. Or maybe she should just stick with "Cowgirl from Oklahoma." After all, cowgirls survived the wild, wild West, Burt thought cowgirls and butchers went well together, and if that's what Burt thought, that was good enough for her.

The day after Christmas, Ken, Cassandra, and the boys arrived at the Manfords to meet their three new family members. Cassandra could only say, "I don't believe this." Craig and Sheryl watched as Cassandra repeated the words through the tears that she let rain first onto the head of Mutt, then onto the nose of Grady, and the rest, which she buried deep into the silky neck of Sarah, who licked her face until it was dry.

It was clear to the Manfords that the dogs instantly took to Cassandra and to the boys. Although it was bittersweet for them to meet the family—the woman—under whose wings they would surrender their beloved pets, they had no doubt they would be kept safe and well and that their prayers had been answered.

This young family became a reassurance to the Manfords that even in the midst of their trials and suffering, God still had His eye on them.

Part Three

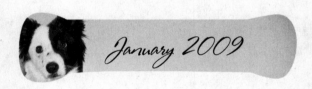

January 2009

Twenty-Nine

After Leo and Margret returned from their Montana visit with Leo's parents, after the first of the year, they invited Irene and Carl over for a roast beef dinner. "We have something important to tell you," Margret said on the phone during her invite. "But so you don't jump to the wrong conclusion, no, I'm not pregnant."

"I already knew that," Irene said.

"How?"

"Champagne."

"I was going to say I could never pull something over on you, Mom. But then, I still have *decades* of material to surprise you with, just when you think you have heard it all." She laughed.

"NO!" her mom yelped in mock distress. "I can't *stand* to hear any more about your youth."

For the rest of the day, Irene convinced herself that her daughter's news might be an impending adoption. Instead, she and Carl learned over dessert that, unless God pulled a fast one on all of them, there would be *no* grandchild for the Bambeneks.

"We've had time to digest this." Margret rose from the table and hugged first her mom, then her dad. "I know this will take you some time too. But I hope it helps you to know—and please believe us when we say this, because it is true—that we are peaceful in our decision to let go."

Irene picked up her napkin and dabbed at her nose. "Honey, I believe you. I've noticed a new, more relaxed spirit in you for some time now. I'm just glad you're at peace."

That night Carl and Irene held each other as they shed tears together and tried to allow their heartstrings to uncurl from their dreams. After they crawled into bed and Irene turned out the light on her nightstand, as usual, they said their prayers together. They thanked God for each other, for their daily bread, and for His hand on their lives. They each expressed their concerns and asked God to empower them to conform to His will. They always closed with general prayers for world peace, something they never gave up on. But tonight, before the "Amen," they asked God—*beseeched* God—to help them let go of what was not to be and to recognize what would fill the gap, knowing full well that God never closed one door without opening another.

"Help us find a place to pour all this saved-up love, God," Irene said, breaking into a heaving and surrendering bout of tears.

"Oh, Margret," Cassandra said into the receiver, "I feel like I'm living in a bubble of grace." She'd just put the boys down, Ken was at the computer, and Sarah lay at her feet.

"No disasters yet? That's hard to believe."

"Sure, things are a little crazy, but not nearly as bad as I thought they'd be. You gotta come over and see the boys with them. The dogs are settling in, but they're still a little overwhelmed with all the activity and tentative about so many things." She laughed, recalling a vision of Grady racing through their house. "The first time I turned on the garbage disposal, Grady ran to the Everything Room. We could barely get her back to the kitchen. But since the last time you and your folks were here, at least Sarah seems more at ease. Mom could hardly believe it. She and Burt dropped in yesterday. They brought a giant bag of dog toys. Burt said it was a belated Christmas gift for the new family members. He'd wrapped some frozen bones from his shop, complete with baking instructions. Mom actually giggled when Burt read them to Mutt. *Giggled*. Did you catch that?"

"Sure did. Very cute."

"It *was* cute. *They're* cute."

"Speaking of cute, you should see the pictures I took of the boys and the dogs the other day. I'm putting your Christmas gift to good use; who knew that even I could figure out a digital camera!"

"Listen, Cass, I have got to get to bed early tonight, and I still have a financial report to review. I'll try to stop by this weekend, but no promises. Life's crazy busy at work right now, I'm behind on housework...and just about everything else. But I'm so happy for you. I'm happy for Ken too. He was tormented over the decision, so I'm glad it all worked out. It just goes to prove that God is God, and that He works in mysterious ways—even if He had to use a snowglobe, three dogs, and a gutsy husband to do it."

Cassandra's eyes welled. The arrival of the dogs had tapped a new well in her soul, one ever-ready to overflow with tears of joy. Each river of tears released another corner of years of pent-up critter love. When one of the dogs was in the proximity of the snowglobe, prayers of gratefulness sprang forth. *Thank You, Lord. Thank You. Thank You.*

"Margret, until the day I die, I will never be able to explain what happened with that snowglobe. All I know is that it was meant to be. Every ounce of drama was worth it." As if on cue, Sarah stood and leaned against her. Cassandra scratched her behind the ear and kissed the top of her silky head.

Cassandra knew her honeymoon with the dogs was over the day she blew a fuse and banished the two larger dogs to the garage for the first time. She felt utterly defeated, like she let Grady and Sarah down with her lack of patience, especially since they spent most of her day-care hours out there.

Special safety precautions had to be taken when the day-care kids were present, until much warmer weather allowed the kids or the dogs to be outside. Ken and Cassandra agreed that liability was a serious issue. The Higginses needed to make *more* than sure there weren't any hidden problems lurking, especially with the bigger dogs who stood face-to-face with the children. Mutt, however, had already proven himself to be kid-friendly and small enough that he couldn't push anyone around, not even Bradley. He was ever present, no matter who was in the house.

The heated garage was by no stretch a dungeon, with both vehicles pulled outside, a bucketful of dog toys, bones galore, the mound of blankets they shared for lolling, and the large kennels Ken bought for each of them as "personal spaces" and to secure them when the family was out. It was at least a two-star accommodation.

"Consider what your alternative might have been!" Cassandra said, shaking her finger at them before she closed the door on their first banishment. But she immediately reopened the door and rendered a teary, "I'm sorry." She couldn't believe such a horrid thing had even slipped out of her mouth. She went to the giant bag of dog biscuits, handed one to each, and tossed the squeaky hotdog between them. "I'll let you back in after I calm down," she said, gently and with a smile. "Clearly, I am almost out of my mind."

The guilt she felt was the same as when she complained about her kids in front of Margret.

Cassandra thought about Margret for a moment. Something was up with her, but after Christmas, Margret and Leo left for Montana, and their brief visits were chaotic and rushed. They'd found no private face time to talk for way too long and that needed to change.

Later, when Cassandra and Ken lay in bed after the lights were out, she confessed, "I just had to take a break to get a hold of myself. The day-care kids were so wound up, and after they finally left, Grady and Sarah started a tag team against Mutt and Chuck, so *something* had to give. I was afraid it was going to be *me*." She almost felt like she was mentally back in the confessional of her youth again, admitting her sins against the critters. But thankfully, for the most part, her long-held guilt was lifting—aside from this temporary backslide. She was determined never to get stuck in guilt again. Still… "If one more thing got knocked over, I was afraid I'd go *ballistic*! When the entryway floor lamp crashed and busted, I grabbed hold of Grady and Sarah's collars and all but dragged them through the kitchen. Grady's tail was tucked so far between her legs, it looked like she didn't even have one. You know how sensitive she is. When we got to the garage, Sarah licked her face, as if to say, 'I feel your pain.'"

"Hon, I'm proud of you."

"Proud? *Proud* I lost it?"

"No, I'm proud you knew what you needed to do, and you took action. Saying 'I need help,' and 'I need a break' are not signs of weakness and failure, Cass," he told her now, as he had on numerous occasions.

"They're some of the strongest words on the planet, and wise people know how to wield them. The people who go the furthest in business are the ones who aren't too proud to call in help when they need it, or to take time-outs for themselves."

Cassandra laughed. She was aware she sometimes suffered from a slight martyr syndrome, wherein she fought things out in moments when it would be best to surrender.

"You think that's funny?"

"No. I think it's brilliant...and comforting. That wasn't why I laughed, though. I was laughing at me. Here I was so angry at the dogs about the lamp. But after I got the mess cleaned up and took it to the garbage can in the garage, I gave Grady a *thank you* kiss. I hated that lamp. It's needed to go for a long time."

"It'll be better when spring arrives, it finally warms up, and I can get a big dog pen built in the backyard, and the kids, or the dogs—or all of them—can be tossed in.

"Honestly, though, Cassie, I've never seen anyone as natural with dogs as you, and I'm not just saying that. Since I've watched you with the dogs, I love you even more, and I didn't think that was humanly possible."

Tears welled in her eyes. "Even with all the chaos, I feel like I've finally come home to myself. To our dying day, you will *never* be able to top your 2008 Christmas gift. As much extra work and trouble as they are—and there is no denying that some days my crew, and that's including the boys *and* you—," she said, playfully poking him in the ribs with her elbow—"border on too much. But the truth is," she said, rolling on her side to face him, "the blessings are a millionfold. Even for you," she said, surprising him with a rocketing kiss.

During their Christmas day together, in the chaos and gaiety of the celebration, the Higginses never had much of a chance to tell the Bambeneks the story of how the dogs came to them. They hadn't talked about how ill the Manfords were or what a terrible financial circumstance they were in. One afternoon, Cassandra spilled the whole tale to Irene on the phone, mentioning that she hadn't even told Margret all the details yet, but Ken maybe had.

"I had no idea. Margret and Leo haven't said anything about it," Irene said. "I just assumed Ken had found them at the shelter."

Now that Cassandra had met Craig and Sheryl, been to the kennels, into their home and gotten to know them, she was full of empathy for the Manfords, wishing she could help them further. She shared as much as she could remember with Irene, this mother of her heart, who would listen as long as Cassandra kept talking.

After Irene hung up, Carl asked what all the "oh, that is so sad" talk was about. She told him about the Manfords and their horrible circumstances.

"Is there anything we might do to help them?" she asked. "Maybe sponsor a fund-raiser or something?"

The Bambeneks were known throughout Wanonishaw and the surrounding communities for their generosity. They'd often opened their stately home or their glorious backyard, hired caterers, even a harpist, for fund-raising occasions. In cosponsorship with Bambenek Enterprises, they would pay for everything, donating their personal expenses to the cause. A few local businesses would sell tickets, pull together silent- and live-auction items, and all proceeds would go for the charity or cause. The family or organization in need found help, and the community enjoyed a great time out and the chance to support their neighbors. In this day and age, more people than ever suffered with financial problems, especially due to health issues. The needs were endless. Carl and Irene couldn't take on every request, but something about the Manfords' circumstances really struck both of their hearts.

"First, let me find out a little more about them," Carl said, knowing that both Cassandra and his wife could be bleeding hearts of the most vulnerable kind.

Thirty

Patty stood behind Betty, who sat ramrod straight in the salon chair, a drape cloth wrapped around her neck. Betty studied the large posters on the wall, trying to keep from making eye contact in the mirror for fear Patty would detect her trepidation.

What a tangle of humanity, she thought, frowning at the posters. Women and men, most of them wearing *ridiculous* hairdos, some with red streaks the color of raw meat, stared back at her. *Raw meat?* She concluded she had been hanging around Burt too often. She'd seen those frightful sprigs of hair sticking up this way and that on the young stars filling the pages of *People* magazine. She wished she'd not succumbed to the vice of the pricey gossip rag, but she couldn't seem to resist when passing through the checkout counter at the local grocery store. On an otherwise lonely evening, each issue was good for at least a couple of hours of entertainment, especially if she made herself read every word, even about the stars she'd never heard of. Burt teased her plenty when he first noticed a few issues tucked down in the magazine rack near her favorite chair. "I was just…I didn't…," she stammered. He laughed at her inept attempt to make some excuse, then admitted that he, too, liked to read *People* when he was in the doctor's or dentist's office.

Still staring at the posters, Betty jumped as though she'd been shot with a water cannon when Patty spritzed her head. Patty rested her free hand on Betty's shoulder. "Sorry. I should have warned you." She spritzed a few more times.

Betty, now staring at the bright blue water bottle, wondered what kind of a hair wash this was. Having never been to a salon before, how was she to know such oddities took place in them? It hadn't been Betty's idea to come to the shop, but if she'd turned down or not used Patty's gift certificate, Betty was afraid Burt might be offended. He was very proud of his daughter's talents as well as her generous, thoughtful heart.

"Let's get a look at you," Patty said, gently resting her splayed fingers on each side of Betty's head and lifting it straight toward the mirror. "I assume you don't want too much of a change, right? Maybe just a little evening up?"

Betty's eyes flashed to the mirror and briefly locked on Patty's. She felt humiliated by the implications of her self-induced haircuts. "Yes, thank you." She looked down again. "This is so kind of you. Really, it's not necessary. But I am grateful."

"Just relax, okay?" Patty went to work, combing Betty's hair this way and that, pushing it forward, pulling it behind Betty's ears. Betty was uncomfortable, the intimacy of the action and touch keeping her on edge. Although there wasn't much hair to work with or any hint of a natural wave, Patty said that a little shaping, maybe just a little layering, would do wonders to soften Betty's look. Whatever that meant, Betty wondered.

"Okay, let's get to the shampoo bowl. You can leave your handbag here."

By the time they were back to her cutting station, Betty felt a little more at ease. There *had* been an actual shampoo!

"I haven't really had a private chance to thank you again for inviting me to your Christmas gathering, and for giving me such a lovely surprise gift. I still feel bad I didn't have a gift for…anyone." For the past several months—since Burt gave her the extra sausage—Betty had been working especially hard to remember to say thank you. She fretted over why casual conversation felt so difficult for her. She didn't want to seem unfriendly, though, so she tried to think of something else she might talk about. Thankfully, Patty jumped in and spared her further torment.

"Betty, you've thanked me several times now. Truly, I was just glad you came to the party on such short notice. And mercy—we would have never expected you to buy a gift for someone you didn't even know. We were glad to have you, and it sure made Dad happy." She parted Betty's hair down the middle, and Betty's eyes widened. "Don't worry. This center part has nothing to do with a hairdo. I'm just sectioning it off."

Betty's shoulders dropped a fraction of an inch.

"Tell me about your job," Patty said. "I bet it's interesting."

"It's nothing, really," Betty said, feeling inferior. "Factory work doesn't require much. Anyone could do it." She realized her quick attempt to breeze over the topic came out as snappy. Her cheeks reddened.

Before she could apologize, Patty jumped in. "I beg to differ. I wouldn't have a clue how to run a machine. Machinery intimidates me. I don't even like my mixer! I think you're very brave."

Betty swallowed and looked down at her hands, but the tension in her shoulders began to ease as Patty's fingers unexpectedly, tenderly massaged her scalp.

According to Ken, hints of spring arrived in the nick of sanity-saving time in early April. Day after day of forty-degree, sunny weather had the local weather reporters doing happy dances and melted the snow, leaving only a few dirty piles. But then winter returned, bringing back the snow and ice, causing folks in Wanonishaw to cover spring's fragile sprouts of progress and sending Ken back under his sunlamp for what he termed a "refuel."

The same type of seesaw battle continued throughout the entire Higgins household, but theirs was a three-way struggle, with Mutt, Sarah, and Grady frequently declaring victory over the rest of the residents. Their chaotic chases through the halls often left one child or another on his behind. On a daily basis, Cassandra caught Bradley drooling mouthfuls of dog food, and she wondered if it tasted better than teething biscuits. Water bowls spilled as often as the boys' milk. Muddy paw prints laid trails on every square inch of floor, up onto furniture, and tracked the bedspreads as the Higginses struggled with the dogs to set and maintain unfamiliar boundaries, since they'd had the run of the Manfords' house.

Monkey Man had to be disciplined when he tried to hang on one of Grady's long-but-fragile legs, and Cassandra repeatedly warned him to stop teasing the dogs with bits of human food. Bradley pulled on doggy ears. Howie started crying when they ran off with his toys— often. Chuck? He had to constantly be reminded that yelling at a dog to stop a behavior was not the same as using a firm alpha-dog voice.

Mutt's ongoing and restless whining could cause anyone to raise the white flag. Cassandra understood that of the three dogs, Mutt missed his old master the most and needed more time than Sarah and Grady to feel at peace, but this didn't lessen the irritation of his high-pitched whining. And *then,* when all the dogs started barking at whatever noise, and Chuck yelled at them to BE QUIET! and Howie cried because it hurt his ears, and the combined commotion woke Bradley from his nap too early…yes, the dogs often won.

But not always. Sometimes it was a seesaw draw, each dog, like each human resident, offering forth a mix of downsides and pure goodness.

Border collies were bred to work, so Sarah needed lots of exercise. If she didn't burn off some steam every day, she found trouble—like digging in the trash can and chewing up the kids' favorite toys. But Cassandra marveled at her herding instincts, and she and Ken would laugh at the way Sarah tried to corral all four boys into the middle of the Everything Room sometimes. She was also what dog lovers lovingly refer to as a "butt dog," backing up to her people so they could scratch the top of her backside.

Since Grady was seven *and* a greyhound, she was pretty mellow. But she was just so darn tall. Her nose and tail found plates full of food, accidentally whipped glasses to the floor, or wagged Bradley right in the eyes. She was happiest when she could shadow someone—anyone— and she was so gentle with the kids.

Like Sarah, Grady needed to follow her instincts. So when Sarah and Grady got to chasing each other, their genetic speed burners kicked into high gear. Their churning legs reminded Cassandra of the melting tigers in the childhood book *Little Black Sambo*. She remembered how the four tigers ran around and around a tree so fast that they turned into butter—just the type of blur Grady and Sarah left in their wake.

These bouts of craziness left Cassandra wishing Wanonishaw had a dog park; she'd read about them in the two dog magazines she now subscribed to, devouring them cover to cover as she read in bathroom snippets. It would be wonderful if they could just get out and run, the way Craig said they had out on their farm. But the dogs lived in a community now. Too many cars, too many corners, too many reasons for their curiosity to lead them astray. And what if they tried to run back to their countryside home? No, for now, frenetic household and muddy backyard runs would have to do—and as much walking as the family could endure.

Mutt was another story entirely. After he first arrived, he didn't show many signs of happy tail until Ken walked through the door after work. It was clear Mutt was a Man Dog, and that's all there was to it. But the minute Ken arrived home, an earnest tussle began as to who got his attention first: Bradley, Chuck, or Mutt. Of course, where went Mutt—especially when he garnered attention—so went Grady and Sarah, unless one or both of them had been sent to the garage for a time-out.

But no matter how bad the day went or how big the cleanup job, the dogs continued to work their miracles.

One night when the kids went to bed early, it was particularly clear. Grady assumed her now-customary nighttime encampment spot on the braid rug in the room of the two youngest. Ken was on the computer, Mutt on the floor beside him. Cassandra sat curled up in a lounge chair, running her bare toes through Sarah's fur, occasionally bending down and letting her silky ears slip through her fingers. It was such a peaceful moment. How, she wondered, could she be so blessed? How could she have allowed herself to *live* this long without a dog?

She still felt undeserving, yet she sensed that something deep within her—so deep she could not even fathom the depth and breadth of the damage—was starting to heal. She could feel it. The dogs were seeing to it.

Although her boys didn't need healing, Cassandra watched the dogs help them grow. Grady had immediately bonded with three-year-old Howie, and she called them Team Sensitive. Howie sounded so animated when he was telling Grady all about something. When she'd watch Grady follow Howie around, it was like watching her own sweet relationship with Toby unfold—witnessing her own vulnerabilities and fragileness through her child. For the first time, she understood her lack of power to have made things any different than the way they'd played out. Now she could *see* it.

And Sarah, smart and cunning girl, curled up at Cassandra's feet every time she sat down. The dog warmed her ever-cold toes, licked away her occasional tears of frustration, and poured huge doses of a magnificent grace-filled balm into the terrible aches of her past. And watching Sarah with six-year-old Chuck, whose sulking face immediately brightened when she'd follow his commands, was amazing. She'd laughed when she'd told Irene, "I don't know who barks louder: Chuck or Sarah!" Chuck now had someone other than his brothers to boss around, and she could see Sarah teaching Chuck the value in teamwork.

Craig had been kind enough—no doubt for the sake of Sarah—to write down a few basic herding commands and whistles. He'd even spent some time demonstrating them to Chuck, putting Sarah through some amazing drills. "Walk up." "Way to me." "That'll do." Watching Chuck spew out the commands and watching Sarah comply put Cassandra in the mind of the movie *Babe,* which she adored. In fact, since getting the dogs, they'd watched it several times, just to see the dogs and pig in action.

As for Mutt, when he wasn't whining or dreaming up mischief, like dragging their dirty underwear to the front door for the day-care parents to see, he was a pure, wonderfully entertaining, willful goofball. He twirled, whirled, and performed Craig's list of "Mutt's tricks" masterfully, plus anything Ken, Cassandra, or the boys could dream up to teach him. This included a few naughty things Chuck delighted in coaxing him through, like hiding in his closet.

Yes, the dogs were a seesaw of comfort and chaos, but always, *always* a blessing. If only her Grandpa Wonky could see her now. When she allowed herself to think about the miraculous, inexplicable way the dogs had come to her, she had no doubt he'd been up there in heaven, pulling some strings to make it happen.

For Cassandra, some of the happiest yet teariest times were when Craig, Sheryl, or both of them came by to visit their faithful friends. Watching the dogs bound to their sides, seeing the delight in the Manfords' eyes to observe how well the dogs were doing, was of course bittersweet for all of them—on many levels. But Cassandra felt every ounce of gratitude the Manfords left behind.

During one visit, Harry asked Sheryl why she coughed so much and Craig why he was so "kinny."

"Harry!" Cassandra said, not knowing what else to say. Craig squatted down, called him over to his side, put an arm around his waist, and said, "Sometimes, Harry, even grownups get sick. I know you've had a cold, right?" Harry nodded. "Well, it's like Sheryl has a real bad cold and it won't go away. And me, well, I'm skinny 'cause I don't eat enough vegetables." This was true, but only because treatments left his appetite missing. "That's why you better eat yours!"

Harry stuck his tongue in his cheek and thought about that. "Do I gotta eat brokki so I don't get kinny?"

"What kind of monkey doesn't eat broccoli?" Craig asked, sounding utterly astounded. "You *especially* have to eat broccoli, man. How do you expect to grow strong enough muscles to hold on to your dad's leg when you get another ten pounds heavier?"

Harry nodded, then took off chasing Mutt, who'd taken off after Sarah, who chased Grady to the Everything Room. In lickety-split time, their train came barreling through and lit out again, but this time Mutt stayed. Since Craig was still squatting, Mutt lapped at his face like he was trying to lick it off, very glad to see his master again.

Cassandra had to turn away, heartbroken, but grateful to be able to share the moments with the Manfords.

As for the cost of the dogs... *Jeny Kochany!* She thanked her lucky stars they could afford it and thought about her poverty-ridden childhood. Her mother had to stretch a dollar—and sometimes there simply wasn't a dollar to stretch. Cassandra now realized the literal costs of keeping a dog, which gave her a hint of insight into her mother's decision about Toby. *Who knows. Maybe that decision hurt Mom too.* How, she wondered, watching her boys with the dogs, could it not have?

Before she even thought about it, she reached for the phone and dialed her mom.

"Mom...I didn't wake you, did I?"

"Goodness, no! Burt was just leaving."

Cassandra heard a "Hi, Cassandra" in the background, then a "Bye, Betty and Cassandra."

"Mom, would you mind if I drop by for a short visit?"

"Now?"

"It's barely eight thirty. I won't stay long. I want to talk to you about something."

"Sure. I'll see you when you get here."

Thirty-One

"Would you like a cup of coffee?" Betty asked. "I put a pot on for Burt before he stopped by on his way home from dinner with his daughter, but he said he was 'coffeed out' today."

"Sure, but only a half cup. Your dark-brewed coffee would keep me up half the night."

"It's decaf."

"Decaf? You're drinking decaf now?"

"There's a lot you don't know about me these days," Betty said, smiling.

"Maybe there are some things a daughter *shouldn't* know about her mother." Cassandra raised an eyebrow. "After all, you are a grown woman, and—"

"Goodness! I wasn't talking about anything like *that*," Betty said, her neck flaming.

"To tell you the truth," Cassandra took a deep breath, "there is something I'd like to know about you, though. It's the reason for my visit. And sure, I'll take a full cup of the decaf."

After the coffee was poured, the women sat across from each other at Betty's kitchen table. Cassandra mentioned she liked Betty's new colorful floral tablecloth.

"It was time for that ancient oilcloth to go," Betty replied. "And speaking of going, how's it going with the dogs?"

"Funny you should mention that." Cassandra took a sip of her coffee, then stared straight into her mother's eyes. "I'm here to talk to you about Toby."

Betty felt a chill sweep through the room, but hot tears sprang into her eyes. In an attempt to ignore them, she moved her hands from her lap to her coffee cup and back to her lap again.

Finally, she spoke. "I had no idea how long your heartache would last, Cassandra. No idea." She brushed away a tear. "I knew how much you loved that dog, but I just saw no other way around it. After your grandfather died, all the hard choices were mine, and I…" She bit her bottom lip.

"You *what*, Mom?"

"I just didn't know what else to do." A few great heaving sobs racked Betty's body. She picked up a napkin and hid her face. Cassandra froze, eyes wide; Betty felt embarrassed to be caught so vulnerable in front of her daughter.

"We had to survive, Cassandra. I just knew you'd starve yourself to death before you'd watch Toby go hungry…and his shots were due, and… We had to survive." Again, the tears poured. "Cassandra, I know I've given you reason to mistrust me, but I am so truly happy that Ken got you those dogs. I am honestly sorry to have given you such cause for…" She bit her bottom lip again, swallowed, sighed, then continued. "I have spent a good part of my life wishing things could have been different—a lot of things. But now, we are where we are." To her dying day, she would thank Burt for helping her understand the truth in that simple expression. "And I'm honestly happy for you. I am grateful," she swallowed hard again, "that you and the boys have taken in pets. I hope that one day you can believe me…and forgive me."

For the sake of the heartache that threatened to crumble her and empathy for her daughter, whose face looked filled with questions, Betty stopped talking.

After a long silence, she watched her daughter slowly stand, then silently turn and leave, her nearly full cup of coffee still sitting on the table.

In an emotional rendering, Betty told Burt the details about her evening meeting with Cassandra. He wrapped his arms around her and suggested she stop wasting time rehashing it.

"Don't let Cassandra's response get a stronghold on your emotions," he firmly warned. Yes, he admitted, it *would* feel terrible to have your own daughter walk out on you like that, especially after such an honest moment. But he reminded her that it was an important moment, and they had decades of pent-up hurt leading up to it, which likely could not be *un*done in just *one* moment. Now, he said, the moment was past, and it was time to figure a way to turn it around.

After much discussion and some thought—and learning Betty was due for her hair appointment the next day, her new bimonthly routine with Patty—he came up with a plan.

Although Burt hated to use his daughter to circulate information, he knew how quickly things traveled within, and then outside, a beauty salon. His late wife had been a stylist too. After careful planning and practice, he encouraged Betty to casually mention something to Patty, where it was overheard by her employee, who mentioned it to several others, one who passed it around until Naomi got wind of it.

Naomi couldn't *wait* to tell Cassandra when she dropped Ben off for day care that obviously *nobody* was prouder of her daughter than

Betty Kamrowski. Someone had said, that so-and-so had said, who heard it at the salon, who heard it straight from Betty herself, that her daughter, Cassandra Kamrowski Higgins, had a natural born *gift* with animals. "Who better to take in those poor dogs than my daughter?" Betty had said.

"It seems your mom," Naomi told Cassandra in a breathless gust, "is telling *everybody* that—and this is a direct quote—'My Cassandra could have been the best veterinarian in the whole state of Minnesota, but instead, she chose to care for children. And now she's taken on dogs, too.'"

After they'd gone to bed and turned out the light, Cassandra vented her anger to Ken. "After all those years of Mom telling me, 'Wishing doesn't make it so,' now she tells me that *she's* spent a good portion of *her* life wishing things could have been different. And I can't believe she is using my grandfather's words to impress Burt's daughter and her new friends. After all that hurt she caused…all those years!"

Ken just listened. Even after she wound down, he remained quiet for a long time. He tried to understand Cassandra's questions, her wounds, her fury. And yet one thought kept rising to the top of his consciousness, one he felt compelled to share with her. He turned on the light.

"Hon, what if she's saying all that because she means it?"

Cassandra sat up, threw the covers back. "She *never* thought I was smart enough to be a vet! How can you say such a thing?"

"Did she ever tell you that—in those words?"

Cassandra sifted her memory. "Well, not in those words, but she implied it. She was *always* telling me how smart my brothers were, how clever this person was, or talented that one seemed."

"I hate to tell you this, Cass, but that doesn't sound like a *bad* thing."

"No? Well, she never said those things to *me*."

He had no answer, so he just quietly added, "Still, that's not the same as telling you that you aren't smart."

Cassandra tossed and turned a good part of the night. Try as she might, she could not argue Ken's point.

Was it possible, she wondered, that her own academic inability had filtered her perception about a lot of things? Was it possible that, as her mom had said, she truly *had* been sorry about Toby—or was Betty just being patronizing? And if it was true, why hadn't she just accepted her mom's apology? Why had she just gotten up from the table and walked away like some kind of ungrateful brat? Here her mother was, *crying*, and she hadn't even reached for her hand. Still, her mom had been the queen of the dictum, "No crying!" even during the cruelest of times.

And the whole time her mother spoke, Cassandra kept trying to imagine telling one of her boys that their dogs had to go. There was no way she could have. They were so in love with them. *Who could do such a terrible thing?*

But if she truly believed that, for the survival of just *one* of her children, all the dogs had to go, there would be no question. The dogs would be gone.

Lord, have I been mistaken, about so many, many things? And if I have, what am I supposed to do about it?

Then came the Voice. It uttered one word. *Forgive.*

~∞~

Cassandra and Margret drove along the Mississippi River, destination unknown. All Margret knew was that when Cassandra had called her earlier in the afternoon, she said Ken was watching the kids and that she needed to go for a ride, "as in *need* to." Margret drove, waiting for her friend to spill the beans.

"Margret, I need you to be honest with me about something. Do you think my whole life has been a lie?"

"What? Have you been watching Dr. Phil *and* Oprah?"

"Seriously. Do you think it's possible I've misunderstood much of my life's experiences?"

"In what way?"

"In countless Betty ways."

"Oh. It's Bad Betty time, eh? I need to find a place to pull over." Right ahead, she could see the exact spot she and Leo had stopped at when they were headed to the Mayo Clinic the previous September. So much had transpired since then, so much about their lives had changed. She turned on her turn signal, sidled up next to the fence, and turned off the engine. "Spill it."

"Tell me what you know to be true about my mother."

"Wow. It *is* Bad Betty time."

"Okay, let's start with that. Is she bad? Was she ever?"

"Honesty only, right?"

"Absolute."

"Let me think a minute." Margret ran the index and middle fingers of her right hand around and around the steering wheel, then reversed them for a few rounds. "Now that I'm older and so much more mature…" She smiled at her friend, who looked so uptight that Margret decided to straighten up. "Okay, here's the truth. I think your mom has always been more sad than bad. How could she *not* have been sad? Just like you, she suffered a lot of terrible and hard losses in her life. I mean, both her folks, her husband…her sons moving away when they were barely out of high school. She's always worked her tail off—"

"So," Cassandra said, jumping into her sentence, "was she *ever* Bad Betty? Do you think I just invented that persona to make myself feel better?"

"Whoa! First, you did not invent the nickname. I did. I'm the clever one, remember?" Margret grinned. They had to lighten up a little. "Second, what do you mean when you say to make yourself feel better? About what?"

"About being embarrassed by her and blaming her for making me feel dumb, and…for Toby?"

"I think, Cassie, that relationships are way more complicated than you're trying to make this one out to be."

"What are you talking about?"

"Now you're trying to reason that Betty not being bad means that you are." Margret sighed. "You know, if you want honesty, here's something for you: you two are way more alike than you are different. That's so clear to me now. You've *both* been through hard things. And now, you're both in better places. You have Ken, four sons, and three dogs. Your mom has at least some of her grandchildren nearby—who, by the way, my Mom and I both noticed on Christmas morning are very fond of her—and she has Burt."

"You think Mom and I are alike? Please tell me you don't mean that."

"I know you are. Look at you two, Cass. You both suffer from some kind of inferiority complex, neither of which is warranted. I mean, holy cow, look at you. You are the kindest, most motherly, empathetic woman I know! You can do anything you set your mind to—and don't give me that 'couldn't be a veterinarian' bunk, either." Cassandra's eyebrows shot up. "Do you think I don't know about that? Let me tell you something. Your Grandpa Wonky saw what I see—what your *mom* sees in you—what everyone who knows you sees. A vulnerable, kind, caring person with natural instincts for kids and critters. So what that you're not a vet? Lots of people who do good for animals aren't. By the time you were twelve, you'd already rescued more animals than most people do in a lifetime, and now you're back in the rescue business again. Give yourself a break, girl.

"Cass, you've rescued me more times than you'll ever know. You have always been there for me…" Margret's voice cracked. "And your mom? Holy cow, Cass…she's landed Burt Burt! He's the most desirable older bachelor in Wanonishaw." Margret chuckled through her tears. "You both needed more laughter in your lives, and now you've got it. And you sure as heck both needed to get over Toby. Cass, I watched your mom's face when the boys showed those dog pictures around on Christmas morning…she was fighting back *tears,* she was so obviously relieved and happy for you.

"It's time to count your blessings, Cassandra Kamrowski Higgins, and if I were you, I'd count your mom among them and move on. Sometimes, you just have to make up your mind to get back to living."

Cassandra bit her bottom lip, then chewed on a fingernail. She folded her arms across her chest and closed her eyes. She burst out laughing—and laughed until she cried. "Thank you, my friend, thank you. This is such an enlightening…shock. Yet such an affirmation. While I'm counting my blessings, guess what? I *will* count my mom among them, but I'll count you, too, and that snowglobe. Think about it—if it hadn't been for my *flurrious* experience with that *snowglobe*..."

"That just gave me the chills."

They sat in silence for a few moments, staring at the river. Cassandra started sniffling, then she spoke. "You know, I feel terrible. I don't want to go into it, but I...I was horrible to my mom. Turnabout is not fair play; it's guilt producing and sinful. I am unwilling to ensnare myself in another guilt trip, so thank you for helping me *allow* myself to love my mother again. I can't tell you what a relief this..." She sobbed. Margret reached for her hand, bringing home how terrible it must have felt for her mom to break down and get nothing in return. "The horrible, honest truth is...it's so clear now...same as I didn't allow myself to get back with the critters, I didn't allow myself to forgive me *or* my mom. It's like I was punishing both of us for things that were out of our control."

Margret leaned over and hugged her best friend as they cried together.

Finally Cassandra pulled back, sniffed, and said, "Since we're all about honesty, how about you come clean with *me* now?"

"About?"

"About why you haven't talked to me about you and Leo and babies."

Margret stared at the same stand of trees where she and Leo had watched the eagle disappear. "Why are you bringing that up?"

"Because...because I've added a few things up, and you never mention it anymore. That's not like you."

"We've decided to stop trying to get pregnant, and before you say anything," Margret said, holding up her hands, "you need to know we're both at peace with that decision. When I told my mom, she asked me if I'd mentioned it to you yet, and we both agreed you didn't need to divert an ounce of your emotional energies from the dogs right then. I knew you'd feel bad, maybe, likely, even tell me about some article you read about the latest in fertility whatever. But I'm glad Leo and I are back to living the life we've been given, Cassie. That's why I'm such an expert now at passing along that sage advice." She smiled and spread her arms wide for one more hug.

"No more sadness and no more articles. I promise. Besides, I have dog magazines to read now," Cassandra said, a chuckle bubbling through her lips. "I'm with you, I'm for you, I love you."

"Like when we were teens, it still takes both of us to make the perfect woman, doesn't it?" Margret wiped tears from her eyes. "Look at us. Between the two of us, we've got husbands, dogs, kids, banking careers, stainless-steel appliances, collectibles—"

"And enough happy tears to raise the river!" Cassandra said, a flood of relief washing through her.

On their way home, Cassandra asked Margret to stop in front of her mom's house. "Wait right here. I'll be back in a minute."

Margret tried not to watch when Betty opened the door and the mother and daughter began talking, but she couldn't help herself. She saw Cassandra's head bob like it did when she was emotional, then she swiped her face with her left hand. Next she saw Betty Kamrowski put her arms around her daughter, the first time Margret could remember witnessing such a thing, and the two of them embraced. Right there on the front porch, in broad daylight. They shared another brief exchange of words, then Cassandra came bounding back to the car.

"What'd you say to cause Bad Betty Kamrowski to risk her decorum out there on the front porch?" Margret asked.

"I said…drumroll, please… 'I forgive you—and me.'"

That night, Cassandra had a remarkable dream. She was a little girl, lying in deep, white snow. She wore no hat, shoes, coat, or gloves, but she was perfectly warm. As the sun started going down, she watched the entire sky turn a dusty blue. Out of the woods, an animal came running straight at her, but she wasn't afraid. It was just dark enough that she couldn't tell until it reached her that it was Toby. He twirled around a few times and lay down beside her, resting his head in the crook of her arm. She closed her eyes and felt like she was about to fall asleep.

"There you are, my Cassie girl," she heard Grandpa Wonky say. *"I hoped I'd find you two together."* Eyes still closed, not quite awake, she could hear his voice circling her and Toby. When she opened her eyes to smile at her grandpa, she noticed he was walking straight and tall and that it was her mother's head on her arm, not Toby's. Around and around he walked, singing a happy Polish song. Toby followed her grandpa, his tail wagging. She started laughing…and then she woke up.

Ken was leaning over her, smiling. "That must have been some dream. I've never heard you laugh in your sleep before."

"You know, Ken," she said, tears springing into her eyes, "I don't think I *was* dreaming. I think I was visiting heaven."

Thirty-Two

Irene had no idea what her husband, Mr. Almost Retired as she called him, had been doing in his home office all morning, but after she fixed him a bite of lunch, he asked her if she wanted to take a ride.

"In this weather?" she asked, looking out the window. It was snowing again, one of those Minnesotan spring snows that comes out of nowhere, doesn't last very long, and yet causes many a groan.

"Look to the west. It's clearing up."

"A ride to where?"

"The Manford Animal Rescue and Shelter."

She had no idea what Carl was up to, but from the renewed vigor in his voice, she decided to just get in the car and go for a ride.

What they saw when they got to the shelter, what they learned, hijacked Carl's heart and utterly devastated Irene's. They spent an hour with the Manfords, hearing them out, listening to their wishes—and praying with them before they left.

"What do you think, Reenie?" Carl asked her on the way home.

"I think that is one of the saddest situations I've ever seen. They need more than a fund-raiser, which I'm thinking about already. Surely there's something more somebody can do to help bail them out."

"I was hoping you'd say that. In fact, I was counting on it. I've been doing some investigating, online and with several Realtors. I've already got our corporate lawyer checking into a few things too, like tax exempt 501(c) status—can you believe Craig and Sheryl never applied for it? Didn't even know about it? Licensing, regulations, and permits..."

"Do you know of a buyer?"

"Yes."

"Who?"

"You're looking at him."

Irene did not respond. For several miles, they drove along in silence. Irene pictured those sweet doggie faces, thought about all the work a kennel would take, still felt the coldness in her fingers from the frigid barn air, pictured Sheryl sitting curled up on the end of that terrible avocado-green couch looking like death warmed over. She wondered if either Sheryl or Craig might still beat their diseases, even though they hadn't been given much hope. What on earth could they do about that? How long did this drive from town take, anyway?

Then a thought caused her heart to zing. Did Carl expect her to—move? Into that drafty old farmhouse? To leave their stately old home in Wanonishaw and their only child's neighborhood? Did he expect to isolate them out in the country? At their ages, there was no way they could take over everything the Manfords managed. She was too old to start shoveling that much dog poop on a permanent basis; it was too late in their lives to undergo a change that drastic.

But those dogs, all just waiting for someone to help them out, to shower them with attention, to pour some love into their lives.

Oh, my goodness! Hadn't they *prayed* for a place to pour all their saved-up love?

Surely You're not trying to tell *me, God…*

"Surely," she said aloud, unaware her mouth had actually opened, "you're not expecting us, at *our* age, to give up our lives and run a dog rescue, are you, Carl?"

He laughed, a bright laugh. "Surely not, my dear!"

"Thank goodness, Carl…you scared me for a minute."

"However, what I expect and hope you're prepared to agree to is buying the whole estate and finding someone to move into that old farmhouse and manage the kennels. Or rent the farmhouse separately, although that might not be ideal. Or maybe even sell off the parcel the house sits on. I'd have to look into zoning laws more carefully. Craig said he and Sheryl once sold off five acres; that's how they ended up with that small horse farm so close by."

"Might the Manfords be able to stay on and take care of things if they were out from under the financial burden?"

"I asked Craig about that while you were in the living room talking with Sheryl. He said neither of them is supposed to be physically exerting themselves like that now or being around so many germs. In fact, he didn't know *how* they were managing. On some days, they can barely care for themselves."

"Did I understand correctly that they have no health insurance?"

"You did."

"I can't even imagine…"

"Neither can I. The only thing I can imagine is what a relief it would be to them to know the dogs are taken care of, and how a cash sale might alleviate a portion of their financial mess."

"What if we can't find someone to run the kennel, Carl? Do you have anyone in mind?"

"Not at the moment."

"When are the Manfords moving out?"

"He said they need to get into town, closer to the doctors and hospitals, as soon as they can. He was hoping by the end of the week. They already packed up what they could fit into his wife's cousin's duplex. He'd already talked to a vet about putting down the dogs…"

"It's so awful."

"Irene, I feel like God has put a call on my heart. I'm ready to dig into this. After I learned the Manfords didn't even have a 501(c) in place, that they didn't utilize the Internet and weren't savvy about fund-raising, I *knew* this was a good match for my skill set. It was great to feel the old fire in my gut."

"If we don't step in, Carl?"

"Manfords will move, the mortgage company will take over the estate, the dogs will be put down—and you'll have a retired old fogey moping around the house all the time." He smiled at her. "They sure can't afford to pay anyone to take care of the dogs while the place is for sale. Craig did have another offer from someone who wanted the land, but not the dogs. The guy is apparently interested, but lowballing him now, since he understands their desperation. Being a shrewd business person myself, Irene," she nodded her head in agreement, "I know that's just the way it goes. But it grinds my hide how the little guy *always* loses—especially if there is another option, you know what I mean?"

"You betcha, I know what you mean."

"So, what do you think?"

"I think, Carl, that I am reminded why I love you. Your heart is in the right place, and we might be able to help. But I also think we need to make sure we don't bite off more than *these* old dogs can chew." She reached for his hand.

They rode with fingers interlocked all the way home. Carl went straight into his office and researched the possibilities, not even stopping to eat dinner.

When they prayed that night, they asked God for a sign. "Just keep us from making a terrible mistake here, Lord."

Neither of them slept very well, they were so haunted by Gomer, Dozer, and every other floppy- and pointy-eared, yapping or nonyapping dog they'd seen. But the thing that haunted them the most was the look in the Manfords' eyes when they'd walked through the kennels together.

"I figure it this way," Craig had said, stopping halfway down the aisle. *"Maybe me and Sheryl and the dogs would be better off if they just put us all down together."* He'd laughed, of course, as if making a big joke, but for Carl and Irene, those words had clinched the deal.

Thirty-Three

B etty could hardly believe it was income tax day again. Her life had drastically changed in the past several months, and she continually found herself trying to make sense of her emotional roller coaster, to stand strong and trust in her newfound insights and love.

Work was more exhausting by the day. There'd been rumblings about the company's sending some of its business offshore, which would mean layoffs. Frustrated union energies were ramping up, which historically made Betty uncomfortable. She hated hearing murmurings about possible layoffs, a strike, or pink slips and fretted about the lack of control she had in her own financial security.

Since the children had long ago flown the nest, she'd been able to eke out a tight-reined yet stable living for herself. Still, her nest egg didn't yet allow for a sudden income stoppage. One day, when she *could* retire, between social security and her pension she should be okay. Something she heard more and more of these days was the sudden withdrawal of health insurance for retirees. One never knew. In this economic climate, promises meant nothing. The predicament of that poor Manford couple made her cringe. It also made her grateful she had *any* type of insurance coverage.

At the Bambeneks' fund-raiser for the Manfords, the first philanthropic event she ever attended—and only because Burt couldn't believe she *wouldn't* go—she'd watched Carl take the microphone and talk openly about the Manfords' physical and financial plight. She leaned over and asked Burt what possessed people to share such personal details. He explained that Carl was just being candid and working hard to get the attendees to be generous with their contributions. "He's doing a bang-up job!" Burt said with enthusiasm, as he reached into his back pocket. His bigheartedness inspired Betty to dig into her wallet too.

Learning about the Manfords' financial plight washed up some of Betty's past trials. Yet their story was a perspective slammer. At least she'd never lost it *all*. However, these days even *with* insurance coverage there were limits and loopholes. Every year the portion of the premiums she was required to pay went up. Burt told her she should thank her lucky stars she didn't have to take any prescription drugs. Although he was fairly healthy, albeit about twenty pounds overweight, he did take a couple of blood-pressure medications. His copay set him back a good penny too. When she'd heard how much he had to put out for health insurance, she uttered not another word of complaint.

As Betty continued to assess her life, she laid out its polarizing elements. Hopefully her job remained the same. She was in a wondrous and growing relationship with Burt, a surprise that continued to confound her and lift her spirits.

Then there was the relationship with her daughter. They'd definitely turned a corner, but they still had a ways to go. Same with her sons. Although they didn't live nearby, she had taken to calling them every week, talking to their wives and the grandchildren, whom she felt she barely knew.

Chutes and Ladders, indeed.

But even as she and Cassandra continued to work together through the complicated shadows of their relationship, one plagued by guilt and misunderstandings, there appeared brilliant flickering lights of hope. They communicated far more often and seemed more comfortable around each other than they had since before Gerald's death.

And the growing relationship with her Wanonishaw grandsons: what blessings! Truth was, if it hadn't been for Burt modeling how much fun grandchildren could be, how they could even help *her* remember how to play, things would be so different. Without their bright energy, presence, and tutoring, her very *life* would be so much less than it was.

Burt's love for her—yes, he declared he loved her—had changed so very many things. She'd even started attending church with him, right there in Wanonishaw. It wasn't the same church her daughter attended, nor the church of her past. It was the church of a man whose faith was strong and whose love was abiding, a church in which she experienced the sweet balm of spiritual healing too.

What she realized was that she hadn't found church again; perhaps for the first time in her life, she'd come into a real faith. One she could express and receive within—or outside—the walls of just about any ecumenical establishment. When her grandsons were involved with church plays or pageants, she and Burt attended their Lutheran church, and likewise for his grandkids—even though one of Burt's sons had married and broken with the traditional family faith and "had himself submerged in the Baptist indoor pool." (Burt winked when he said that.) Much to Betty's surprise, she did, however, feel a gnawing longing to become a part of a church family, as Burt referred to it. She'd spent a good deal of her life living as a loner; it was time to consider a new way. Where that church family might be, she wasn't sure yet. But for now, worshiping and praying, free as a cowgirl riding across the range, had continued to nurture her longing to get to know God better. She felt personally drawn to the One she was coming to know as the *loving* God, not just a judgmental God who thundered around waiting to damn a person to eternal hell. This loving God, she thought, must have been the same God her father knew and loved.

Even her comfort level with Burt's robust and oft-gathering family had grown. She couldn't be sure, but perhaps that's what drew her toward a bigger family—a church family. The Burts had adopted her. And for the first time, she understood why Cassandra had so enjoyed the Bambeneks all these years. Sometimes it was the family of another that made you feel most welcome, where you had a clean slate, and they helped you grow—helped you yearn to show love to your own family a little better. She was actually enjoying her regular hair appointments with Patty. It was decadent, and Betty insisted on paying full price, but it also felt right. Patty's soothing hands massaging her scalp helped her relax, and she and Patty had grown to know each other through their visits. Everyone loved the new hairdo she'd given Betty. They claimed it gave her a softer look.

"Softer." Betty heard the word regularly now. She hoped what people noticed was really a reflection of what was happening *inside*.

Thirty-Four

With a huge sigh, Irene Bambenek plopped down on Craig and Sheryl Manford's ratty avocado-green couch. She looked around the room. The whole place radiated the Manfords' hippy-dippy essence. As much as the chaos disturbed her, it also haunted her. It *was* true, she thought: *The last few months have proved a wild, provocative, heart-bending yet rewarding ride. No wonder I'm so tired.*

Within sixty seconds she was sound asleep, and it was just two in the afternoon.

When she awakened on the terrible green couch in the hippy-dippy house, she couldn't believe she'd slept as soundly as she had. She had told Carl that ratty old piece of furniture should be burned, along with just about everything else the Manfords left behind. Every item in the house was scratched, wobbling, broken, threadbare, chipped, or just plain horrid. They'd obviously put every spare penny into feeding the dogs. They were the most selfless people she'd ever met, and now their whole world was crashing down around them. Even so, when they'd sealed the deal, both Craig and Sheryl had sat at the big kitchen table and cried like babies, they were so grateful for the rescue of their dogs.

The last nap Irene could remember taking was fifteen years ago, the time she had pneumonia. Today's exhaustion stemmed from six straight hours of cleaning kennels and walking dogs. It was the kind of tiredness that made her thankful she could still work that hard, the kind whereby she knew she'd used every ounce of her physical energy for something that really mattered.

Cassandra recently said she didn't think either of the Manfords had very long to live, that the last time the couple was scheduled to come to their house for their weekly visit with the dogs, Craig came alone.

"Aside from the spark that flickered in his eyes when the dogs came running," she told Irene, "he looked lifeless—especially when he said Sheryl would likely not be back again but she insisted he visit. She's under hospice care now, he said. It was all I could do to keep from breaking out sobbing, right on the spot.

"After he left, Chuck asked me if we could take the dogs to visit Sheryl. Imagine... I'll see if that's possible. I don't know...germs, dog hair. All I do know for sure is that dogs possess healing powers."

Sadly, not even the loving licks of the three dogs was enough to save Sheryl from the ravages of cancer. Sarah, Grady, and Mutt had gently, as if they understood her frailty as she lay in the hospice-provided bed, showered her with affection, and it was obvious that their unconditional, bountiful love helped ease her pain, at least for a time.

For nearly four months, Irene, Carl, Cassandra, Ken, Margret, Leo, the Higgins children, members of Burt's family, a gracious vet, and every other sign-up volunteer they could muster, had struggled to keep the dogs in the Manford Animal Rescue and Shelter safe, fed, exercised, and as healthy as possible. Irene, who was most often available to help out when someone had to cancel, caught the brunt of the duties. Catching a nap on the green couch quickly morphed into one of the luxuries of her day.

Over the course of this brief time, they'd lost two of their dear shelter dogs: one to old age and the other to a sudden cancerous attack that could not be stopped. True to Craig's predictions, shortly after, in the middle of the night, somebody left two older dogs tied to a tree in their front yard.

The Higgins boys held funeral services for Dozer and Gomer; they buried them in the pet cemetery behind the barn. During Carl and Irene's first visit to see the place, when Craig had first told them about the cemetery, as only he could, he jokingly added a comment about digging a couple of extra holes and just leaving them available. He admitted he didn't know how he and Sheryl were going to pay for their own funerals. But the Bambeneks got the Manfords connected with a cremation group and had funds earmarked for that purpose from the fundraiser, another huge relief for Craig and Sheryl.

Although everyone was grieved to learn that Dozer and Gomer had died, Ken admitted to Irene that he was grateful things hadn't gone differently during his first Christmas visit. Had he chosen one of them, this early loss would have been way too hard on Cassandra. She surely gave him no argument.

"God's ways are mysterious," she told him, "and best."

Something was always going on at the rescue center. Carl finally got all the 501(c) documents in order and now owned all the property, but in parcels. Between the township, the county, and the state, everything took considerably longer than he'd speculated. He'd also been putting more hours in at his company. Bambenek Enterprises had acquired a new client, complete with nervous, high-maintenance executives whose jobs were on the line if new ad campaigns couldn't boost their sales, and mightily. They needed all calming resources available. He was glad to help, but it proved one thing to him: although it felt good to be needed, he realized he *was* ready to move on to the next thing, one that garnered more personal and spiritual satisfaction. Irene was already plugging for a dog park, and they'd rescued four dogs from an unbelievable situation.

Since Sheryl had passed and Craig was now under hospice care, Carl felt a greater urgency to report to Craig that *all* was well with the kennels and the land. He wanted to tell him that their long-established dedication to saving and protecting innocent dogs was guaranteed to remain in place for years to come. It was the best gift he could give the man.

Still, what to do about the old house on the property? Carl was tempted to put it on the market and sell "as is," but he kept hoping they'd eventually find a marriage between the kennels and farmhouse residents. He decided that when the barn upgrades were complete, they'd host the next fund-raiser right there on the property, maybe tie in a rededication service too. A major event like that might even attract the kind of people who'd be interested in moving in and running the whole thing.

These were the types of things that pulled at his heart now, much more so than his business. Even though Irene sometimes complained about her weariness or her mildly aching back ("Shoveling poop takes its toll," she'd told him), she, too, admitted that she had no doubts that what they were doing was the right thing. "I've never felt more rewards for my labors, Carl. Now, if we can just sort out a few details."

Like, *was* there a way to host a dog park? How Macy, Minie, and Moe loved romping around on the farm grounds, but Irene worried when they ran out of sight. Thankfully, they'd always come back. Could just a couple of lush acres be fenced? Cassandra was sure rooting for one too.

Carl told them to be patient. "One step at a time. First let's get the barn upgraded, then figure out something with the house. *Then* we can talk about a dog park…maybe," he cautiously added, after Irene clapped her hands with delirious pleasure, thinking of Minie and Moe safely running themselves into happy exhaustion.

Thirty-Five

Cassandra stood with the snowglobe in her hands. It was late, she was tired, and Ken had already gone to bed, but she needed a few minutes to herself. After this sweltering July sweatbox day, fraught with the chaos and frustration of misbehaving kids and energetic dogs, the idea of mentally losing herself into a cool, snow-white blanket of serenity held great appeal. *You've come a long way with this snowglobe, baby! Perhaps it's even better to admit it's come a long way with you.*

She turned on the end table lamp, stretched out on the couch in the Everything Room and held the orb above her face, turning it in her hands, watching the snow rotate, the grace-filled symbols of Christ's body, broken for her entire family. She now understood her flurrious experience to be the beginning of extraordinary healing and mercy in her life. That mercy touched the life of her growing relationship with her mother and, in a way, the lives of Sheryl and Craig, the Bambeneks, Leo and Margret. So many lives, touched by the flurries.

She smiled as she set the globe on her stomach and interlaced her fingers over the top of it, pondering the breadth of her journey. She'd gone from getting knocked in the head, complete with broken nose, to the *flurrious* moment, to fainting in church, to thinking she was crazy, to hearing the Voice, to yelling at her mom, to getting three *real* dogs, to forgiving her mom *and* herself, to peace. She closed her eyes and uttered a sort of rambling prayer, something she was taken to doing more often lately.

God, I have no idea what really *happened with this crazy thing, but thank You. I'm going to keep it forever so that I never forget. Why is forget-ting so easy to do, especially when I'm cranky and overwhelmed like I am right now? Life is so complicated.*

Feeling herself beginning to doze off, she checked her wristwatch. 11:05 p.m. She was so comfortable. Why bother crawling into bed now? She could hear Ken snoring.

Sarah padded over and rested her head next to the snowglobe on Cassandra's stomach.

"Lie down, girl."

Sarah blasted a dog sneeze right at her, then curled up on the floor next to the couch.

"Thanks!" Cassandra said, wiping a few droplets from her face. She let her hand drape over the side of the couch and rest on Sarah's side. She raked her fingers through the dog's fur as she speculated as to the whereabouts of the other two critters.

The dogs had spent a lot of time in the yard since the completion of their new outdoor kennel. Their yard fence turned out to be tall enough, even for Grady, who wasn't prone to leaping. She had, however, worn a path around the perimeter of their yard.

Cassandra pictured Grady running full-out on the rescue-center property, beautiful and powerful, a blur of legs, Sarah and Mutt doing their best to keep up with her.

Sarah usually chased after Grady for only a short spell though. She had work to do, never seeming more satisfied with herself than when patrolling the grounds. Craig was glad to hear she still had a chance to work her route, as he called it. After first checking each room in the old farmhouse, looking for Craig and Sheryl, Cassandra speculated, she'd duck through the dog door off the porch and go straight to the kennel, then all around the property, making sure everything was where it belonged. Then she'd start all over.

The Higginses hadn't been out to the shelter for a couple of days, but Sunday they were scheduled to clean and fill the water bowls. Maybe she'd see if Leo and Margret would like to pick up a bucket of chicken and join them for a little picnic under that beautiful, sprawling maple tree in the backyard. The first time the boys saw it, they'd begged for a tree swing. Carl and Irene were going to work on the farmhouse this weekend too. They'd probably enjoy the company and a chance to picnic. Cassandra couldn't help but marvel how they'd thrown their lives into the entire project.

They'd *all* been so busy. Maybe Cassandra should invite Burt and her mom too.

Oh, geez! What date is it today? Thursday, July…23? Saturday is mom's birthday! I wonder if we can do double-duty and turn the picnic into a belated birthday party? We could take a cake and paper supplies… The boys would love it! Then she wondered if maybe her mom already had plans with Burt's family. Burt and Betty were all but inseparable on Sunday afternoons, often busy with one member or another in Burt's large family. She was glad her mom enjoyed them—although much to her shock, she realized she felt a twinge of jealousy.

I wonder if that's how Mom felt all these years about my relationship with the Bambeneks?

She'd have to call Betty first thing in the morning. One more thing to add to her list.

Sinking deeper into the couch, Cassandra continued to shift between sleep and a blurry twilight place, where thoughts hijacked her mind, jolting her awake again and again. She finally reached up, turned off the lamp, tucked the snowglobe under her neck, and stretched out on her side. As her eyes adjusted to the darkness, the utter chaos of her surroundings came into view. Dog toys, discarded magazines, Legos, a half-built fort made out of chair cushions and a sheet, a pizza box from the evening meal, one of Bradley's blankets he dragged from here to there. When the day-care kids were present, there barely seemed a corner left in which to breathe. But as she nodded off, she thought how much she loved this place, and she could not imagine her life any other way.

Cassandra and Ken sat across from each other at their favorite ice-cream shop. They hadn't been on a "Friday Night Mommy and Daddy Night" for a couple of months. They'd finally escaped yet still found themselves talking about the boys.

"I wonder," Ken said, pausing to slurp the quickly melting ledge of ice cream before it ran over the cone's edge, "what we used to talk about before the boys?"

"Having them?" Cassandra smiled and licked a couple of rounds on her own cone.

"Right."

"I'm worried about Mom handling all four of them alone, but between her *and* Burt, I'm sure they're managing. Sweet of them to offer."

"You made the right call, kenneling up the dogs."

"How long do you really think that lasted after we pulled away?" She raised an eyebrow.

"Hard to tell. I'm not going to worry about it now, though," he said, "not when I've got ice cream melting faster than I can lick it." He worked adeptly to consume the overflow; the bottom of the cone was already getting soggy.

Cassandra took one more lick of her cone, then dumped the rest of it in the trash. When she sat down, she wiped her mouth and rested her chin on her propped arms.

"Full?" Ken asked.

"No, but I don't want to stay out too late, and I do want to talk to you about something. Please know this might sound...odd, or...odd. And that you can't have a wrong response, okay? I've already had some time to think about this."

Ken's eyes opened wide. The last time she'd started a conversation like this, she followed it with the announcement that she was (surprise!) pregnant with Bradley.

Cassandra immediately dispelled what she could tell he was thinking.

"This might sound even more shocking."

"Impossible." He popped the last bite of his cone into his mouth, chewed, and swallowed. "Shoot."

"You know last night, how I slept on the couch?"

"Yup. It's not like you not to make it to bed. Nothing personal, but you were really snoring when I checked on you at two thirty, so I left you alone. Such a disturbing snore that I think our kids will one day add it to their Sad games." He grinned his goofy, charming grin. "For the record, I did try to remove that snowglobe from under your neck. You were clutching it so tightly that it looked like the base was digging into your windpipe. But you hunched around it tighter, so I just left it."

"I had this dream."

"About that snowglobe? What showed up—or disappeared—this time? Elephants? I absolutely forbid elephants in the house. You need to know that right now." He chuckled, but in truth, the whole inexplicable snowglobe phenomenon never set well with his calculating brain. He wasn't opposed to the idea of miracles, what Cassandra chalked the experience up as, but when he examined the snowglobe, the thing occasionally gave him the creeps. But it did seem at the root of so many good transformations.

"No, nothing showed up in the snowglobe," she said. "I just fell asleep with it and...

"Oh, my goodness, Ken! Maybe there is a connection between my dream and the snowglobe. I didn't think of that. That gives me goose bumps. Before I fell asleep, I was lying on my side, looking around the room, at all the chaos. We had pizza, remember? The pizza box was still on the coffee table... HEY! Maybe that's why I had such a strange dream—blame it on the pepperoni!"

"Sounds like a movie."

"So," she continued, "I looked at the pizza box, the toys, and...just the general mess." She paused, nervously rolled her napkin into a snake. "Truthfully, Ken, I've been feeling a little overwhelmed lately, and some of it has to do with the fact that, well..."

"Just say whatever it is, Cassie."

"I'm feeling boxed in."

"What do you mean by boxed in? Like you need a vacation?"

"Not really, although that would be dreamy, wouldn't it?" He nodded. "More like—and I never thought I'd say this because you know how much I like our house—like our house feels like it's...shrinking. The boys are getting bigger, and now the dogs."

"Makes sense. Is that what you dreamt about?"

"Not exactly. I dreamt I was walking through a house—you know how dreams are, I think it was our house, sort of—and I kept discovering rooms I didn't know we had. A lot of rooms."

"You know what they say about house dreams."

"No, what?" she said, curiosity rising in her voice.

"I don't know either. I do know there's something about house dreams, though. Maybe exploring yourself or something?"

She studied him for a moment. "Maybe. But here's the thing: every room was so warm, the sun shining in the windows just so. And every room had different critters in it. One had a bunch of birds—some singing and some with splints on their wings. Another room had rabbits, including one that looked just like Clipper."

"Clipper?"

"He was a baby rabbit I found in our backyard, back when Grandpa Wonky was still alive. He built a pen for Clipper, and I kept him out in the shed. I had to go out there all the time and try to give him a bottle. Well, it was an eyedropper thing from one of Grandpa's medications. Grandpa warned me that Clipper likely wouldn't make it, but he did."

"Why'd you name him Clipper?"

"Because that's what he told me his name was. I don't care if you don't believe me, but it's true."

"Out loud?"

"No!" she said. "Somehow I always just knew the names of my critters. How else would I have known if they didn't tell me?" She shot him a playful smile, but she still remembered how fervently she used to believe that. "It *was* magical, the way their names were suddenly just there in my head. It was the same with Toby.

"Anyway, another *huge* room was filled with all sizes and colors of dogs, kind of like out at the shelter. Another room housed a crazy raccoon, then there was a… Doesn't matter. Let's just say the whole place was wonderful. When I got to the kitchen in the dream, there was a giant old table—kinda like the one in the farmhouse at the shelter—and all the boys were talking and laughing and passing giant bowls of food. I mean giant, like the bowls were basketball-size."

"Sure this wasn't a pepperoni-induced nightmare?" He raised his eyebrows. "I mean all those animals and kids and stuff."

"It was the opposite of a nightmare. It was a slice of pure heaven, Ken. Here's the most wonderful part: I woke up humming. Ken, I was *humming*, the way I used to hum to calm Toby. I swear, it was that same tune. I hadn't thought about it in years. And," she said, her voice lower, "I was crying such happy tears again. Just before I woke up, I was look-ing into the eyes of a dog I'd never seen before. They were such beauti-ful, grateful brown eyes. When I woke up, opened my eyes, *humming* and *crying,* Sarah had her nose right in my face." She put the flat of her palm up to her nose. "She looked straight into my eyes the same way the dog in the dream had. It's like my humming must have awakened Sarah, and she came over to lick away my tears."

"That is some dream. Some story." He ran his fingers through his hair.

She swallowed. "Here's the shocking part. Since the dream, I keep getting this feeling that it was a sign or something."

"A sign? Like, a sign for—"

"A sign we should move into the old house out at the shelter. The boys would love it, and you know the dogs would!" He raised his eye-brows. "I know, I know this seems nuts. And I didn't mean to say we should move. Bad choice of words. Let me think of a different way to say this.

"Maybe we could consider what an opportunity it might be for…"
She put her hands over her mouth. "This is going to sound so selfish."

"What, Cass? What were you going to say?"

She slumped, the wind knocked out of her sails. What had she been
thinking? All these years Ken had loved her, given her everything she
wanted, helped them get the house just so, and she was actually going
to suggest they should pick up and *move*! Because it would be good for
her? She started to cry. When had she gotten so completely selfish? Margret had been right; she was more like her mother than she thought. She
reached for the remaining napkin on their table and covered her eyes.
She'd almost forgotten they were in a public place. She pulled herself
together, dabbed, and looked at him. To her amazement, her dear husband was smiling.

"Wanna know what I think about your dream? About your harebrained idea that we should pick up and move out of our house, out
into the country?" He paused just long enough to notice her lip begin
to quiver again. "I thought about how wonderful it would be for *all* of
us as soon as I knew it was available, but I never in a million years
thought you'd want to move."

"Really?" Her voice was barely audible. "Oh, Ken! Do you think it
would work? Do you think we'd kick ourselves for making such a drastic change? For uprooting us and the boys from our neighborhood? I'd
likely lose my day-care business, you know. Nobody I sit for would want
to drive that far out of town before work. But I feel ready to let that go
and move on to the next thing. The older the boys get, the more brain
power they take. And with the dogs…"

"With a place as big as that to take care of, you wouldn't have time
for day care anyway. You know, I'm not even sure there's a school-bus

route that far out. Would we have to drive the boys to school? Would we want to?

"I'm glad we're on the same page with the thought, but I don't know, Cass. Maybe we should cool our jets until we get more information. In fact, I'm not even sure how the property is set up. *Could* we even own it—or is it owned by the nonprofit? Plus, the housing market is so bad. Think our house would sell? What permanent part, if *any,* can our family afford to take on with the kennel—in terms of sanity? Certainly we can't do it all, not with four young sons and me working full time. You couldn't stay out of the kennels if you were that close to it. My biggest fear? I'm afraid you'd do yourself in, Cassie. I *know* you."

"You're right. I got ahead of myself. There are too many unanswered questions. But oh, *Ken,* I am *so* glad you're at least willing to explore it! I had no idea you were thinking about it too."

"I wasn't about to mention it because we've been so happy where we are, and you've got enough on your plate."

"How about we talk to Irene and Carl about it this Sunday at the picnic? Mom and Burt will be there, and we'll be celebrating her birthday, but maybe we can get a moment to see what the Bambeneks have to say. I know they're out there working on the place now. It could be that the opportunity no longer even exists. But I can't help but believe living in the country would be wonderful for the boys. Have you watched them when we're there?"

"I sure have. In fact, that's what started me thinking. When they asked about putting a swing in that tree, I could picture it, hon."

"Hey, you been sleeping with my snowglobe too?"

Ken shuddered, then grinned. "Hardly. One kook in the family is enough."

Thirty-Six

Betty thought her heart would pound out of her chest, leap through Burt's truck window, race down the country road, and not stop till it reached Canada. She twisted her hands in her lap, fiddled with the seat belt, turned off the radio, then twisted her hands some more.

Burt took his eyes off the road for a moment to study her. "Betty, it'll go fine. It's just a picnic and a birthday party out under a big tree."

"You *know* that's not what I'm fretting about, Burt! I don't know how you can be so calm."

"I can be calm because you're nervous enough for both of us. If I added one ounce of anxious energy to this vehicle, it would hop off the road like a giant jackrabbit."

"I'm sorry. I just can't help myself."

"I know," he said, leaning over and patting her arm. "I know. Who should do the talking, you or me?"

She drew her lips inside her mouth. "Well, I certainly don't think my mouth is going to even work."

Burt smiled. "Your mouth," he said, "certainly works plenty good enough for me. In fact, if I weren't driving, I'd have it give me a kiss, right here and now."

Betty turned crimson. "Oh, Burt! *Please* don't kiss me in front of the kids!"

He laughed so hard she thought me might drive them into the ditch. "Okay," he said. "I promise not to kiss you in front of the kids— at least not more than once and only for a very short time." He turned and winked at her. "But the question still remains: which one of us do you want to tell them?"

She squeezed her hands together so tightly, her knuckles turned white. She finally said, "It should be me. It's my family."

"I didn't ask who it *should* be. I asked who you *want* to do it. Bet, honey, is it gonna take the rest of our days together here on this earth to retrain you to think about your own wants?" He flipped on his turn signal and headed up the driveway to the shelter. "Speak now, or forever let me blab. We're almost there."

"Don't I know it," she said, her voice sounding small and defenseless. "Maybe it's not a good idea to tell them today," she said, reaching for the ring finger of her left hand, thinking she might just put the engagement ring in her coin purse for now.

"Don't you *dare*! Since when does a little thing like this scare a bona fide cowgirl from Oklahoma?" Betty couldn't help but giggle. He always knew how to make her laugh, just when she needed it the most. And the way he'd proposed—it was too wonderful to ever, *ever* forget.

On her birthday, the day before, he'd arrived at her house with a rectangular box about four inches wide, two inches high, and a foot long. It was, of course, wrapped in white butcher paper, and the bow was made of butcher string. "You can't open it till after dinner, though," he said. "Just leave it here on the table for now. As promised, we're going out for the ultimate steak dinner."

Betty thought she'd die when a whole band of waiters and waitresses came to the table, the lead guy carrying a brownie sundae with a candle on top, all of them singing "Happy Birthday." When they arrived back at her house, he told her to go get the box. They sat on the couch together while she unwrapped it. She stared at it, then shot him a quizzical look. It appeared to be a box of business cards.

"Did you get yourself a gift for my birthday?" she asked, thinking he'd had new cards made for the butcher shop.

"Nope. Even better. Take one out."

She could not believe what she saw. Across the middle, in all-caps red lettering, it boldly read, BETTY KAMROWSKI BURT and underneath, in smaller letters: A cowgirl wife from Oklahoma.

Her mouth dropped open as she stared at the card. BETTY KAM-ROWSKI BURT. When she looked up, Burt was down on one knee.

"Betty," he said, grabbing hold of her hand with the card in it, "I love you. Will you be my cowgirl wife, to have and to hold, to quit your job and come help me serve Burt's Durves on Thursdays, till death do us part?"

For a long while, she was utterly speechless. Utterly. Quit her job? Live *where*? She couldn't help feel tickled, even in her shock, that he remembered their conversation about business cards and cowgirls and used it so creatively. Unbelievable!

She looked at the kind and dear face of the man kneeling before her, the man who had brought so much *life* back to her life. While her head swarmed with questions, in her heart, she felt the buoyant and powerful winds of new promise. Like she actually *could* be a cowgirl from Oklahoma. It was as if the slate of her dark past had been wiped clean and she'd found a new identity—rooted in the unconditional and patient love of Burt Burt and God.

"Will I be your cowgirl wife? *Certainly!*"

❧

"What a great day," Burt said to Ken, as they walked around, picking up the last of the birthday cake plates. "I'm glad the humidity and the worst of the heat finally broke, at least for a little while."

"Me too. I'll tell you, it was so hot this week, I didn't even get the hot sauce on my Durve last Thursday. I was afraid it'd melt me."

Burt laughed his big, wonderful laugh, and Ken laughed too. "How did you like the Durves I brought today?"

"Great, as usual."

"Those little pumpernickel breads make anything taste good, including my special liver sausage. The trick is to get just the right sliver of thickness to the slice of onion."

Cassandra walked over and sat next to her mom. "Isn't this place wonderful? The boys just love coming out here." They watched the dogs and her three oldest sons flash from here to there. The boys had been given a short-but-intense set of instructions: stay within sight and for *sure* stay out of the kennel unless an adult is with you. Thus far, they'd been good, although Chuck had tested them a few times, just to see if they were watching.

Betty looked at Bradley, who was fast asleep in a playpen at the base of the big tree. He was lying on his tummy, his little butt up in the air, knees drawn under him. "Fresh air is so good for kids. I was always glad for those woods behind our house. I think you and your brothers spent more time back there than anywhere else. Children need room to run." She sounded like she was going to add something, but her voice cracked and she stopped talking. Cassandra looked surprised.

Truthfully, Betty was thinking about how difficult it would be to abandon that beautiful view of the woods from her kitchen window. So many memories. Especially of Cassandra enjoying time out there, for the woods were ripe with critters.

Betty could still remember the day she saw Cassandra carrying Toby. Her little face was beet red and sweat dripped off the end of her nose. She looked utterly exhausted, but she was consumed with saving him. Betty had stopped at the edge of a neighboring garage and watched. She remembered thinking, *One more mouth to feed...how?* But somehow, her father had talked her into letting Cassandra keep Toby. For *both* of them—it had been the first step to a terrible end.

Now, by the grace of God, her relationship with her daughter was mending, thanks to the dogs. Her life was so completely different than it had been just last year, and it would continue to change. She would move in with Burt, whose kitchen window boasted a view of his neighbor's cluttered yard. His house was larger, modernized, and better equipped. It was full of color and life, possessing a great family room that could fit nearly all their grandchildren. Even though he didn't have a view of the woods, his yard was beautifully landscaped by one of his sons-in-law, he kept a wonderful garden, and he owned the most delightful porch swing. There would be trade-offs.

"Cassie," Margret walked up from behind her. "Want to go for a walk? The fields look ripe with wild flowers."

"Irene, Carl, could you come over here?" Burt yelled. "Wait a minute, please, Margret. Betty and I have something we'd like to say."

Betty nearly leaped out of her skin. She turned bright red. "Oh, my!"

"Mom, what is it?"

"You'll find out soon enough." Betty clutched her handbag up under her arm and walked over to Burt, who was waggling his come-hither finger at her. When they'd arrived, before they got out of his truck, Betty talked him into letting her take off the ring until they made the announcement. "You know how kids notice everything," she'd said. "*Please,* Burt. Let's at least wait until after the cake."

Irene and Carl came back to the circle of chairs, paper plates still in their hands. "Have a seat, please," Burt said, taking their dishes and setting them on the table. Then he grabbed Betty's hand. "Ken, you too." While everyone took their places, the boys and dogs came bounding back. Chuck started to ask permission to do something, but Cassandra hushed him. "Mr. Burt is about to tell us something, honey."

However, before Burt could open his mouth, Betty opened hers.

"We're engaged." It came out in a whisper.

"What's that?" Carl asked. Irene and Margret had both noticed— and commented on the fact—that he suffered a slight hearing deficit, one he absolutely would not admit to.

"Mom!" Cassandra yelped. "Did you say you're engaged?"

"She did," Burt said, his eyes twinkling as brightly as the ring Betty was fidgeting to retrieve out of her coin purse. "This cowgirl from Oklahoma has agreed to be my wife!"

Betty handed him the ring and he slid it back onto her ring finger, part of the deal when he agreed to let her go without it until the announcement. He was so sentimental about such little things.

"What cowgirl?" Chuck wanted to know, scanning the crowd.

"This cowgirl right here," Burt said, putting his arm around Betty and giving her a little squeeze. "You didn't know your grandmother is a cowgirl from Oklahoma?"

Chuck looked at his mom, who looked just as puzzled as he did. Cassandra seemed glued to her chair, so Irene was the first to jump up and check out Betty's ring. Although they had never been close friends, they'd shared Cassandra for years.

"Congratulations," Irene said, hugging Betty, then Burt. She walked over, bent down, and hugged Cassandra. "Congratulations to you too…daughter of the bride!"

Cassandra finally managed to rise out of her seat. Betty held her hand in front of her, the small diamond—the first she'd ever been given—sparkling in the sun. Cassandra raised her mother's palm, lifting her hand for a better look. "Mom...I can't *believe* it!"

"Me either," Betty said. "Me either."

Cassandra threw her arms around her mother's neck. "I'm so happy for you, Mom," she whispered in her mother's ear. "Burt is a great guy."

"That he is. I am so blessed to find love again. After all these years." Her voice cracked.

Burt came up and gave Cassandra a hug. "I suppose I should have asked your permission," he said, "but I figured that even if you objected, Ken would have talked you into it. He'd do anything for free Durves, including marrying into the family to get them." Ken walked up, and the two men laughed, smacked each other on the back, and gave each other bear hugs.

"The sound of happy," Cassandra said.

"Yes," Betty whispered, her face lit with love for the man in front of her, and the warmth in the feel of her daughter's hand in hers.

"Grandma!" It was Chuck. "Let me see!" Betty held the ring down in front of him. He glanced at it, shot her a disconcerting look—one she'd seen in her own reflection—then ran off to play, screaming, "Ew, LOVE! YUUUUUUCKIE!"

"Grandma. Let me see." Howie looked at the ring and said, "Love. Yuck."

The next thing Betty knew, a wondrous new form of love came her way. Harry ran up, looked at her hand, said, "Wuv," then latched onto her leg. *Monkey love,* she thought. *At long last!*

⌒∞

The rest of the waning day was spent celebrating and tossing around wedding dates and possibilities, everyone adding his or her two cents.

The best idea came from the Bambeneks: a casual wedding to take place here on the grounds, out under the beautiful tree. Betty and Burt wanted to marry in September, a favorite time of the year for both of them and a month neither had been married in before.

Burt was the master of casualness. "We've got between now and then to figure it all out, including how to combine our homes. We'll move Betty into my house little by little. By the day of the wedding, we'll be set to cohabitate." He announced this with a devilish wink, pecking her on the cheek, and turning her crimson. Everyone knew she had so few belongings that, in reality, it wouldn't take but a weekend and his pickup truck.

They decided on Sunday, September 20, if all their family was available then. Betty would call her sons later and let them know. Seemed no sense even shooting for a Saturday, what with so many of the grandkids in fall sports and the butcher shop being open.

Much to everyone's delight, Burt announced he'd make Winsome Wedding Durves. Leo said they should be bell shaped; Ken suggested they come with a variety of special romantic dipping sauces to make them "wedding worthy."

Burt wanted to post an invitation in his shop, inviting all the customers. Although Betty was mortified, her mortification did not seem to overrule *everyone's* enthusiasm for the idea. With all the grandkids they hoped would participate and their large families, "What's a few more people?" Burt said. When asked about a color scheme, Betty told everyone to just wear what they wanted.

Margret, who loved cranking up the spiffy new appliances in her kitchen, volunteered to bake the wedding cake—after Howie suggested they serve windmill cookies. As a wedding gift, Leo promised to rent the tables and chairs, and Carl offered to rent a huge tent. Irene said she'd make punch; Margret offered to spike it. Cassandra wanted to take charge of wedding favors, maybe have all the grandkids make a craft item for everyone to take home, deducing that would at least keep them busy during the reception. Just like that, a no-hassles wedding was in the works.

"All you'll have to do is get yourself a wedding dress," Cassandra said to her mother, who appeared as though the scary reality of her engagement and impending wedding had finally set in. "We'll have to go shopping together."

"I already have one picked out." Cassandra's face clouded with disappointment. "But we'll go shopping together for just the right dress for the daughter of the bride to wear."

Betty lay in bed that night, her emotions waffling between unbridled joy and utter terror. It was amazing the way the wedding plans fell into place. And yet from the moment she'd said yes to Burt, it was as if a galloping team of horses pulled her toward the altar and she'd lost the reins. She'd wanted to wait a respectable amount of time after their engagement to wed. But when Burt asked why, she couldn't defend a single one of her reasons. He even called her back the next day, after he confirmed he could add her to his insurance policy. Still, she needed to have *some* control over her life. Yes, she *did* plan on working for a while, she told him. What would she do with herself all day if she didn't? The butcher shop was nice, but what did she know about butchering? Besides, she wasn't *that* good with people, and the thought of too many changes at once—marrying, moving *and* quitting her job—overwhelmed her.

When she told Burt she would at least consider cutting back on her hours, he'd said, "See if you can at least get Durve Day off." She'd laughed, but...serving Durves?

She rolled onto her side and punched her pillow, then tried to picture Burt's head on the pillow next to hers. Her stomach filled with butterflies, and her neck turned crimson when she realized how much she liked what she saw.

What had Howie called him? Burt Durve.

"Mrs. Burt Burt Durve," she said aloud. Then she giggled.

Thirty-Seven

Shortly after the engagement announcement, Ken caught Carl during one of his rare office appearances and invited him to lunch. Carl happily agreed; he could barely stand another business meeting. His lust for corporate management days had died, he was sure of it.

Ken settled back in the high-back restaurant chair. "Cassie and I have been wondering how things are going at the shelter. Life has been so crazy for all of us lately, it doesn't seem like we've had a chance since Christmas to get caught up."

Carl rolled out a lengthy, detailed account of the nonprofit status, the volunteer roster and their dream for additional help, and a list of their needs, which included everything from printer ink and more contributions to old blankets and a few new water bowls. When he stopped talking, Ken still looked like he had questions, so Carl told him a couple of stories about the center's latest inhabitants and two new adoptive "parents."

"Cassie told me about the adoptees. She was really stoked. Sounds like the people who got the Sheltie were beside themselves with joy."

"Word travels fast in the tangled web in which we live, eh?"

Ken nodded.

"Ken, is there something specific you'd like to know? I'm sensing—"

"To be honest, I was wondering how it was going with the house."

"Oh, for various reasons—most having to do with my sanity—I've kept the house and the shelter compartmentalized. It's good of you to ask. The status is that I own a farmhouse that bellies up to an animal rescue. I haven't been able to marry the two, or sell the one, so perhaps the farmhouse shall forever remain my wife's expensive napping station."

"What kind of shape is the house in, basically? I mean, is it sound?"

Carl studied Ken, then his eyes lit up. "Don't tell me that all this time the answer has been right under my nose. No, or I'd have heard about it from Irene, who would have heard from Margret, who would have been told by your wife." Ken didn't reply, other than to tilt his head. "Seriously? Are you interested in the house?"

"Depends. To be honest, it didn't occur to *us* we were interested until just before the picnic. We were going to talk to you about it then, but…we've all been a little distracted. And we didn't want to get our hopes up if you had something else in the works."

The waitress set their plates down on the table. Ken squirted ketchup on his burger and fries and Carl fiddled with his salad.

"Cholesterol," Carl said. "The only bad part about retirement is that now Irene monitors nearly my every meal. I guess she's got me trained. Talk, son, tell me what you two are thinking."

Ken shared that he and Cassandra were attracted to the place. He said they'd done a little scouting, in terms of school bus routes, et cetera, and answers were in their favor. Cassandra was out there as often as possible, volunteering, nurturing this or that kennel dog, working with behavioral issues, and reporting any health concerns to the vet. Irene was only too glad to take over with the kids, as Carl knew, when Cassandra needed to work with aggressors in attempts to help them become adoptable. Ken also reported to Carl that Harry told him that his mommy was hiding a "sick wabbit and a kittie in the chitten poop," but that it was a "pwize, so don't tell." Cassandra's gift with critters had sprung back to life.

Carl listened and smiled. "That's our Cassandra. She was always special that way. Irene and I are delighted to learn she's using her gifts again—even if she *is* hiding wabbits in the chitten poop!" Carl roared; hearing those words come out of his own mouth struck him as highlarious, as his daughter would say. "But seriously, I can't think of a better use for that old chicken coop than what Cassandra's doing with it. Tell her the secret's out, and that it's fine with me."

"The thing is, I am concerned, Carl. I worry that if we were that close to the kennels, Cassandra might bite off more than she could chew. Look how her involvement is already expanding. She'd be relentless, caring for the boys, the dogs...her undoubtedly ever-growing menagerie. We were going to talk to you together, but I decided since you know her so well, I'd better run this by you myself first.

"So, here it is. Yes, we'd be interested in buying the farmhouse and whatever acreage might be available with it. Cassandra is, of course, already heart-invested in the rescue. But I know you were ultimately hoping for a manager to move in who could oversee the whole place, and that just can't be her—or us. I'm glad to hear about the growing volunteer roster, but seriously, what do *you* think about getting a manager who doesn't live in the farmhouse?"

Ken put his hand up. "Wait...before you answer, there's one more thing. There is no way we could buy until we sell our home, and it's likely we're months away from getting the house prepped for the market, especially with the wedding, then the holidays a couple of months later. Who knows when we could actually close and move in, even if you do think this might work."

"Time to talk business, son. Let me see if I have this straight. You're interested in buying the farmhouse without being saddled with the responsibilities for the kennels. Your wife is already hiding animals in one of the buildings, which is likely a criminal offense." He winked.

"You're asking if I'll commit to selling to you, but you cannot buy until *you* sell. In this housing market, that could take a few months after it goes on the market—and you might not be able to list it until after the holidays. Does that cover everything?"

"Well, if we can work the issues regarding the kennels into an agreement, we're willing to give you earnest money right now. We decided it's a risk we're willing to take. I know we're all friends, but business is business."

"How long would you want me to keep the place off the market for that earnest money?"

"I was afraid you were going to ask me that. In an ideal world, we'd want to wait until Chuck's out of school, so we'd have until June to sell and start moving. But with the market what it is…"

"Ideal world. What an interesting concept. If only, eh?"

Ken nodded his head. "It's what we have to offer. No offense if you decline. But if you do, I'll sic my wife on you. And how can you refuse a woman who thinks of you as nothing less than her second father?"

Carl took a few bites of salad and a large drink of iced tea. "I *know* I couldn't resist that beautiful wife of yours, and if I tried, my wife and daughter would have my scalp. But there is one caveat: you have to trade me half of your hamburger for half of my salad, and then I guess we have a deal." He wiped his lips with his napkin, then jutted his hand out in front of him.

Cassandra blew her allergy-tweaked nose using a floral paper napkin Margret had set out, the kind that looked beautiful but smelled stinky, felt uncomfortably stiff, and didn't work well. "These are useless as schnoz wipers."

"Did you stop by just to give me grief?" Margret said, handing Cassandra a box of tissues from the countertop. "Mom and I have been sampling things, attempting to coordinate the wedding cake decorations with the paper goods. I think I'm gonna do white-on-white frosting, maybe with a hint of colorful ribbons between the flowers. I shall take your napkin assessment under advisement, since I'm assuming you'll have at least one meltdown during the wedding."

"Can you believe the wedding is only one week away! Seems like Mom and I have been baking cookies and freezing them for a year now. I could smack myself for agreeing to windmill cookies for the wedding favors...but it made Mom so happy. Margret, for the first time that I can ever remember, I stood next to my mom in the kitchen and we baked something—together. I haven't seen her look like this since...ever. I have never seen my mom like this. I feel like I barely know who she is."

"Maybe this is the first time you've had an opportunity to finally meet the real Betty instead of Bad Betty, the Sad Betty."

Cassandra looked thoughtful for a moment, then she started laughing. She laughed so hard, she could barely speak.

"What's so funny about *that*?" Margret asked.

"It just occurred to me that Bad Betty rhymes with Sad Betty which fits into the Sad Game Ken and I play."

"I have no idea what you're talking about."

"Doesn't matter. It would take too long to explain. Plus, I doubt I actually could. Let me just give you the punch line and we'll move on. I can't *wait* to tell Ken that I no longer have to worry that our kids might inherit the Bad Betty gene, since it's now mutated into a glad one, so I don't have to bring it up during the Sad Game."

∽∾

At the culmination of a crazy week spent cranking out Winsome Wedding Durves, during which Burt also ran the butcher shop, served Thursday Durves, and endured endless, good-willed ribbing from his customers, it was at last his wedding day. He pulled into the driveway of the shelter in a truck filled with wedding food. He'd stored the Durves at the shop in his giant refrigerated coolers, using his industrial containers. Betty offered to help him prepare, but he ordered her to do absolutely nothing but to concentrate on being the bride. "I've got plenty of family to pitch in. I have to give them *something* to do; they're driving me crazy."

He had to wind back through a maze of tables and chairs and past the giant tent in order to get anywhere near the food tables. Thankfully, it was a beautiful day, if a little on the warm side for September. He was wearing his favorite black wool suit, a blue shirt, a new striped tie, and a crisp white butcher apron.

"The groom needs a hand out here!" he yelled.

Ken, Leo, Carl, and Betty's sons came bounding down the steps from inside the house. "Thank goodness," Ken said.

"You worried I wouldn't show? That'd be a fine mess, wouldn't it? No Durves *and* no groom?"

"No, that's not it," Carl offered. "We're just glad you rescued us from that whirlwind of estrogen in there. I've never seen such fussing. Well, not since my own wedding, then Margret's. What do you need?"

"I need to get the Durves where they belong. Hopefully, someone in the estrogen brigade told you exactly where that was supposed to be, at least for now."

The men went fast to work, doing as they were instructed.

Burt then checked in with Cassandra. She counted and recounted the sandwich-bagged elements for the windmills, each bag containing a cookie, beef jerky stick, paper plate, miniature marshmallow and napkin. She showed Burt the small printed notes that would go on each plate and teased him about what he'd started when he'd told her mom how to make these cookies. "Welcome to the fresh winds of new beginnings," the notes read. After the children made each windmill, Cassandra said she would instruct them how to attach the notes before handing them out. Burt gave her a big hug and thanked her for her generosity—and her mother.

At the sound of Burt's booming voice, Betty peeked out her bridal-room window. The Bambeneks had moved all the Manfords' old furniture out of the farmhouse, so Margret and Cassandra transformed one of the upstairs bedrooms into the perfect room for Betty to prepare for her big deal, and she was glad to have a moment to herself. She'd never been so fussed over.

Burt looks so handsome in his suit and crisp white butcher's apron! She was extremely nervous, but at the same time, she never in her life had felt more sure about anything. Burt was only a part of it. The sounds of her family and her soon-to-be extended family working together, joking, laughing, and sharing in one another's lives was pure grace. At least that's what she now believed grace to be: a wonderful, inexplicable gift.

She took another look at herself in the floor-length mirror Irene brought from her home. She started at the top of her head and worked her way down. Her hair looked magnificent, as did everyone's in the wedding party. The Beauty Barn gave them all free 'dos since they were family now. She and Gerald had eloped, so she couldn't help but feel this wedding was over the top with luxuries!

Betty wore a bright blue dress with a double string of red wooden beads. The beads had been her grandmother's and came with her from

Poland. Like Burt, she, too, wore an apron. It bore her mother's best handiwork. For the wedding, at Burt's special request and to her deep delight, she would enter to *"Jesienne Róse,"* "Autumn Roses." Cassandra found it on a CD by surfing the Internet. It was the best wedding gift her daughter could have given her.

At last, everyone and everything was in place. Cassandra and Ken sat in the front row. Burt and his grandchildren flanked one side of the wedding trellis, which was decorated with a hundred real, little windmills, all sparkling and whirling in the sun. Burt's grandkids came up with the idea after they heard about the windmill cookies. The music began, and out of the house marched the first of Betty's five grandsons and two granddaughters, poking and prodding one another playfully. When Betty learned both her sons and their families were coming, she'd cried and cried, which she was trying not to do right now and ruin her makeup. They carried tiny windmills, their arms waving to make sure their windmills were whirling. Betty watched Chuck and Howie poking each other, which made her laugh. Ken leaned toward them, brows furrowed.

With a nervous zing, she suddenly realized she needed to get in place, and then, at last, she stepped through the doorway. To the shock of everyone including Burt and especially her daughter—along with her dress, beads, and apron—Betty wore a cowgirl hat with magnificent colorful ribbons trailing off the back of it. She knew she looked silly and that the finishing touch was completely "unBetty," but she simply could not resist. After all, her business cards said she was a cowgirl bride from Oklahoma, and it was her wedding day. She kept her eyes right on Burt—who broke into happy tears when he saw her.

After the cake was served and the windmill favors were assembled (for the most part) and handed out (for the most part), Carl took the microphone.

"Just one final important thing," he said, then realized the mike was off. He flipped the button. "Before I begin, I'd like everyone to know that we have Burt and Betty's blessing for sharing with you the following commercial, of sorts. In fact, they insisted."

Margret's eyes met Cassandra's. She was already dabbing at her nose, which caused Margret to well with tears too.

Carl swallowed before speaking. "Ladies and gentlemen," he said reverently, "as you know, we gathered here today to celebrate a wonderful blessing. A unique gift of love, given by our Creator God, the marriage of Burt Burt and Betty Kamrowski."

"Cowgirl Betty Kamrowski *Burt*!" Burt hollered.

"RIGHT!" Carl paused for the ripple of laughter.

"But before we crank up the music and open the dance grass, we'd like to celebrate one more unique gift of love. Speaking on behalf of the bride and groom, Irene and I, and the Higgins family, we'd like to take a moment to honor the memory of Craig and Sheryl Manford. The heartbeat of this entire estate is the Manford Animal Rescue and Shelter, started more than twenty years ago by Craig and Sheryl's tireless and sacrificial acts. Both of the Manfords were taken from us by cancer earlier this year, and later, in a private ceremony, we will spread their ashes in the cemetery behind the kennel. If you haven't figured it out by now, the sounds of the barking dogs—our unofficial welcome to the wedding committee—came from the kennels in the barn.

"Before the dancing, we'd like to extend an invitation for a kennel tour to anyone who's interested. If you're not interested, relax, enjoy a few more Durves, and visit with your neighbors until we return.

"If you do come on the tour, you'll see for yourself the fruit of the labors of those special folks who were given natural-born hearts for the critters.

"Here is our brief pitch: the shelter is seeking volunteers. We have pamphlets for you there by the barn door. Please feel free to take one, give it a read, and see if you might be moved to either chip in, or fit in, or both. Some of you might not know that the Higgins family will be moving into this beautiful old house. Although they're already big-time volunteers here at the shelter, many more hands are needed. So, anybody interested, please follow me."

Not a single person remained in their seats.

When Betty saw the overwhelming response, she said a silent prayer of thanksgiving. For her and Burt to be able to extend this opportunity for the well-being of the critters and also her daughter felt like an unexpected gift. The grateful look of love in Cassandra's eyes confirmed it.

"Surely goodness and mercy will pursue you all the days of your life." The words from the morning's church service rang in Betty's head as she held tight to the hand of the man she loved.

After the reception ended, everyone departed but the family members and the pastor. They'd asked him to remain since he performed the wedding ceremony and he was the man of the cloth who conducted the public animal blessing at Burt's church every year. Carl gathered everyone while his wife retrieved the urn.

Cassandra, who'd been watching the trellis full of windmills whirl and sparkle in the sun, suggested they first move the trellis to the pet cemetery where the Manfords had requested their ashes be deposited.

Carl and Cassandra took turns walking past the tiny grave markers for the dogs, pouring the ashes as they went. Pastor Creeley and the rest of the family followed behind, praying aloud, thanking God for the humble service of the Manfords, and asking Him to bless the future of the shelter and all who set foot on it, whether they be human or animal.

When they were done, they set the empty vase under the trellis, gathered around it in a circle, and held hands. Pastor Creeley led them in one final prayer, ending with "Lord, *hear* our prayers."

After the *amen,* the wind picked up, setting the windmills into whirlwinds of twirling, refracting flashes of sparkling sunlight that raced across faces and played throughout the cemetery. Betty's cowgirl ribbons, each matching one of the bright colors in her mother's apron, waved in the winds. It was as if God had blown a powerful breath to stir up His unmistakable acknowledgment that, yes, their prayers had indeed been heard. The glory of it held them all spellbound, and goose bumps raced up Cassandra's arms.

When the wind settled, she was left breathless but leaned over and whispered to Ken. "My *flurrious* moment with the snowglobe was *like* that! Thank goodness we're all still here."

Make Your Own Burt's Durves!

Have any three of these ingredients on hand? You've got DURVES!

Mix-and-Match 'Em

Sweet pickles

Dill wedges

Ham, bologna, pepper cheese, sharp cheddar—some thin slices, some ½-inch thick slices

Hot mustard

Sweet mustard

Horseradish

Cream cheese, milk, and fresh-squeezed garlic; beat till easy smearing consistency

Crackers (any will do, but Burt tends to be a Town House man)

For fancy Durves, use a crinkle cutter for everything, including the pickles.

Crinkles also hold dip well.

Recipe suggestions:

Tasty Durve

Spread garlic smear on thin slice of ham (or bologna, or cheese, for you vegetarians).

Wrap around sweet pickle. (Or dill—see how this works?)

Secure with toothpick.

Serve with mustard dip of choice.

Crinkle Durve

Crinkle cut thick-slice bologna and pepper cheese into cubes.

Put one cube each on toothpick.

Mix horseradish with any mustard for dipping sauce. (Burn me, Babe!)

OR

Crinkle cut meat and cheese into thin slices, spread crackers with garlic dip, and pile the goodies on.

Durvey Duo

Wrap thin slice of meat around pickle of choice.

Serve smear of mustard. Or a smear of different mustards. Or mix together, and maybe add horseradish sauce. Use as dipping sauce.

READERS GUIDE

1. When she was a child, Cassandra's beloved Grandpa Wonky declared that she'd "one day become the best veterinarian in the whole state of Minnesota." Disappointment with herself over this unrealized dream drives how Cassandra reacts to many things in her life. Discuss specific areas and other characters that were touched by Cassandra's perception of this failed expectation. How was Grandpa Wonky's belief realized, even if Cassandra couldn't recognize it? What other characters in *Stray Affections* deal with the tension between expectations and disappointment?

2. What does the snowglobe represent for Cassandra? Do you have anything in your life that triggers such an emotional and spiritual response in you?

3. Betty Kamrowski is known by the people of Wanonishaw as "Bad Betty." Cassandra describes her to Margret as "Our Lady of the No Wishing, Wanting, or Being." How do you think Betty sees herself? What do you think Burt Burt sees in her?

4. Margret and Leo make an important decision regarding their family. At one point she says, "But I just have this feeling it's time to let go of a baby so we can get back to *living*." What do you think this means? Have you known friends or family who have faced similar decisions?

5. What do you think happened to the little girl and the three dogs in the snowglobe?

6. Ken takes a big risk, according to Margret, on his Christmas gift choice for Cassandra. Why do you think Ken felt it was critical to take this chance?

7. Burt Burt shows Bad Betty that she is still lovable after so many years of being alone. How do you feel about Betty's difficulty in accepting Burt's affection? Why do you think it's such a challenge for her?

8. Cassandra and Ken's sons play a key role in bridging the gap between Betty and Cassandra. Can you think of a personal story where the *next* generation served as catalyst for change in family dynamics?

9. Margret and Cassandra have a very close friendship, yet both keep from fully sharing with her best friend the changes they are experiencing. What is holding them back? Discuss why friends don't always choose to rely on each other when faced with tough circumstances.

10. Because of Margret and Leo's decisions, Irene and Carl Bambenek are facing different retirement years than they had imagined for themselves. How would you adjust to this transitional period? Do you think you'd likely take the same approach as the Bambeneks?

11. Suicide is a terrible tragedy with long-term consequences. Do you understand why Betty and Cassandra dealt with Gerald's death as they did? How do you believe Betty could have dealt with it differently? What could Cassandra have done as an adult to repair the years of brokenness with her mother? How was she trapped, keeping her from doing so?

12. At the point of Betty and Burt Burt's wedding, many of the characters in *Stray Affections* come to understand themselves and their relationships differently than they understood them when Cassandra went to the Collectors' Convention. In your opinion, whose perspective changed the most? How can you imagine Cassandra growing as her family lives on the shelter property? Betty as Burt's wife? Irene and Carl tackling their new endeavors?

Acknowledgments

When God first impregnated my heart with the seed of an idea for a series revolving around mysterious snowglobes, He gave me everything I needed to begin: curiosity, love of story, joy in my craft, and goose bumps. But God didn't stop there. Each step of the way, He gave me exactly what I needed, exactly when I needed it.

✓ A brilliant, hard-working, encouraging, morale boosting agent. Thank you Danielle Egan Miller! I cannot imagine my professional life without you and your "happy-happy" reminders. Well, I can (WHAAAA!), but I choose not to. You are the best. Again and again, you are the best.

✓ An editor who listened to the seedling concept, caught my vision, and acquisitioned the series. Thank you, Shannon Hill Marchese! I've never worked harder to get better, and that is a supreme compliment. You helped focus my story, sharpen the pace, and yet never once lost faith in the Mystery and the messages within. Or your point of view. (wink-wink)

✓ Ears to hear and eyes to see the new characters walking into my head (I don't outline; I'm a story chaser), and a computer to keep track of what they said and did— whether I liked it or not. Imagine my *flurrious* surprise when I started watching/listening/writing this first book in the series, and the "three dogs mom" showed up rather than the "sense of place woman" I thought I'd be writing about. I ADORE it when God does that!

✓ An absolute love for the state of Minnesota, where it quickly became clear the characters in *Stray Affections* resided.

✓ Through the awesome memory of Kari Knutson, I was led to Dick and Irene Heibel. ('Twas a breathtaking "coincidence.") They allowed this babbling stranger into their home to barrage them with questions. To the best of my knowledge, Dick is the sole snowglobe repairman in the country. He walked me through his workshop and shared so many details... Every fact he put forth ignited another burst of imagination.

✓ Thank you, God, for Bret Lee Haskins, Brian George Baumbich, Katie Ann Baumbich, and Bonnie O'Hara Nuttall. In our family, love abounds, laughter rings, adventure lives, and family is RIGHT-ON! The blessing in that grace encouraged me to desire the same for *Stray Affection*'s Cassandra and her mother, Bad Betty. But this I knew to be true: I cannot make my characters do other than what they will. And so I wrote and prayed for them.

✓ My giggling grandgirlies ever reminded me that life is fun, fragile, energetic, feisty, exciting, best when honest, and filled with silly and JOY! Thank you, Bridget Ann Baumbich and Colleen Ann Baumbich, for teaching me what it's like to be a child in today's world. Cassandra Higgins (one of my characters) thanks you too, for helping your Grannie B to portray *her* children in a real manner, even though Cassandra's munchkins are boys. As were mine.

✓ Members and volunteers at the Winona Area Humane Society give their hearts to the critters. Because of them,

Kornflake, my bliss-inducing dog (What kind is he? A big red kind!) was parked at my feet for most of the writing. When I needed inspiration, or when one of my character's situations made me cry, I buried my face in his neck, and he always came through. Thank you God, for WAHS—rescue folks everywhere—and Kornflake. And thank You, too, for Jake, Widget, and Sage, three more dogs who make our family members exceedingly and waggingly loved.

✓ Sunday mornings at Homer United Methodist Church in Homer, Minnesota, continuously fed my soul and helped keep my eye on the wondrous grace and endless, stalking love of the Divine. Thank you, Pastor Christine Robinson, and all who worship there. Pastor Christine blessed Kornflake, and therefore also blessed me. Thank you, God, for helping me pass along the special blessings of the critters through the power of story. What a satisfying way to pay it forward.

✓ When I learned my main characters descended from Kashubian Poles (because they told me), who better to help me with their history than the knowledgeable and passionate volunteers at the Polish Cultural Institute of Winona, Minnesota? They were lavish with their time and spirits. Thank you, God, for the hearts of those wonderful people and their resources, and thank you, volunteers. I hope I got it right. If I didn't, it sure wasn't your fault.

✓ Joanna MacKenzie, thank you for personal efforts. Your enthusiasm to dive in when asked a question is always so refreshing. And thank you Lauren Olson, also at Browne

and Miller Literary Associates (GO TEAM!), who fielded
a few of my hysterical calls.

✓ One after the next, folks at WaterBrook Press stepped forward to cheer me on and to help get this book into your
hands. Copyediting, production management, sales and
marketing, publicity, and on and on, your careful and
enthusiastic attention to excellence is remarkable. A few
names that come to mind: Amy Haddock, Allison O'Hare
(all those A names), Pamela J. Shoup, and Steven Herron.
Thank you, God, for instilling such hearty spirits in each
of them.

✓ God especially saw this project through by giving George
John Baumbich, my husband of forty years, the strength
to stick with me while at the same time freeing me to
chase my stories. As always when I'm writing a book, I disappear for weeks on end. Or I'm here crabbing around.
Distracted. I mutter about people he can't see. I make
messes. I'm frantic. I'm tired. And George? He's standing
back, stepping up, doing laundry, and cheering me on.
Thank you, God, for the love of a good man.

✓ And now we have you, the reader. God, YOU ROCK!

There is no end to God's giving. May we be wise enough to hold
out our hearts and hands and receive it with abandon.

ABOUT THE AUTHOR

Charlene Ann Baumbich is a popular author and speaker ("fascinating" would be her word of choice) and an award-winning journalist. Her stories, essays, and columns have appeared in numerous magazines and newspapers, including the *Chicago Tribune,* the *Chicago Sun-Times,* and *Today's Christian Woman.* In addition to her Dearest Dorothy series of novels, she has written seven nonfiction books of humor and inspiration. She lives in Glen Ellyn, Illinois with retired hubby, George, and Kornflake, her big red dog. Kornflake was adopted from the Winona Area Humane Society in Winona, Minnesota. He helped her write much of this book by cheering her on, taking her for muse-inducing walks, and keeping her toes warm while she typed.

To keep up with Charlene's new book releases and receive her sparkling thoughts, subscribe to the *TwinkleGram.*

✓ Share your stories with her via e-mail.

✓ Find link to view pictures of Kornflake.

✓ Find link to upload pictures of YOUR dogs and snowglobes.

✓ Stay in touch!

You can find instructions for all of the above by visiting **www .charleneannbaumbich.com.**